MONSTROUS LITTLE VOICES

ABADDON BOOKS

T0051776

WWW.ABADDONBOOKS.COM

MONSTROUS LITTLE VOICES

New Tales from Shakespeare's Fantasy World

Jonathan Barnes ⮞ Adrian Tchaikovsky ⮞ Emma Newman
Kate Heartfield ⮞ Foz Meadows

An Abaddon Books™ Publication
www.abaddonbooks.com
abaddon@rebellion.co.uk

First published in 2016 by Abaddon Books™,
Rebellion Publishing Limited,
Riverside House, Osney Mead, Oxford, OX2 0ES, UK.

10 9 8 7 6 5 4 3 2 1

Editors: Jonathan Oliver & David Moore
Design: Sam Gretton & Oz Osborne
Marketing and PR: Rob Power
Head of Books and Comics Publishing: Ben Smith
Creative Director and CEO: Jason Kingsley
Chief Technical Officer: Chris Kingsley

Cover Art by Sam Gretton, based on
On Nocturnal Dance of Fairies, in Other Words Ghosts,
Olaus Magnus, 1555. See p. 297 for a full list of
woodcuts used in internal illustrations.

UK ISBN: 978-1-78108-393-2
US ISBN: 978-1-78108-394-9

Printed in Denmark

In memory of
Lisa Anne Jardine, CBE FRS FRHistS
(1944 – 2015)

Note from the Editor

THE DEDICATION TO this volume honours the memory of Professor Lisa Jardine, who passed away in October 2015 after a lengthy battle with cancer.

Professor of Renaissance Studies at UCL and founder of its Centre of Interdisciplinary Research in the Humanities, Lisa had a list of appointments, honours and awards from institutions around the world too long to list here. A Fellow of both the Royal Society and the Royal Historical Society, she was a world authority on the renaissance who spoke eight languages, ancient and modern, an impassioned political advocate and a regular guest on TV and radio. She was also the lecturer for Queen Mary University of London's Shakespeare course in 1997-1998, when I studied under her.

My enduring recollection of that course—aside from her clearly prodigious knowledge of the subject, and her passion and candour—was her enthusiasm for teaching Shakespeare in a modern context. We studied revisions and updates; we examined Shakespeare's language in his own time, and ours; we interrogated his politics. I remember she taught *Romeo & Juliet* almost entirely off the Luhrmann film, and spent half a lecture looking at a shot of a guardsman weeping silently at Princess Diana's funeral to discuss emotion and eloquence.

I'd barely thought of Lisa for years when I heard the news, and while I have no particular superstitions about coincidence, the fact I was working on this volume at the time struck me as timely. I can't say if Lisa would have approved of the book you're holding, but I hope so. She wanted to give Shakespeare to today's world, and I believe Foz, Kate, Emma, Adrian and Jonathan have done that, and done it some justice to boot.

Her voice—never little, and rarely monstrous—will be missed in the world.

David Thomas Moore
November 2015

$\mathscr{P}$rologue

Venice, 1598

THE REVELS IN the fairy court of Oberon are, it's said, less glamorous than those of his wife's bower, but more wild. But it was early yet; a hunter's moon glowered over a copse in the woods overlooking Venice, throwing bloody light over a few satyrs wooing nymphs, a band of ogres playing heavy drums and goblins capering through a riotous gavotte. Later, the wine would flow and there would be duels and a hunt.

The King of the Fairies, reclining in a couch of bones and roses, had yet to join the festivities. He drank deeply of dark, bitter wine and watched his courtiers as he listened to his emissary Nightshade's report.

"So the Medicis make war?" asked Oberon, staring into space. He wore an antlered form tonight, twice the height of a man and half-bestial. The revel promised to be savage.

"'Tis true. Ferdinand, the younger, sues the elder for the Tuscan throne."

"Aye, and Ferdinand's wife is Aragon's niece, and so Pedro will rattle his sabre and offer hot words, though in truth he cares not whose throne it is."

"And Francesco the Duke is wed to Orsino's niece," said the younger fairy, the crimson moon glittering in his featureless black eyes, "and so Illyr joins the debate." He smirked. "Both brothers, it's said, trouble the Wizard of Milan, but neither has had satisfaction."

"And France?"

"Oh, Henry'll none of it. He grants his lords to fight on this side or that as takes 'em, to seek honour and glory."

The King threw up his hands, heedless of the wine splashing from his goblet. "Then will all the world fight?" he asked.

The goblin leaned back on his haunches and grinned. "Is't not the nature of mortals to war?"

"Aye," said Oberon darkly, holding out his cup to be refilled by one of his buzzing attendants. "Well, my thanks for your report, good Nightshade. You may return to your duties."

"My lord..." ventured the fairy, nervously.

"Yes, fairy?" The King arched an eyebrow, surprised at his servant's temerity.

"It seems to me... the Serenissima will find common cause with Aragon. And your Queen still resides in Illyria, where she woos Orsino..."

"Aye?"

"My king, it were best if the fairy courts did not take part in a mortal war."

"Hmm." Oberon mused for a moment. "You're right. Choose a dozen fairies of good character and send them to the mortal courts as emissaries. Give a message of peace."

He tossed his newly-refilled goblet on the moss, stood and sighed. "I will go and speak to my wife."

CORAL BONES

BY FOZ MEADOWS

Full fathom five thy father lies.
Of his bones are coral made.
Those are pearls that were his eyes.
Nothing of him that doth fade,
But doth suffer a sea-change
Into something rich and strange.

The Tempest, Act I, Scene ii.

Act I
My Father Lies

Naples, 1580

"HE MAKES YOU *sleep, you know,*" *said Ariel, then. She—it was she, that day—kicked her airy heels against a convenient boulder.* "*When he tires of you. He makes you sleep.*"

"*I know,*" *I said. And then, when her faint expression saddened,* "*Don't all good children sleep? Don't all living creatures?*"

"*They do,*" *said Ariel.* "*But not like that.*"

FEVER WRACKS ME as storms do ships. I cannot stay ahead of it; delirium blows me in narrowing circles, over and up and back again, yet doesn't unmoor my body from its bloody pulse of pain. Miscarriage, the physician says, is a betrayal as wife, as *woman*, yet I feel more betrayed than betrayer. Or perhaps, like Caliban, I am merely the monstrous, wild creature that they say I am, as red of tooth as I am of hair—red, red. The sheets are red, and I twist against them, fevered and rimed with sharp, sweet salt that doesn't know the sea.

"Will she live?" asks Ferdinand. He stands out of sight, but not beyond hearing. Is that his design, or by accident?

"She might," the physician hedges. "The womb's waters ought to protect against the incursion of foul humours during pregnancy, but in this state, with the waters gone"—I feel, more than see, the wave of his hand—"she is vulnerable." He lowers his tone, but not his volume. Coughs. "Though it pains you to hear it, my lord, there is some correlation between women who eat scantly in childhood and women who struggle to bear in turn, and after being raised on an island—"

"Raised by a sorcerer, Ceasare. Raised by a duke and a wise man both."

"A wise man who, by his own admission, cannot conjure food, no matter his pure intentions. My lord, I mean no slight to the Princess Miranda, but though she is surely beautiful, she is slim-hipped, small. She has no fleshy reserves with which to fight this fever, and if it continues to burn, I fear the worst. And even if she survives"—gently, over Ferdinand's gulping—"you must consider the high likelihood of her future barrenness. Early miscarriage is often a predictor of such things, in my experience."

"Barrenness? Truly?" Ferdinand's voice is angry, blanched, and in that moment, I hate him as I have never hated anyone, not even the cruellest court ladies.

Those are pearls that were his eyes, my Ariel once sang, and through my rage I laugh at the thought, for my woman's pearl was all in Ferdinand's eyes; my chastity was the oyster he prised open in his pursuit of it, and now I fade, fade, fade to nothing, fevered and thin and red.

"She stirs! Ceasare, look!"

"I see her, my prince. Ah! Let me fetch some water."

They press the cup to my lips. I do not drink.

"I suppose it makes sense." I drew my child's knees to my chin, considering the problem. "After all, it would take an awful concentration to put every fish in the sea to sleep, and every ant and bird and mouse—unless it's done in groups?"

Ariel shook her head. Her form was modelled on mine, though her hair moved with the buoyant lethargy of kelp in a current, coiling slowly around her face; or my face, rather. Ours.

"Does father sleep, then?" By my own logic, I supposed he must, though I'd never caught him at it.

"He sleeps when you sleep, so that you won't wake him."

"Wake him?" I wrinkled my nose in puzzlement. *"How could he wake before he's ready? Sleep doesn't work like that."*

"Natural sleep does."

"I don't believe you."

"Shall I prove it?"

"If you can," I dared.

(I often dared, then.)

BETWEEN ONE BLINK and the next, they leave. Or maybe more than a blink; my awareness, like my flesh, is shivershaken, unreliable. I stare at the ceiling: vaulted stones and painted angels. Will I ascend in death?

Something stirs beside the bed, a gust of air solidifying out of light and shadow.

"Miranda?" The voice is mine, but not-mine.

Ours, then.

"Ariel?"

I turn my head, and there she is—or there I am—or there we are, though her copy of me is unfevered and whole, her languid halo of bright red hair like fire around her (*my, our*) face.

"Oh, child." A pale hand hovers across my brow. "I am so sorry. I shouldn't have left you here. I abandoned you."

"It's not your fault. I wanted to come. I thought—" My throat goes dry, and I break off, sweating and shuddering at a fresh burst of pain. "I never thought it would be like this."

"How could you have known? You knew nothing of men."

I close my eyes. "I knew a little."

"A little," Ariel echoes softly. "But still. Not enough for this."

* * *

AT MY CHALLENGE, *Ariel became a leopard—or the shape I knew as leopard, without reference to an original—and invited me onto her back. Her pelt was soft, but translucent, blue-limned like a fire lit with salt-warped wood.*

"Be silent," she said, her voice a low rumble, and bore me up through the warm air, through the island's green heart, until we found a colony of sleeping mice curled in a tree-knot. To my surprise, they stirred when I stroked them, waking with tiny squeaks.

The mice themselves delighted me, though I was sorry to have distressed them. I said as much to Ariel, who flew us back to the beach, assuring me that, once we'd gone, the mice would resettle themselves. No magic required.

"WHY HAVE YOU come here, Ariel? Why now?"

"At first, I was busy. Fairy business. I was on that island for a long time, child. I had to return to Titania's court, to make my obeisances, pardons, pledges. I had to report and explain my absence. But after that—" She falters, looks aside. "After that, I was ashamed. And hopeful, too, just a little; I thought you might adjust, given time."

"I could adjust, perhaps. But as *they* will not, I cannot—or if I did, there'd be no point to it."

She doesn't ask who *they* were. There's no need.

"Do you love him?" Ariel asks, softly.

"Compared to what?" It comes out harsher than I intend, a pant of rage as pain saws through me. My father impressed on me the value of feminine virtues, and when the ship came— when Ferdinand came, and I finally had an audience—it was surprisingly easy to embody them, as though my flesh and feelings both had only awaited their function. But the world in which it was easy was a small, unvarnished one, as utterly distinct from my present state as shells from sapphires. If such a woman truly exists, she is not me, nor have I met her like, here in this place where my every move is scrutinised for the failings of barbarism. "Compared to how I once loved my father? Compared to how I should love myself? I do not." Tears slip down my cheeks. "I do *not*, and now it's all too late."

"It doesn't have to be." Ariel kneels, or gives her airy form the semblance of kneeling. "You can leave this place, Miranda. Go where you will."

"As a woman alone? One marked as spurned, or barren, or runaway from her lawful lord, and whose father in any case would drag her home again? Such choices you offer! Pearls to make a pauper rich." My lucidity slips like a lady's veil, restored by the cooling brush of Ariel's hand.

"What if," she says, and stops. On the island, I had no true glass, but this past year, I've grown enough accustomed to the sight of my face to recognise its expression now as one of fear, and grief, and defiant apology. "What if they thought you dead?"

"NATURAL SLEEP, LIKE *natural life, is precarious,*" *said Ariel, alighting on the sand. Her leopard-voice was a rumbling purr. "Remember that, Miranda."*

"I will, but what does precarious *mean?"*

Ariel paused in the act of washing a paw. She twitched an ear, then popped back into our shared girlshape, toying with a curl. "It means unsafe, and subject to change. Like a sandbar moved by waves."

I nodded; I was an expert on sandbars. Then, unbidden, a strange thought came to me. "The mice moved when I touched them," I said. "Do I not move in my sleep?"

"You don't," she said. "No matter the provocation, you stay still."

"Oh," I said. "That's... comforting, I suppose." My skin felt strangely cold. "Is it comforting, Ariel?"

Her eyes were mine, yet older than mine. "That depends,"
she said.
"On what?"
"On the provocation."

"THERE IS A spell," says Ariel, when I say nothing. "A glamour
of sorts, though a little more complex. All who know you here
will think you dead of your childloss fever—which I can cure, in
either case," she adds, quickly. "You will live, Miranda. I owe
you that much. But if you wanted—"

"Yes," I say. I exhale relief like poison. I don't know where
I'll go, if Ariel will take me there or merely provide me with a
chance at departure, but I cannot stay here. My island was not
wild, compared to this.

There are such monsters in a palace.

$\mathcal{A}$ct II
Fathomless

"WHERE DID YOU *come from, Ariel?*"

"*From the fairy court of Queen Titania,*" *Ariel said. He—for Ariel was boyshaped that day, or so he said; I had no basis for comparison, and had had to be told—scratched absently at a skinny, scabbed knee and stared into the distance.*

"*No, I mean—where did you* come *from? How did you come to be?*"

Ariel's narrow gaze sharpened. His eyes were thin and folded at the edges, his skin the colour of wet sand. No hair, though: just a dark scrape of stubble. A borrowed shape, I assumed, as when he borrowed mine, though whose it was originally I didn't know.

There was a lot I didn't know, then.

"*Are you asking about fairies in specific, or me in particular?*" *he said.* "*Or about the genesis of creatures generally?*"

"*Are the answers not the same?*"

"*Not remotely.*"

This surprised me. "*Truly?*"

"*Truly.*"

"*Give me an example, then. Or better yet—show me!*"

ARIEL'S CURE IS a nostrum that tastes of moss and sunsets, scratching my throat like swallowed earth. It sits in the core of me like ice, a steady coolth radiating outwards, soothing my fever; soothing *me*. I stare again at the painted angels overhead and wonder how unlike them I must be, that I can leave my father and husband to think me dead. But if I stay—

"I asked them to teach me," I say, to the gold smoke of Ariel's current form. It eddies in acknowledgement, sparks flying out as the glamour takes hold. "We came here, and I wanted to be a scholar. And Ferdinand aided me, at first. He thought it novel, and maybe right, that a girl raised in isolation would want to learn. But when I wouldn't restrict my interests to suit him—when I wanted to learn physiognomy, astronomy, history, and not just music and manners—his humour for it faded." I step from the bed with more strength than I've had in days, and into the tub of waiting water, conjured by Ariel. Sweat and blood slough off like scabs.

I do not talk about Ferdinand; about the child we lost, or that child's begetting. I am not ready for that. Not now.

Not yet.

When I am clean, I dress in clothes of Ariel's choosing— stolen clothes that render me boyish, breasts bound, hair hidden—and wonder at myself, that I'm not afraid. Or I am afraid, rather, but not of this; not of the unknown, and not of Ariel.

"Are you ready?" Ariel asks. Her form is mine again, though traces of gold smoke linger, limning our hair like a halo.

"Yes," I say, though I'm not sure for what, and as she sets a hand on me, I feel the spell of my disappearance settle on us like ashes.

"See, here?" Ariel pointed at the eggs, three pale-shelled things the size of small fruit snugged tight in a woven nest. "Baby nightjars hatch from these. The mother lays them, and they hatch on their own."

We'd climbed the tree together—no leopard-flights today— like the children we both resembled, but only one of us was. The shells were warm to the touch, and as we made our way back to the beach, the feel of them lingered on my fingertips.

We didn't speak; Ariel was in the middle of a lesson, and the silence between us was a companionable thing, worn easy with frequent use.

At the edge of a promising tidepool, Ariel dropped to his haunches, dark eyes darting as he sought out a subject. "There!" he proclaimed. "Do you see it?"

"The starfish?" I asked.

"Yes, yes! Such strange things—if you cut off one of their arms, not only will it grow back, but the severed limb will turn into a whole new starfish. But then, we have the neighbouring seahorse—there, can you see?"

I squinted into the water. "The fat one, with the stripes?"

"Exactly!" Ariel beamed at me. "It's pregnant, and male. When his babies are born, they'll burst from the pouch in his stomach like a puff of dandelion seeds on the wind, a flock of little seahorselings."

Another child might have disbelieved him; but I lived alone on an island, and could hardly have known that this wasn't the usual way of things. "Is my father like a seahorse, then? Did I come from him?"

"You came from him, but not that way," said Ariel, suddenly solemn. "Your kind is born from a mother—"

"Like the nightjars?"

"Yes, but not from eggs. You grew in a womb, within her body, and when you were big enough, she pushed you out into the world."

I frowned at Ariel. "If I have a mother, then where is she? Why isn't she here?"

"Your father could tell you that, but I cannot."

"Because you don't know?"

Ariel sighed and rocked on his heels. "Because he's forbidden me to."

*   *   *

"TAKE ME TO Titania's court," I say, suddenly.

Ariel stills. "You don't want that."

"Why not?"

"You just escaped one court!" She waves her hand at the palace behind us, stark grey lines against the evening sky. "Why trade it for another?"

"Because," I say, and hesitate, trying to think it through while so enamoured of the prospect as to imperil any rational examination of its consequences. "Where else can I go? I want to learn, to study, and I cannot do it here; not without a male patron, and as I am now feigning death in order to avoid such oversight"—my throat tightens sharply—"that option seems an especially poor one."

"I thought," says Ariel, softly, "that you might want to return to the island."

I stare at her. "With you?"

"Perhaps. If you wanted. Or alone, if you did not." She sighs, shoulders tightening, and stares out into the human dark. "I still go there, sometimes. Often. I have made a truce of sorts, with Caliban. In the end, we were both captives."

Hearing that name aloud is an unexpected pain. "I hated him, once. And then I pitied him."

"And now?"

"And now I know better. He was a reflection, Ariel." I cannot keep the bitterness from my voice. "His lusts were mimicry. Nothing more."

We are both silent at that. There is no comfort in it.

"Take me to Titania's court," I say again, when my voice returns. "Save for this past year, my whole life has been lived in magic, and at least there, I need not hide it." I look at Ariel and smile. "Perhaps I might even venture to be myself, whoever she is when you're not wearing her face."

Ariel flinches. "I'm sorry. I can change—"

"No. Don't." I lay a hand on her (my) arm and give a gentle squeeze. "I didn't mean it like that."

Another silence, softer than the first. We are relearning ourselves, it seems.

"I cannot take you," Ariel says at last. "Not because I don't want to, but because I have duties elsewhere—duties I have already prolonged for the sake of your rescue, but which I can stay no further."

I lift my chin, defiant. "Then I shall make my own way there."

Ariel laughs, proud and pleased and sudden. "What, all the way to Illyria, alone? And why not? But let me furnish you with a guide, at least, to give you an introduction. As it happens, I have a friend who's travelling that way. Mind, he's an impish thing—though not all imp, if you'll credit it—but he'll keep you safe and see you entertained besides, or I'll eat my name."

"Eat your—" I begin, but abandon the query as unimportant, fixing on what matters. "Who is he, then? And where can I find him?"

In answer, Ariel closes her fist. When she opens it again, a tiny red-breasted bird is nestled in the dent of her palm, chuffing its feathers against the cold. Its eyes glow bright, and with an impatient chirrup, it shoots off like an arrow, trailing a tiny phosphor-wake through the air behind it.

"Come on," says Ariel, and together we follow the bird, out through the city gate—still spelled silent, unseen, unknown—and onto the dusty road. Whenever it gets too far ahead, the bird circles back to chirp at us, until we've followed it over hill and briar, past ridges and stones to a thicket of trees and a smallish clearing within them. A cheerful fire crackles in a makeshift pit, and next to it sits a long-limbed man with a pair of horns peeping out from his tightly-curled hair.

As we step into view, the bird flies straight at him, cheeping. He looks up, startled and happy all at once, then laughs as the bird alights on the tip of a horn. It gives a final chirp and dissolves in a shower of sparks.

"Ariel!" he exclaims. "And—what's this? A human child?"

"Well met, Puck," she says, smiling. I feel suddenly shy, and let Ariel guide me over, taking a seat by the fire as she clasps Puck's hand. He looks at me with obvious curiosity, noting our shared features.

"This is Miranda," Ariel says. "My island charge."

"Is she, now? And here I'd thought the story half a myth." He leans on his hands and grins at me. His skin is a light, warm brown, and the curls of his hair are copper in the firelight. "A pleasure, I'm sure, though what you might want with me, I've no idea."

"She wants to go to Titania's court," says Ariel. "And I want you to take her there."

"DID YOU ASK him?" Ariel said. They were a leopard now, but whether that meant male or female wasn't clear. "About your mother?"

I frowned, confused, and sat down on a rock. I felt strangely empty, light, and the hairs on my arms stood up. "I don't know," I said, slowly. "Why? Should I have done?"

Ariel's whiskers rippled. "You went away to ask, and now you're back. Did you change your mind?"

"My mind?"

"Miranda? Are you all right?"

"I can hardly say." I hugged my knees, but let them go as Ariel laid their head in my lap, their velvety paws stretched out beneath my thighs. "I feel so odd. What did I mean to ask about?"

"Your mother."

"I had a mother?"

"You did."

"Oh. That must have been nice."

Ariel chuffed in distress. "If I was unbound—"

"It's all right."

"It's not, Miranda. You know it's not."

"Do I?"

"You do. You did."

"Still." We sat together, looking out at the twilit ocean. *"It's a lovely evening, don't you think?"*

Ariel didn't answer.

"You want me—*me!*—to take this child as a votary to Queen Titania?"

"I do."

Puck looks flatly at Ariel. "Have you forgotten why I'm wanted at court?" He turns to me and says, wryly, "Queen Titania is less than delighted with me at present."

"And why is that again?" asks Ariel, amusedly.

"You know why."

"Miranda doesn't."

"Miranda isn't asking."

Both fairies look at me. I flush, not knowing whether to laugh or flee, but can't resist the temptation of knowledge. "Why *is* Queen Titania wroth with you?"

"Because," says Puck, "I am King Oberon's envoy—or one of them, anyway—and as certain of the Queen's attendants took it upon themselves to mock me in that capacity, I took it upon *myself* to make them regret it."

"What Puck means to say," says Ariel, "is that he made Moth fall in love with a tortoise and bound Mustardseed's hair to a willow-tree, and as both fairies failed to see the humour in his trickery, King Oberon has sent him to make reparations—for the hurt to their dignity, and to the dignity of Queen Titania's court."

"Exactly!" Puck says. "I'm in disgrace, and as undeserving as I am of such acrimony, I hardly see how Miranda could benefit from my stewardship."

"That's because you're looking at it backwards," Ariel says. "Queen Titania holds her votaries—and their presentation—sacrosanct. Bringing her Miranda will be seen as a show of good faith on your part—and as a penitent offering, too, as you might just as easily have taken her to the King. Miranda won't share your shame, you foolish imp; she'll lift it."

"A pretty politician you are," says Puck, and when he smiles, I see the points of his teeth, as needlemouthed as a deep-sea fish. "And why, pray tell, would you do me such a favour?"

"The favour is for Miranda," Ariel says, with weary patience. "You know as well as I the rules surrounding human votaries: they must approach the court on foot, by mortal means, instead of being spirited there by the fairie roads. I have no time to walk that path, but you, in your penitent state, must take it regardless."

"And more's the pity," Puck grumbles. "My feet *ache*."

"I am a font of endless compassion."

"You're a font of endless something, 'tis sure."

I laugh at that, the sound startled out of me like birds from a copse. How strange these fairies are! And yet I delight in their bickering the same way I delight in my newfound lack of pain and duty both: as a freedom once longed, but unlooked for.

"Will you take her, then?"

"Oh, Ariel, Ariel—best of spirits! Airy friend!" Puck wags a finger. "Must you be so transparent? By your own admission, I'd be doing *you* the real favour, as you value the child and cannot shepherd her yourself. And as moved as I am by your paean to the use of votaries in appeasing your Queen, it would—as I'm sure you can appreciate—go against my nature to accept your charge without bargaining."

Ariel bares her throat to the sky, as though in supplication to the firmament and its bright adjudication. "Bargain with me, then."

"I could do that," says Puck, and flicks his gaze to me. "Or I could bargain with *her*."

My heart begins to pound, but my voice is steady. "What manner of bargain, sir?"

"Miranda—" Ariel warns, but Puck cuts her off with a laugh.

"As I'm a magnanimous Puck, that's entirely up to you, child. What's your preference—chance, skill or trade?"

"What's the difference?" I ask, feeling bolder than I sound.

It's Ariel who answers. "Chance means betting in a game of luck; if you lose, he won't take you. Skill is a game of, well, skill; and again, if you lose, he won't take you. And a trade means you offer him something valuable of yourself—a favour, most likely—in return for his help. Though of course"—and here she glares at Puck again—"you'll have to haggle for it."

"What sort of trade? I have some coin, but somehow"—I meet Puck, whose eyes gleam—"I feel you have little use for such currency."

"Just so," says Puck, and yet my hand still moves to the purse at my borrowed belt. I ought, perhaps, to feel awkward in men's clothing; some acknowledgement of a transgression which, at the very least, should shame me in its brazenness. But then, I am already an unnatural thing, and whatever else can be said of me, I've always had a practical streak.

"If not coin," I ask him, "what is it you want?"

"Memories," he says. "Or else—"

But I don't hear what comes next. Fear drags me down like an undertow.

The stars vanish.

I STARED AT *the wall of the cave, at the writing scrawled across it, shaky shale script on darker stone.*

"I don't remember," I whispered. "I don't understand it, Ariel. Why?"

Ariel, shaped as a white-furred she-wolf, leaned against my leg and whined.

I slid to my knees and buried my face in her glowing fur, anemone-soft and just as mobile, rippling as if in some unseen current.

"He fears you," Ariel said. "It's in the nature of sorcerers to covet knowledge more than company. He fears what you might learn; what you might do with your learning."

"And so he steals it from me. Over and over. Like water eroding stone."

Ariel whined again, low and sad.

"What if he comes here, too? What if he wipes the wall?" With my memory unreliable, it was all the true record I had of my conversations with Ariel; of what I knew about the world beyond my father's lessons.

"Then I will remember it for you," Ariel says, with a wolfmother's fierceness. "I'll help you rewrite it, again and again, like the tide that builds the sandbar."

A fragment of memory came to me, and I choked on a laugh.

"Sandbars are precarious, Ariel. You taught me that."

A wet nose bumped my collar. "True," she said. "And yet, correctly placed, they can wreck galleons. Remember that, too."

"I will," I whispered. "If he lets me."

"CAN YOU SPEAK, child? Are you here with us?"

A soft hand strokes my back. I open my eyes, and firelight rushes into them—warm air, warm light. My throat is raw as an uncooked fish.

"No memories," I rasp. "I will not trade them. Not for Titania's crown."

The hand on my back—Ariel's, of course—continues its gentle circuit. "Of course not," she murmurs, apologetic. "Forgive me. I should have thought—"

"It's not your fault."

"Miranda—"

"*Miranda*," Puck says, suddenly. Belated recognition sweeps his features—bright, then dark, the sun obscured by clouds. "You're *that* Miranda. Duke Prospero's daughter."

Something in me hardens. "I am more than my father's child."

"Clearly, as you are here." He looks at Ariel, almost contrite. "One child is much like another. You told me of your island charge, I knew of Duke Prospero's return, but didn't connect the two."

"And would it have changed things, if you had?"

"Perhaps," Puck admits. "And yet..."

"And yet." Ariel snorts, derisive. "Go on, then. Make your bargain."

Puck looks at me, assessing. His gaze is a weight, but unlike the stares of some of the men at Ferdinand's court, it holds no barbs: no lust, no disparagement. As though his sight can sift the grains of my soul like sand through an hourglass.

"Miranda," he says, "in deference to the inherent mischief of your escape, in trade for my services as protector, friend and guide, I will accept no lesser payment than the colour of your hair."

I blink at him. "Is that a literal offer, sir, or a metaphoric one?"

He laughs, delighted. "Literal, dear child, though if you're to deal with the fairy courts, you'd be wise to keep an eye out for such promising loopholes in future. Well? Do we have an accord?"

My hair is bound beneath a cap, invisible to me; yet Ariel still wears my face, her red mane drifting lionish about our jaw, cheeks, chin. I think of my bloody sheets (*red, red*), the tearing loss of what might have been my firstborn child, and decide I have russet enough to spare.

"We do," I say, and extend my hand, as a gentleman might and a lady ought not; *but perhaps*, I think, sudden and lightning-sharp, *I am both those things, and neither.*

"Done," says Puck, and clasps my palm. His grip is warm, and a tingle of magic threads between us, fine as ravelled silk. It feels as though we cradle a spark between us, something in the hollow where our hands are joined, and as its heat intensifies, I flick my gaze to Ariel.

"Oh!" My free hand flies to my lips. I startle and smile behind my fingers, but don't quite laugh, watching as Ariel's ruddy hair turns white as snowfall, its brighter colours leeching away in time to the pulse of Puck's magic. Even her brows and lashes fade, which makes me wonder if, when I next undress myself, I'll learn other, more private changes. (Like so much else, the thought should make me blush, I suppose. But it doesn't.)

Something pushes against my palm, and as the last hair on Ariel's head turns pale, Puck makes a satisfied noise and gently pulls away.

"There," he says, and in his open palm is—not a bird, as Ariel's earlier trick half lead me to expect, but a russet-red gemstone, opal-bright, as perfectly round as an owl's eye. Almost, it seems to beat like a heart, but before I can blink and look again, Puck spirits it into his pocket, grinning impishly.

"I am now, officially, at your service," he says, and offers me a more perfect bow than even the primmest courtier could manage, horns and all.

"At last!" Ariel cries, and with a shiver, her body changes, rippling from its copy of mine to the form of her blue-limned leopard. In this feline guise, she bumps her velvet head against my trembling knuckles, just a whisper of purr in her farewell. "I will see you again, when my errands are run."

My throat feels oddly tight. "I know."

"I'll look for you, at Titania's Court. And if I can't find you."—she blinks at Puck, her tailtip twitching warningly—"I'll know who to blame."

"Then I shall, as ever, be blameless," Puck says, and sketches a bow no less courteous than the one he offered me.

Ariel growls in what I know from long experience to be a fond, exasperated way, and with a final glance at me, she turns and stalks off into the air. Her silhouette steadily blurs in the gloaming, and then she's gone from sight.

"I CAN'T GO on like this."

Ariel curled her arms around me, face pressed into the back of my neck. She wore my girlshape, as was more and more her habit, leaving us tucked together like twins. We slept that way, sometimes, but only when my father was out of sight; experiments in natural sleep, we called it, unaided and unforced by magic.

I had come to love dreaming.

"I'm sorry," she whispered. "Miranda, if I could—if I wasn't bound—you know I'd help, you know*—"*

"Don't worry," I said, and shut my eyes. The darkness didn't scare me, when I chose it. "I have a plan."

Act III
Something of Her That Doth Fade

"HERE ARE THE rules of the votary's path," says Puck, arms swinging as we walk. The sun beats down on both our backs, though where a cap conceals my hair—now gleaming white, as verified by my reflection in a convenient rain-barrel—his head is bare. A glamour, he says, conceals his horns from all human sight save mine. Not that he'd find less welcome as a fairy— even the most fearful man knows better than to slight one—but Puck, it seems, of a piece with his mischief, savours anonymity. "Are you listening, Miran?"

It isn't quite a masculine name—or at least, it's no proper variant—but like my bound breasts and borrowed trousers, it serves to disguise the truth. And in any case, I find I rather like it.

"I'm listening," I say.

"Good. There are three rules—we're fond of threes, we fairies. Rule the first: all supplicants must reach the court by mortal means, though this does not preclude fairy guidance, as you see." He grins and gestures at himself. "Rule the second: if importuned by any fairy, spirit, god or ghost en route to the Court—and votaries, where anticipated, are often importuned, the better to judge their character—you must escape unaided, or else wait three full moons before reattempting your pilgrimage."

"Am I likely to be importuned, then?"

"I wouldn't think so," Puck says, blithely. And then, at my raised eyebrow, "Or, well. It's not *entirely* unthinkable, but as I'm not a member of Titania's court—and as I'm neither known for shepherding votaries nor expected, on this occasion, to bring anything other than my charming self—you should be safe. It's me who'll have to watch for harassment."

"And should your harassment not worry me, too? I'd hate to be deprived of my guide."

Puck laughs, warm and pealing. "Your concern is touching, but deeply unnecessary. Did Ariel not tell you, child? I'm a trickster, and though my enemies try as they might, it's tricky to trick a trickster with even the trickiest trickeries. And in any case, should anyone try to trick me"—his smile turns vulpine, sharper even than his teeth—"they must do so in the knowledge that I'll trick back."

"A boastful thing, aren't you?"

"Modesty is for saints, which I most certainly am not."

"Indeed? You shock me, sir!"

"Excellent! I do so love to be shocking. Which brings me, via roundabout means, to rule the third: that, should the Queen accept you—and there's no guarantee of that, whatever Ariel might have said—she will do so either by offering you a boon, or, more likely, by asking you for a service. And whatever she asks or offers, your refusal means your ejection from the Court. She will not consider you again."

A shiver runs through me. "What if she asks for something I'm unwilling to give? Can I not bargain with her?"

"Some have tried," Puck says, with a sidelong glance, "but seldom successfully. When boldly done, she respects the attempt, but values her will above a new servant's wishes."

"But could I still stay on, if she said no?"

"It depends on the circumstances. If she rejects your supplication outright, she may still let you remain as a human visitor. Your access to the court would be restricted, and you'd have no formal place, but it would be something. If you refuse her, though—then no, I cannot imagine she would do other than cast you out. It would be an insult, child, and as my current predicament attests, the fairy courts do not take insults lightly."

I bite my lip. I have a sudden, pointless urge to turn and look behind me, back to Naples and what I've left. The city is no longer visible, and yet I feel the tug of it behind my navel, grief and guilt and grime.

"You can't go back," Puck says—lightly, such that it ought to seem a question, and yet we both know he's not asking.

"Ariel cast a glamour," I say, forcing myself to stare at the road ahead. "They think I'm dead. They think"—I hesitate, stumble on the truth like an unexpected stone—"they think the miscarriage killed me."

Puck's silence is an alchemical thing, as though his very presence transmutes the air. Softly, he says, "I sometimes forget how young you humans are. How brief your lives, and how very perilous their various inceptions." He blinks, as though considering something, and when he looks at me again, his eyes are more alien than Ariel's ever are. "Should I be sorry for you? Or sorry with you? Or should I be something else?"

"Why should you be sorry, when I am not?"

The words, though mine, surprise me to a standstill. Puck halts, too, but doesn't speak.

"I'm not sorry." The words feel strange in my mouth, like moss. "I'm something, certainly. I grieve, though I don't quite know what for. But I'm not sorry. Does that make me monstrous, do you think?"

"I have met many monsters, child. You resemble none of them."

"It's just—I should." I hate my tears, the mess they make of me. "I should feel worse than this. About leaving. About what I've done."

"At whose insistence? Surely you don't *want* to feel worse?"

"No, but—"

"Is anyone demanding it of you? Am I? Is Ariel?"

"No, but my father, my lord husband—if they knew—"

"But they don't know," Puck says, cutting me off. "That's the whole point, is it not? Unless I miss my guess, it seems to me that, even had you stayed, they would have wanted you to feel other than you do, be other than you are. That being so, your departure hardly makes a difference: if they realised the trick, they'd require the same as if you'd never made it—which is *why* you made it, and why their ignorance frees you all. You see? It does no good to dwell." He pauses a moment, as though to grant me space enough to comprehend his logic, then thumbs the tears from my cheeks. The gesture is gentle, a shocking intimacy; and yet I smile at it. Puck grins back, then spreads his arms and shuffles an impatient jig. "There, now! Though grief has its place, I am, as you see, a merry Puck, and Illyria is not so near a march that we might dawdle. Come, come! Run, run!"

And off he shoots like Ariel's conjured sparrow, sprinting down the road.

I have not run since the island. *Ladies*, Ferdinand said, *and princesses especially, have no cause to run.* My father agreed.

I launch myself in pursuit of Puck. My laughter is my rebellion.

My FATHER SLEPT *when I slept, so Ariel said, in order that I not wake him. And when I slept—unnatural, still—it was because he made me.*

But what if I slept unaided? What if, when the time came for his rest, I slept already? Would he deepen the slumber? Or would he—lulled by his own sense of power—see no need to take that extra measure?

"How drowsy I feel!" I said, and lay down in the afternoon sun.

I closed my eyes.
I waited.
Slept.
And slept—
—and woke.

* * *

THE INN IS small: by no means does it resemble a palace, but next to an island's comforts, the straw ticking in my pallet is luxurious indeed.

Puck, however, does not share my sentiments.

"The ground was more comfortable," he mutters, wriggling against his own pallet. "Straw just pokes. And itches! I'd sooner nap on a sleeping crocodile."

"Ariel was a crocodile once. He made himself all gold and blue, and swam me down the river on our island."

"He?"

"He was he that day."

"Huh," says Puck. "Huh."

"What?"

"You just answered a question I didn't know was in need of answering."

"How so?"

"I have always thought," says Puck, "that mortals are natively predisposed to think of themselves—and therefore of every other living creature—as immutably male or female. I'm much older than you, remember, and I've never seen anything to make me doubt it. But you, Miran-Miranda"—a strange thrill goes through me at this double-naming, though I can't articulate why—"seem perfectly amenable to the truth of things. It gives me pause. And as you may intuit, I am seldom given to pausing."

My pulse feels abruptly loud. "Ariel raised me more than my father did. I never understood why he insisted on calling her only *him*, regardless of shape or preference. He tried to explain it once"—I swallow the memory, hot and sharp—"but I didn't understand."

"Indulge me," Puck says, but so gently as to belie insistence. "What was his thesis?"

"That most spirits, most fairies, were male, and only appeared otherwise as a means of tricking mortals into licentious perils, though he never quite explained why that was such a wretched fate, either."

"And how, pray, did he justify this conclusion?"

I clench my hands in the ticking. "That magic is powerful, and men are more inclined to power than women. More suited it, and capable in its wielding."

"Your father," Puck says, "is an ass."

I make an inelegant choking sound. "Puck!"

"You disagree? You think the appellation an insult to ass-kind?"

"*Puck*."

"If you're going to employ that tone of voice, you might as well use my long name, too. Like this: *Robin Goodfellow*." His mimicry is flawless; I snort against the pillow, pulling the blanket up over my head to hide my obscure embarrassment.

"I don't know why I'm laughing," I say, slightly muffled. "It isn't at all funny."

"Sometimes the gravest things must, of necessity, become the most comic. It's how we know they haven't destroyed us."

"My father," I say. I tug the blanket down again and blink at the ceiling. Everything is dimly shadowed. My stomach turns. "Must we discuss him at such an hour?"

"Not in the slightest," says Puck.

We fall to silence.

Sleep is a long time coming.

THE BOOK WAS old and heavy, the pages salt-warped into scalloped waves. I'd seen it before, of course—and carried it; dusted it; watched my father read from it—but never been permitted to sneak more than a glance at the contents. And yet, of all his precious tomes, I still knew it was the one.

I'd seen him use it often enough.

My father rumbled in his sleep—snoring, Ariel called it. Heart tripping triple-time, I carried the book outside, sitting crosslegged beneath the lamp I'd made with Ariel, thin branches woven into a ball, lined with pale, dry seaweed and filled with fireflies, hung from a branch beyond the cave. It glowed like a tiny jaundiced moon, just bright enough for the purpose. Human magic wasn't the same as fairy magic, I knew that: what Ariel did effortlessly, as an extension of her self and nature, took my father years of study, time and will and sacrifice to achieve a lesser outcome.

I opened the sorcerer's book, and began to read.

ILLYRIA IS FAR away by any means, but farthest of all by foot. Puck's pace, I suspect, is meant to go gently on me, but the gulf between fairy stamina and the mortal kind is evidently vast enough to remain unbreached regardless of his consideration. My body aches, but with a fierce sense of utility. A full year spent in Ferdinand's court without running, moving with no let and plenty of hindrance through narrow spaces, fettered by expectations and heavy skirts both, and now—

Now, I am returned to the world, and thence to myself. My muscles burn with pleasant use, a good ache in my arms and back when Puck consents to let me carry our provender—"Like a two-legged mule," I say to him, and pride myself on his laughter—and when I sleep, though our bed be grass, it is deep and dreamless.

And alone.

We talk, Puck and I, to pass the time, but safely—about the towns and hamlets we traverse, the woods and fields, the fickle rules of Fairyland; about the gentle mischief he makes with the people we encounter. Or mostly gentle, at least: our third night out from Naples, a sneering freeholder refuses us a bed in his barn, muttering lewd remarks about the nature of shiftless young men more fond of each other's company than of right behaviour.

My face flames at the indictment, and though Puck's response is more personable—he bids the man goodnight, then leads me away—he swiftly cloaks us both from sight, then spends a merry hour first persuading all the cats on the property to abandon it, then coaxes in a dozen odd families of mice, encouraging them to sleep in the selfsame barn whose shelter was denied us.

"He could starve," I say, as Puck, still chuckling to himself, makes camp beneath the vasty spread of an ancient, field-adjourning tree. "If the mice eat his crops—"

"He's a man alone," says Puck. "No living wife, his children grown and gone. Every mortal with a grain of sense knows better than to rudely refuse hospitality to travellers in fairy country—which, as any fool also knows, this is. I merely repaid his ill-wishing in kind."

"The consequences of your prank will long outlast the effects of his rudeness."

"Does he know that? For all he cared, we might have died of exposure or been set upon by brigands."

"But we're fine!"

Puck glares at me, the first true flash of anger I've seen from him. "*We* are, yes, because of what *I* am. Which is why my retribution is scaled to rebuke the worst possible outcome of his actions—because, as you rightly say, *he didn't know that*. And not only *didn't* he know, Miran, but he didn't *want* to know, in case it upset his precious mortal dignity." A sizzle of lighting licks between his horns, as though the ivory twists are a chemist's alembic. "I will never understand this bizarre fixation modern mortals have with sex. You weren't always like this!" He shakes out a blanket, fabric snapping sharply. "You *used* to have orgies!"

The noise I make is utterly inelegant. Puck jerks his head sharply, then seems to recollect my presence. He snorts softly, lips twitching. "Apologies," he says.

"Not at all. You make a, ah, compelling argument."

Puck laughs and sets the fire. We sit before it, backs to the broad trunk of the tree, and share the sliced ham, apple slices, bread and cheese we purchased that morning, as pleasant a supper as I've ever had.

"I've always learned quickly," I say, slow and soft, the words coming out of their own accord. Our small fire burns brightly, red-gold on black, the rest of the world a blurred silhouette beyond. "And on the island, my father made sure... that is, he tried to teach me manners, propriety. Feminine virtues." Puck chuckles at that, and I half return it. "I learned very well. But we had no cutlery." I gesture with my last heel of bread. "That was considered a grievous fault, at court; that I had no table manners. Such a strange thing to matter! And I had no fashion, either no sense of how hair or clothes should be styled, for whatever obedience I'd been taught to show, such things were the providence of women alone, and for all his knowledge, my father neither could nor would have enlightened me about them."

Puck tosses a piece of apple aloft and catches it in his mouth. Chews, swallows. Glances at me. "I had heard," he says, as though discussing nothing more personal than tomorrow's weather, "that Duke Prospero's daughter went willingly to her marriage."

I stare at the fire. "What is willingness without knowledge? Without true choice in the matter? All my life, my father had taught me one set of truths, and Ariel another. And on the island, inasmuch as I could, I cleaved to Ariel's wisdom, for it at least pertained to my personal circumstances, to my *self*, and not to some abstract world beyond all access. But then the ship came, and Ferdinand—"

I break off, stomach twisting as if to rid itself of supper. Puck waits me out, and when I speak again, my voice is barely louder than the crackling of our fire.

"Ferdinand was the perfect audience. I performed for him

that version of myself I'd been taught was owed to men, and he replied exactly as I'd been told he should, with courtesy and smiles and confessions of love. He married me even before we left the island, did you know that?"

"I did not."

"Well, he did. And I thought... I thought, after so much doubt and tension as to what I should be and how to live, after all I'd endured, it almost felt a relief to know what to expect. That if I behaved a certain way, the outcome would be predictable. That I could leave the island. That I could be safe." I bow my head, tears trickling down my cheeks. "But it wasn't that. *I* wasn't. And by the time I began to realise... I was more marooned at court than I'd ever been by the ocean."

"You would not be the first wife to feel so."

"You'll forgive me if I think that makes it worse, not better." I try to smile, though even in the attempt, I know it for a failure. "He would... as a husband, he would *take*, and I was obliged to, to—lord, I want to say *endure*, but can it be that if sometimes I found pleasure, too?"

"One meal is not all meals," says Puck, so levelly as to betray that he's keeping his voice in check. "That a dish please you one night does not prevent poor appetite or preparation—or, dare I say it, both—from diminishing its appeal the next."

I nod, though scantly. Later, I know, I'll linger over Puck's absolution, but right now, any greater acknowledgement will crack me open. "I think—" I say instead, and stop, the words too big for my mouth. "I often felt, with Ferdinand—that is, there were times, and maybe if I'd not been raised with Ariel, the thought would never have occurred, but as it did—I often felt that such, such pleasure as I found in him, in his body, was as much envy as desire."

I hug my knees and brace for a condemnation that does not come. Puck looks surprised, but not hostile, and into this flushing silence, the truth flows out of me like water.

"I am—I know I am new to desire, and all my husband taught me was that wanting should be his province alone, with granting those wants my chore. Certainly, I envied him the decision, but it was not—is not—the whole of it. On the island, there was hardly need to think of myself as *girl* or *woman*, except inasmuch as my father told me to, for I had no real source of comparison. Caliban was inhuman, my father defined himself as a sorcerer more than as a mere man, and Ariel could be anything she pleased. But then there was Ferdinand, and for his sake—and for my ease—I took the role I'd been told to take, but though I tried to obey, it was... I wish I could say it was just the skirts, that I chafed only at the expectation of manners, but it wasn't that, Puck, it was language, the words, the *feel* of them. I never knew words could be so sharp, until the wrong ones cut me. But they weren't *always* wrong, that's the worst of it; some days I revelled in being called *lady*, but then the day would pass, the sun would rise and fall again, and the same name felt like a collar, bringing me to heel; or else a corset, squeezing me into wrongish shapes for the adoration of strangers.

"But are they wrong? I still don't know. But, oh, I wish—*I wish*—I could change as Ariel does, that flicker-flash between girl and man; I wish my form could be all the forms my heart desires! The moon has phases, does it not? We call it *full* and *half* and *harvest*, but through its wax and wane, it remains the moon, and we love it no less—must I be any different? I must not, for I am not. My heart is a moon, and some days I am full and bright within myself, a shape that fits my name, and then I fade, and mirrors show only a half-light shared with a silhouette, an absence my form reflects; and then, in the dark, I am dark altogether, until I regrow again. Why should such a thing be any more difficult to grasp than the fact that some think me dead, and yet I live? The contradiction is only in their perception of what I am; and though killing me would perhaps solve it to their satisfaction, it would not undo the truth of me."

I sit back, trembling with an exhilaration near to relief. I look at Puck, and his smile is the softest part of him I've yet seen.

"Miran-Miranda, I would not undo the truth of you for a thousand years of life, and anyone who would is an utter fool."

I am crying still, but as I wipe my eyes, I find their salt has no sting. I smile at Puck, and with a gentle shrug, he flicks his gaze to the fire, long legs stretching as he shifts.

"You're quite right, of course. Forms and hearts and names—we build ourselves with words, but a tool is not the same as the substance it shapes; and if the substance changes, then why not the tool?" He flashes an insouciant grin. "Consider, for instance, my northern cousin, Loki, who once gave birth as a dapple grey mare. He is what he is, and if that be many things instead of one, then who are we to say otherwise? Fairy, god or mortal, I see no reason why anyone should define themselves by a single flesh alone, when such seemings are always subject to alteration. As well to say a grown man is unnatural for cultivating the beard he lacked at birth as to call you anything ruder than your name for desiring what you weren't born with. Why should one change be called natural, and the other not? Crowns and shoes don't grow on trees, and yet we alter ourselves with the wearing of them. Mortals! Such nonsensical creatures." He makes a gesture half-fond, half-disgusted, and tips me an apologetic wink. "Present company excepted, of course."

"Of course," I say, and something in me opens like a once-clenched hand, the better to grasp new things.

KNOWING WHAT I needed and obtaining it were two different things, and only through Ariel's agency was I able to succeed. He spoke to the wind and summoned, on a distant breeze, the feathers I needed—eagle, crow and dove—and stole the crucial lock of hair from Prospero's sleeping head. When my own hand faltered, Ariel spilled my blood in the carved stone bowl, sparked fire to burn the feathers, hair and herbs, then brought me the purest, whitest sand from the far side of the island.

It was Ariel who became a bolt of storm-lightning, arcing down into the ash and sand to fuse it into jagged glass, and Ariel who helped me shape and smooth a single flat piece of it, small enough to fit within my palm.

But when the moment came, it was I—and I alone—who wielded what we'd wrought.

Act IV
Seachanged

I WAKE TO the tug of cold, thin fingers against my arm. For an awful second, I'm paralysed; and then I scream and lurch upright, and someone swears, and someone shouts—and then the world turns gold and purple, black and silver, stars and embers whirling into a warp of air as someone tugs me down and sideways, up and through. The world's veil lifts like a theatre curtain, passing me from *here* to *there*, and when I blink the shock from my eyes, I find I'm no longer in the mortal realm.

I stand within the fairy roads, and stare at the ones who took me.

There are two of them, both fairies, seemingly male and female. One is mottle-skinned, whites and browns in a calico patchwork, her kinky black-and-silver hair pulled into a multitude of tight, short knots. Her curves are wrapped in a flowing dress that leaves one shoulder bare, a gold torc circling her upper arm. The other is tall and lean and olive-skinned, his straight hair bound in thin, brown braids that hang to his middle back. His tunic is mustard-yellow over bird-brown hose, and both their feet, like mine, are bare.

A recent memory tickles me, and something clicks into place. I lift my chin and laugh at them. "You are Moth," I say, "and Mustardseed."

"Clever child," says Moth, in a withering tone that says she thinks the opposite. "I'd ask who you are, but so long as the Goodfellow comes for you, it hardly matters."

The fairy roads take many forms. This one is earthed in bone-white soil, scattered with red stones. The sky is lilac, as pale as an iris-heart and devoid of sun, moon, stars. Beyond the white road, the red stones cover the ground completely, so that it appears as a jut of white bone against a field of blood. It is not a welcoming place, and the hairs on my neck stand up in animal fright.

"You want him to violate the terms of his penitence," I say—slowly, so as to be sure. "He's meant to reach the court by mortal roads alone, but if he comes for me, he breaks his oath."

"Precisely," says Mustardseed. He has an unctuous voice, and a narrow, thin-lipped smile. "So whatever you are to him—doxy, dupe or dependent—just be a good mortal and wait. You can't escape the roads alone, and believe me when I say you'd be foolish indeed to try."

I draw myself up and meet his gaze. "I am a votary travelling to pledge myself to Queen Titania. By bringing me here, you've meddled with my pilgrimage."

Moth scoffs. "The Goodfellow doesn't bring votaries to King Oberon, let alone Queen Titania. If you're going to lie, at least try to make it plausible!"

"Now sit," says Mustardseed, and only as he draws it do I notice his knife, a piece of antler carved to a wicked point. "Or you will, I think, regret it."

Once before, what feels an age ago, I walked a different fairy road with Ariel. My knowledge is woefully limited, but it's more than my captors think I have. I swallow, gaze fixed on Mustardseed's blade, and force myself to nod.

"I'll be no trouble," I say, and sit down on the soft, white soil, heart pounding as I think.

"OH, MIRANDA. WHY must you disobey me?"

My father's voice was calm, but no less furious for it. I stared him down, clutching my glass so tight, my palm was near to bleeding.

"*I would not need to disobey, if you did not yoke me so tightly.*" My voice trembled, raw with fear. "*What threat am I to you?*"

My father shook his head. "*Disobedience in a woman is a threat in itself. The world has a rightful way of ordering itself, Miranda. And when you act in counter to that, you leave me no choice but to intervene.*"

"*No choice? You have every choice! And what world, pray, do you speak of?*" I waved a shaking hand. "*This is all the world we have! Your manners have no use here, father; no purpose beyond denying that I might choose my own!*"

He sighed, disappointed. "*I wish I knew whence you came by these absurd notions. It would make your life, and mine, much simpler.*"

I could feel myself crying. "*You wish me simple, but I am not that. I am whole, a person—I have my own mind, and I wish, I wish—*"

"*Enough.*" He raised his staff, a crackle of magic in the air. "*You will obey, Miranda.*" And with his free hand, he sketched a rune in the naked air, a tracery of light. "*Forget today. Know peace. Be as you were—*"

The spell took flight, and as I screamed, I threw up my glass, light glancing along its edges.

The magic hit like a thunderclap. My arm went numb, and in the boiling flash of the spell's reflection, I had just enough space to see the shock on my father's face before the force of rebounding magic knocked him down, staff tumbling from his hand. I staggered forward, ears ringing. He twitched on the sand, his eyes rolled back in his head. The glass in my hand was cracked, but I didn't drop it, clinging all the harder as I went to my knees and pulled his head into my lap. He groaned, but his eyes still showed their whites, which meant I had time.

I put my lips to his ear, and spoke.

"*This is my spell for you: forget all spells of forgetting. Forget you ever took my memories; forget my disobedience; forget our feud and its implications." I choked, tears streaming down my cheeks, and forced myself to whisper the last of it. "Forget you ever desired me. Forget your shame, and mine. Forget."*

And then I stood and walked away, the glass clutched tight in my hand.

❧

"He's taking his time," Moth mutters, cutting a glance my way. "Either she means nothing to him, or he's planning a trick. I don't like it."

"Or else I really am a votary," I say, cutting in ahead of Mustardseed, "and Puck therefore trusts that I'm capable of rescuing myself."

"You're not," says Mustardseed, but there's a note of uncertainty in his voice that wasn't there before. "And even if you were—"

I tune him out and close my eyes, fingers sinking into that soft, impossible white soil, questing for a familiar edge. *Please be here,* I think. *Please. Please. Please.*

"I have to hide it, Ariel. The book said if he ever finds it, the spell will come undone."

"You could cast it into the ocean—"

"It might wash back up!" Panic clawed my throat at the prospect. I could scarcely believe what I'd done, such that even having succeeded, all I could think of was what my father would do to me if—no, when—he discovered it. "I can't keep it anywhere he might chance across it by accident. Nowhere on the island, and not in the sea. Somewhere it can't be summoned, can't be disturbed. Somewhere safe, or I never will be."

Ariel stared at out at the sunset. "There is a place," she said, softly. "Though reaching it will tax me. Being bound, I cannot go myself, but I think, if I try, I might yet open a door."

"Open a door? To where?"
"The fairy roads."

"MAKE HER BLEED," says Moth. "He's always had a weakness for mortals, always binds himself to them in some way or another. If you hurt her, he'll know, and then he'll have to come."

Three heartbeats pass before Mustardseed answers. Then: "All right. A simple cut." I hear, but do not see, his smile. "To start."

Here is the truth of the fairy roads: no matter how different they appear—no matter their tricks and changes—at base, they are all one road, a single path between *here* and *there*.

"You hold her, Moth. She'll likely try and bolt."

Please. Come back to me. I need you.

Arm-deep in the snowy soil, my fingers close on a shattered piece of glass.

Glass that was made of mortal earth and mortal blood, and which recalls its nature.

I think of my hair-that-was, the coppery colour now bound up in a gemlike ball as red as the stones on this stretch of road. I think of Puck, who put that gem—a piece of myself—in his tunic pocket, pulsing like a secondhand heart.

I grip my glass, and think of earth, and blood, and red, until the sharp edge cuts a line in my palm, a red seep into the ground.

Moth's hand tugs my cap away, revealing hair as white as chalk, as white as snow on a red-white road.

Home, I think wildly, as Moth grips my hair, *home, home, find Puck—*

"Grab her! Moth, what's she—"

"Gods, I don't know! I don't—"

I fall between worlds like a stone dropped into a chasm.

*　　*　　*

I BURIED MY glass in a field of lilies under a starstrewn sky. Ariel kept her door open for me all the while, and though I hurried, she still passed out when I came back, shaking and panting, reduced to little more than a kitten-shape. I pulled her into my arms and cradled her, crying into the soft white of her fur.

"Thank you. Thank you. Thank you."

Her rough tongue licked the tears from my cheeks, and for the first time in what felt like eternity, I laughed.

I FALL IN an unglamorous heap at Puck's feet. He yelps like a startled fox, stumbling back against our camping tree, then bursts into incredulous laughter, clasping his horns in his hands.

"By every star, I wasn't expecting *that!*"

"Nor me," I groan, rolling shakily to my knees. "Are they following?"

"Not if I have a say in things," Puck snaps, and having helped me up, he starts walking a widdershins circle around our campsite, sparks pouring out of his open palms as he chants beneath his breath. He claps his hands—cementing his wards, I assume—and a sharp thunder-scent fills the air, as if before a storm. It's only then, as Puck returns to me, that I notice the lightening sky, faint lines of peach and violet creeping along the horizon like the livid fever-streaks of an infected wound.

"How long was I gone?" I asked, for time runs differently in the fairy roads.

"Almost a full night," says Puck. He shoots me an appraising look. "How long was it for you?"

"A half-hour or so, I think."

"Only a half-hour!" He looks delighted, dark eyes lit with mischief. "And am I right in thinking that your escape has something to do with this?"

And he reaches into his tunic pocket and pulls out my shattered glass.

I gape at him, unable to comprehend the sight of it. Slowly, I lift my own clutched hand and stare at the contents.

I'm holding the gem that holds the colour of my hair, a faint rime of blood smeared across it.

"It does," I say, softly. "I—I buried that glass in the fairy roads some sixteen months ago, when I was still on the island. I never thought to see it again."

Without discussion or conscious thought, we seem to reach some physical accord. I hand him the gem, and he hands me the glass. Without a word, I bury it beneath the roots of the spreading tree, and then, together, we both sit down. I tuck my feet under a blanket, transferring just the barest patina of white soil in the process, and wait for Puck to speak.

"The thing about magic," my guide says, after a minute, "is that it leaves a residue, for those who care to look, and who know what to look for."

"Does it, now?"

"It does." He rests his wrists on his tented knees. "You, Miran-Miranda, stole your father's memories."

"I did."

"May I ask why?"

"Does it matter?"

"He never touched you," Ariel rumbled. The words were a breath against my ear, the two of us curled in the bower we'd built at the back of my memory-cave. Her form was that of the white-furred she-wolf, warm and comforting. "Not like that. Not more than the barest brush of skin or cloth, and then but rarely."

"But he watched me? Wanted me?" I squeeze my eyes shut, scarcely able to say it. "Touched himself?"

"He did."

"But he won't, now? Not again?"

"He won't."
"I'm truly safe?"
"You're safe, Miranda."

"No," SAYS PUCK. He smiles at me. Ahead of us, the sun comes up. "I don't suppose it does."

Act V
Rich and Strange

"Do you miss the fairy courts?" I asked Ariel, swinging my leg over the edge of a rainworn boulder.

He—it was he that day—considered the question carefully, chin resting thoughtfully on his knuckles.

"I miss the option of their distance," he said at last. "Which is to say, I miss being able to visit them, but only because I was able to leave again."

"That sounds a very complicated relationship."

"Most are," said Ariel, "when not confined to islands."

PUCK'S WARDS KEEP both Moth and Mustardseed at bay the rest of the way to Queen Titania's court—their strength, Puck says, is less than his, though I suspect their sudden disappearance has as much to do with the missive Puck sent to King Oberon as with any degree of respect or incompetence.

"You could at least humour my vanity," Puck huffs, when I point this out.

"I'll leave humour to the physicians," I quip back.

Puck stumbles over a rock.

Two days out from Illyria and the court, we're met on the road by a young, dark-haired man who stares pointedly at Puck's horns—or rather, at where his horns would be, if they weren't veiled from casual sight—and says, in put-upon tones, "It's very hard to recognise you without them, you know."

Puck grins his pointed, toothy grin. "And hello to you, too. I suppose you've been sent to keep an eye on me?"

"I've been sent," says the stranger, "to ask why you're taking a votary to Queen Titania instead of to our lord."

"Because I paid him to," I say. "And because, with all due respect to King Oberon, a dear friend of mine is in service to Queen Titania, and I have promised to meet her at the court, should I be granted the opportunity."

"Hm," says the man. He subjects me to a thoughtful sort of scrutiny, his brow all wrinkled up. He has a slim, straight nose, prominent eyes, and a stubborn set to his beardless chin. "I take it, then, that my recommendation as a votary of Oberon would do little to entice you?"

"I'm afraid so."

"In that case," he says, bowing to the pair of us, "I'll waste no more of your morning. Farewell, for now!" And he heads back the way we've come, vanishing around the nearest bend.

Puck clucks his tongue. "Well, that was interesting."

"Troubling?"

"I didn't say so. But potentially, yes. Master Will seldom shows up without purpose, and the purpose is usually Oberon's."

But though we keep an eye out for any further fairy meddling, none eventuates.

THE SHIP ROCKED *beneath me, calm on the open seas. I ought to have been asleep, but the novelty of seeing my island dwindle into the distance—of seeing a horizon unbounded by trees or mortal limitations—was yet to fade, and so I stood at the prow of the vessel, watching the moon drift by.*

"Miranda?"

"Ariel?"

My voice was little more than a whisper; sound carried on water, the sailors said, and as there were still some of their number on duty, I had no wish to draw undue attention to myself.

"The same." Ariel drifted in the air alongside the ship, wearing

my borrowed girlshape—but not me as I was in that moment, but me as a child, the way I'd been at five or six. She was translucent, glowing the same silver-blue as the ocean, her eyes both fond and sad.

"Are you well? I thought my father freed you."

"I am well. But we had no proper farewell, and I wanted—I came to make sure you are happy. That you want this escape, this path."

I smiled at her, my heart full of possibilities, the doubts so small, I scarce condescended to hear them. "I am happy, Ariel. Are you?"

Ariel's smile didn't waver. "I am, if you are," she said. "I—I wish you luck, Miranda. But if you ever need me, call, and I will come."

Before I could answer, she pressed a cool, brief kiss to my cheek, and vanished.

QUEEN TITANIA'S COURT is nothing like the court at Naples. Living vines seethe over sculpted marble, twisting to accommodate the whims of guests by sprouting trumpet-flowers full of nectar, knotting themselves into swings—whatever the seething crowd of fairies might desire. Everywhere is chaotic variety, wings and eyes and fur and feathers, animal and mortal guises; horns like Puck's and hair like mine are the least of such strange adornments.

"Now," Puck murmurs, leading me through to the audience chamber, "unless the Queen—or King, if he's here, and he may well be—addresses you directly, let me do the talking."

"What do you mean, King Oberon might be here?" I hiss. "You never said so earlier!"

"If I had, would you be any calmer now?"

My silence confirms the point; Puck grins in triumph. Rolling my eyes despite myself, I nod.

"Very well, then. Lead on."

The audience chamber is, I'm sure, a beautiful thing, but whatever its marvels, they are as nothing compared to the beauty of Queen Titania. Dressed in a gown of white feathers, her skin is the colour of burnished copper, glowing against the warmer brown of her wide, bright eyes and the gleaming, impossible gold of her hair. Her kinky curls are bound in braids which, even wrapped in silver wire and studded with gemstones, are long enough to brush her calves.

And beside her, light where she is dark, is a man who can only be King Oberon. Ebony horns curl back from his head; his hair is a long, black waterfall, straight and dark, strung through with tiny chimes and bright red threads. His skin is neither gold nor olive, but somewhere in between, his black eyes folded gently at the edges. He is beardless and bare-armed beneath a single black garment, belted at the waist with silver, living tattoos coiling up the muscles of his forearms.

They are beautiful, and powerful, and utterly imposing. I fight the urge to fall to my knees, and only through the borrowed courage of Puck and Ariel do I keep upright.

"Robin Goodfellow," Queen Titania says, and at her words, the room falls silent, all eyes turning to us. "Are the rumours true, then? Have you brought me a votary in penance for your impudence?"

"That depends, my lady," Puck says, and when he bows to her, I curtsey, heart beating hard against my ribs.

Titania raises an eloquent eyebrow. "On what?"

"On whether you consider abduction to the fairy roads by two of your number, Moth and Mustardseed, to disqualify her current bid to serve you."

Startled murmurs spread through the court. King Oberon's mouth twitches—a small, pleased smile, there and gone like a flash of summer lightning. For the first time, my stomach lurches at the thought that Puck might be playing some game I know not of; that, despite his pledge, he might yet be loyal to his lord ahead of our bargain. But as I cannot know for sure, I swallow my doubts and trust in Ariel's trust in him.

Titania's expression darkens. "*Mustardseed. Moth*," she says. "*Attend*." Her voice is resonant with summoning-power, and scarcely a heartbeat later, both fairies appear.

"My lady," they say in unison, bowing.

Titania scarcely notices. "Is this true?" she asks, voice deadly calm. "Did you take a votary of mine on the fairy roads?"

Moth's voice shakes like her namesake's wings. "We did, my lady. But only because we didn't know what she was! The Goodfellow has never brought you votaries before; we thought her his doxy, and only when she escaped without his aid did we consider that—"

"*Perhaps,*" Titania says, with icy rage, "you might have trusted your liege to punish the reprobate as agreed, instead of taking matters into your own hands!"

Both fairies fall to their knees. It is difficult not to feel some satisfaction at their predicament, though I do my best to keep it from showing.

"Here is my judgement on you: just as Puck walked to my court in penance for his transgressions, so shall you walk to King Oberon's in penance for yours. Leave now, take no fairy roads, and do not return until your term is filled. *Go!*" This last word she imbues with command, and with a startled, fearful cry, both Moth and Mustardseed vanish from the audience chamber, leaving a ripple of murmurs in their wake.

"Oh, joy," Oberon mutters, his voice rich with wry amusement. "I do *so* look forward to chastising them on your behalf."

Titania doesn't reply to this, but fixes her gaze on me.

"Step forward, votary."

Swallowing sharply, I comply—and, after a moment's hesitation, kneel. This seems to be the right decision: Titania smiles down on me and says, in a far gentler tone, "I am sorry for your mistreatment, child. What is your name?"

"Miranda, my lady, though sometimes Miran, and once the Princess of Naples."

At this, both monarchs look surprised. "You are Duke Prospero's daughter?" Oberon asks. "I heard she died of fever."

"Not dead, my lord, but fled." And then, to Queen Titania, "I wish to enter your service, my lady. If you'll have me."

"And are you so set on queenly service?" Oberon asks, before Titania can answer. His interjection is clearly shocking; the whole room goes quiet, and Oberon smiles as though he knew it would. "You seem to have an uncommonly amicable relationship with my Puck. I understand"—he says, with a slight incline of his head—"that you are, shall we say, *committed* to a certain member of this court, but surely that relationship need not preclude your service elsewhere?"

I freeze in place, a rabbit caught by candlelight.

"Really, Oberon?" Titania snaps. "You mean to poach a votary from under me?"

"I mean to offer the girl a choice. That's not against the rules, is it?"

"The letter of them, no, though it certainly defies their spirit."

Both monarchs look at me then, but though I burn to speak, to say I'll serve Titania only, Puck's warning tickles something in the back of my mind, and so I keep silent, staring abashedly at the floor.

One second of silence. Two. Three.

"A boon," says Oberon, suddenly. "Serve as my votary, child, and I'll grant you"—he pauses, as though musing on the perfect gift—"youth eternal. All your mortal days lived out as young as you are now, without age or infirmity."

"And if I may make a counter-offer?" Titania says, sweetly. "Serve *me*, Miran-Miranda, and I'll grant you"—her pause is dramatic, not contemplative—"a form that changes to suit your heart, as a fairy's might."

My head jerks up of its own accord, heat rushing to my

cheeks. I do not mean to speak, but her double-naming of me betrays her knowledge of what I am—and more, through her proffered boon, her acceptance of it. "Truly?" I whisper.

Titania smiles, generous in victory. "Truly."

"Then," I say. I take a breath, and turn to Oberon. "With all due respect and apologies, my lord, I must decline your offer, and accept my lady's, for though your boon is generous beyond my dreams, in hers, my dreams are manifest. I could no more refuse such an offer than walk to the moon."

For a thunderous moment, I fear that the King will be wroth with me. But then Oberon tips back his head and laughs, deep and heartily. "Oh, well played! Well played indeed! I concede both votary and match."

"Rise, then," Titania says to me, and I obey, my legs as shaky as a fawn's. "Let all bear witness!" she calls, her warm voice ringing through the room. "This votary, though importuned in travelling here, escaped by wit alone. Otherwise, she came to me afoot, by mortal means. I accept her as votary; I accept her into this court, and grant my promised boon. And in exchange"—she lifts my chin with a fingertip, the contact shivering me—"do you, Miran-Miranda, once-and-no-longer Princess of Naples, swear me fealty—to serve my interests, and those of my court, to the best of your ability?"

"I do."

"Do you swear to accept my judgement in return for my protection?"

"I do."

"Do you accept the witness of those gathered here, and understand the burden of these oaths?"

"I do."

"Then be my votary," she says, and kisses me lightly on the forehead. "So will it be."

A strange sensation fills me up, like deep-sea bubbles fizzing through my bones. Titania's boon takes hold of me to the sound of laughing, cheering fairies, light in my blood and music in my lungs, and as though I've grown an extra sense, I suddenly *know,* just as I know the movement of my fingers, that I can make my body change; that I might take whatever shape or sex I choose, and wear it without fear of contradiction.

"Oh," I say, and fall to my knees—in love, in shock, in gratitude. "Oh, my lady!"

"Thank me with service," Titania says, her tone both fond and wry. "For as my first request of you, I ask that you serve as my emissary in King Oberon's court, the better to foster unity between us. After all"—she glances sharply at Puck—"you do have fellows there."

"Of course, my lady," I say, still dazed. Titania winks at me, so brief and quick I might have imagined it; and then the interview is done, and Puck is leading me gently away from the dais, out to the brilliant, buttery sunshine pouring into an adjacent courtyard. Sensitive to my shock, he sits me on a marble bench and brings me one of the trumpet-flowers to drink from, holding its rosy petals to my lips. I drink, and the nectar goes down sweetly, tasting half like wine and half like summer.

"You planned that," I say, when the flower is empty. "Didn't you?"

Puck grins broadly, taking a seat beside me. "Oh, I had a hand in it, to be sure. But mostly, it was Ariel. She knew that, if she brought you here herself, there'd be no conflict to force the granting of a boon, but if *I* did it, my liege would likely make a bid for your loyalty, which means a boon, which means Titania would offer one, too—your lady being, I'll admit, uncommonly adept at discerning a heart's desire."

"Thank you," I whisper, and lean my head on his shoulder, momentarily overwhelmed. "And Ariel? Was she truly busy?"

"Oh, she had some chores to run, but I've no doubt she'll be here soon." He kisses my temple, strangely fond. "But until then, Miran-Miranda, how would you like a proper tour of

Fairyland? After all, as a fellow emissary, I can hardly leave you ignorant."

I laugh at that, and the sound bubbles out of me like joy. "Oh, brave new world! No—brave new *worlds!* For I never truly knew there was more than one, and now I plan to walk them all."

"A noble task," says Puck, and gently laces our fingers together. "Well, then. Shall we?"

"Yes," I tell him.

I don't look back.

THE COURSE OF TRUE LOVE

BY KATE HEARTFIELD

Ay me! For aught that I could ever read,
Could ever hear by tale or history,
The course of true love never did run smooth.
But either it was different in blood,
Or else misgraffèd in respect of years,
Or else it stood upon the choice of friends,
Or, if there were a sympathy in choice,
War, death, or sickness did lay siege to it.

A Midsummer Night's Dream, Act I, Scene i.

Act I

Illyria, 1600

POMONA KNEW THE satyr was there. The stunted pines blanketing the slope on one side of the road rustled although there was no wind. In the corner of her gaze, a shadow darted.

The tiresome old monster! Still she could not risk offending him. He was, for reasons no mortal could fathom, a friend of Duke Orsino's. If Silenus were to stop paying for her services, no doubt many others of Orsino's court would as well. Perhaps even the Duke himself. Passage to Milan would cost her every ducat she could earn in a month's hard labour up and down the Illyrian coast, comforting espaliered olive trees and whispering to withered grapevines.

Something flew past her ear: a pine cone. It rolled to rest on the dusty road. From an outcrop of juniper came a peal of laughter.

Pomona stopped walking and leaned on her staff.

"You are kind to flatter me, Silenus," she said. "By paying an old witch the same kind attention you pay, I have no doubt, to the maidens who come to your villa seeking your famous prophecies. But I know full well I am long past such courtesies."

Silenus emerged, pushing the poor juniper out of his way, his hooves kicking up dust.

"I am only making sure you get home safely," he said with a horrid grin. "Today you saved my vineyard from blight, and not for the first time. It would be most ungrateful for me to call an old woman to my vineyard and then let her walk home alone along the coast road to be molested by ruffians or sailors."

Fie. It was neither concern for her safety, nor lechery, that drove him, but sheer delight in her discomfort. He followed her, and threw things, and laughed, because he had nothing better to do, and because he loved to see a witch wince and hold her tongue.

"I have walked this road five hundred times if I have walked it once, and my house is not far. Silenus, I would not detain you."

His raucous laugh flushed a pair of doves from a lump of rock that broke through the scree and scrubland. She shuffled forward, staring straight ahead. She had endured far worse than a satyr's company.

"No road is safe for a woman in war," he said softly. "And the war is coming here, to Illyria's shore."

"Coming here?"

"Coming here, coming everywhere. This is no mere skirmish now, with the fairy king taking up arms."

"The fairy king! But Oberon has kept himself neutral."

"Until now he has, yes. He and Duke Orsino have had a falling out, and Oberon has declared himself for the Spanish. I have it from the Duke's own lips. So you see, my dear Pomona, perhaps you should not be so ungrateful for my company. I know more than you about the intrigues of the world."

Pompous old gossip! If Oberon were to join the war—God's teeth, it was hard to think with that satyr jumping about—no doubt Venice, his ally and long-time home of his fairy court, would as well. And then it would be all but impossible to travel overland to Italy, and sea travel would be even more costly.

She sighed.

"Oh I am unchivalrous, to give a woman such cause to worry," said Silenus. "Forget what I have said, and fill your mind with the simples to which it is accustomed."

How could she rid herself of this bur? Did he intend to stick to her all the way home? It would be another hour's walk, or close to it.

The Adriatic twinkled blue far to her left, and to her right the hills rose. She could hear the Pelting River's faint roar on her right, beyond the slope, running through its canyon to the sea. Some of its rapids were fords that she could happily cross, with a little help from the mosses and weeds. But Silenus, if he was anything like other satyrs she had known, would not be over-fond of water, would not want to try his hooves on the slick rocks.

She did not slow her stride but stepped up off the road and up onto the rocky slope, making for the lip of the river canyon.

Slienus scrambled up in front of her.

"You've left the road, madam," he said.

"Yes. This is the shortest way to my house."

"But you must cross the river somehow. There is a stone bridge ahead on this road, after it curves."

"It is a shallow river."

"A nasty river, fleet and full of rocks. And as you yourself have said, Pomona... I hesitate to mention it, but you yourself have said you are... not young."

He was one to talk, the grizzled goat.

She quickened her pace, as he clambered behind her.

At the low cliff edge, the canyon opened, greener than the dry coastland behind her. The river flowed prettily, far below.

Pomona whispered a quick command to her staff. It obediently shrunk down to a twig, which she stuffed into her pocket.

"I trust this cliffside will give you no trouble," she said. "As for me, I have no hoofs, and must take another path."

That vine would do nicely, curling around that spindly bush. A strong, sturdy young plant. She whispered singsong to it. It grew stouter and longer, wrapped itself around her body and lifted her up and over the edge, into the open air freshened by the mist from below. Silenus stared at her, then looked down at the river; stamped his foot, and was gone.

She laughed aloud but could barely hear it over the roar of the water. Flying must be something like this: to see so much of the world at a glance, to be bound by no bounds. But Hecate had never taught Pomona to fly. Pomona's besoms were for sweeping her hut, and once in a while, for young fools to overleap, hand in hand. No matter. This was better than flying. Safer. The vine held her tight and tethered her to the earth.

The vine set her down on a flat rock at the river's edge and unfurled itself. She thanked it and released it, and it slithered up the side of the cliff and was gone.

Rocks broke through the surface of the river. She carpeted three in moss and stepped lightly across. Here in the green world the headache she had from the glare of the coast road was softening.

The canyon wall on the far side was a little way back from the water's edge, as if the river in ancient times had been mightier here and carved a hollow it had since abandoned. A long, dry floor of rock led to a verdant cliffside, broken here and there by rocky ledges.

On the top of one such outcropping was a very curious sight: a neat, high stone wall, all carved along its top, with boughs of fruit trees peeking over.

What capricious god or nobleman would build a walled garden or orchard halfway up a cliffside in a river canyon? There were no pathways down the steep slope that she could see. The water met the cliffside on either side of the little hollow.

Pomona left damp footprints on the gray rock floor. No stairs were carved into the rock, no ladders or ropes. A few scraggly pines reached out of cracks. She coaxed one down to take her hand. It was a crotchety, stiff thing, unwilling. She had to sing three verses of an old, old song before it would stretch out and up, carrying her with it, until she could just see over the garden wall.

For it was indeed a garden, its white paths shining and lined with orange and lemon trees trimmed into globes. And there the pear tree she had seen. There beside it, a doughty gnarled apple.

A man sat reading at the far side of the garden, on a stone bench beneath an arbour of woodbine. The line of his shoulder and his bent head echoed the lines of the pale musk roses and pink eglantine on either side of his bower. Silver sparkled in his hair and beard. A man of her own age, perhaps, although it was hard to say at this distance. She coaxed the grumpy old pine a little taller and leaned out over the garden wall.

VERTUMNUS WAS MID-SENTENCE when Mab ran her chariot across the page. She stood there in her hazelnut shell, partially obscuring the word *flood*, folded her arms and stared.

His tiny warden was more powerful than she looked. Vertumnus had no wish to wake up blistered cap-a-pie as he had the morning after he'd trod on her hat, although he still said that the tip of a peasecod was not in any universal sense a hat but only obtained that quiddity *post res*, as Ibn Sina would have it—that is, its hatness was only a product of its being seen as a hat, and therefore to Vertumnus, ignorant of Mab's finery and seeing it only as a bit of peasecod, it was not a hat at all.

The argument had ended painfully for him.

He had better take the safer course and swallow his dignity. Who knew how long proud Titania would leave them locked up here together? Mab's tenure as his warden was no doubt some punishment for her, but Titania was, in her own mind, the only being allowed to hurt her servants. If Vertumnus hurt the tiny fairy, Titania would be so furious, she might leave him here for years, or in some less pleasant prison, while the world thought him dead.

He contented himself with grumbling: "If your atomies leave tracks on my beautiful Rumi, I warn you I'll sing loud and off-key for a week."

As if in response, the six skeletal horses, each no longer than a fingernail, stamped and snorted. He felt his eyes cross just trying to look at them.

"You ought to take more care, Vertumnus," said Mab in her tinny voice. "There is a human watching you right now, and if the human spreads word of you, Titania will be wroth."

A human, here? Vertumnus nearly slammed the book shut, out of shock rather than anger; he caught his hand in time. This could be his chance to get word to Oberon, to get himself free. What would Oberon do, given this chance? Or Thistle, or Puck? What would a true fairy do? He glanced around the garden but there was no human visible, and the thin fruit trees and shrubs were not large enough to hide anyone.

"I see no one," he said. "And even if a human were to get into the garden, they'd see me in the form of an old woman. Titania laid that enchantment on me herself. Do you doubt her magic?"

"I do not, you fool, how could I? Am I not the size I am because of her enchantments? I was once nearly as tall as you, Vertumnus, when I was Queen of Connacht. I had a horse that no one else could mount—"

"Yes, yes, but the point is, Mab, you are small now, and I am in the form of a woman, or should be to human eyes, if Titania's magic is still upon me."

"I do not doubt that if a human were in the garden, Titania's enchantment would cloud her knowledge," Mab said, preening. "But the human I mean is *over* the garden, and *that* circumstance I do not think Titania foresaw."

He brushed a branch of gold and ivory blossoms away from his face and looked higher. There! Over the wall nearest the river, a woman clung to a pine branch. He caught her gaze for a moment.

The branch snapped.

The woman lay face down on the garden path as Vertumnus pushed his book, still open, aside onto the bench and dashed toward her.

"Are you hurt?" he asked, kneeling at her side.

She groaned. She lifted a shock of bright henna'd hair, and

looked at him. Bits of white gravel clung to her cheek. She rolled back, leaned on one elbow, and frowned deeper.

"It knocked the breath out of me, that's all. And God save me, my wits, too? I did not see you in the garden. Where is the man?"

So the enchantment was intact. How it galled to be mistaken for someone else! In his earliest days as a changeling, when Titania was teaching him fairy powers, Vertumnus used to take the guise of an owl or peacock and then forget how to shuffle it off again, and he'd be forced to strut around Titania's bower until she recognized him and, laughing, waved her long white hand.

"There is no man," said Mab, hovering in the air beside his shoulder.

"You are a fairy!" the woman said, her eyes wide.

"Yes," said both Vertumnus and Mab at once.

He could tell her all, blurt that he was a fairy ambassador, disappeared from his post, held in this prison-garden of Titania's invention for the crime of insufficient devotion. But even if the woman could get free of the garden before Mab did something unspeakable to her, she could not reach Oberon with word of Vertumnus before Mab reached Titania with word of her.

Better to play his part before Mab, and watch for his chance.

"*She* is indeed a fairy," Vertumnus said, pointing at Mab, wondering how his voice sounded in this enchanted woman's ears. "I am merely an old woman, as you see; and this garden my home."

The woman was watching Mab flit in her chariot from blossom to blossom.

"This fairy is my companion, Mab," he added.

"*Queen* Mab," said the tiny termagant.

"Queen!" said the woman. "If Titania is queen of the fairy court, then what is your domain?"

"Surely you have heard—" Mab started.

"Oh, she is bounded in a nutshell, and counts herself the queen of infinite space!" said Vertumnus. Once Mab got started, there was no stopping her. "The question is, who are you and how did you come to be here?"

The woman took up her battered straw hat where it had fallen on the ground, punched it into shape and fit it onto her head. He gave his hand to the woman and she pulled herself to her feet.

She was small, and of an age to be calling her grandchildren down from trees, not climbing them herself.

"My name is Pomona, and I plead curiosity. I was on my way home by a... shortcut, when I saw this place and wondered at it. It is a strange spot for a garden. I saw—I could swear I saw a man, sitting on that bench, reading. Reading that book that lies there now."

She strode down the path toward the bench.

She'd seen him! Happy accident. Now for her to take that suspicion, and her description of him, out into the world, where it might find Oberon's ear. But Mab must be convinced to let her go, convinced she posed no threat, and so Vertumnus needed to stoke Pomona's suspicions while seeming to allay them. An easy matter, no doubt, for a born diplomat.

If only Vertumnus were one.

Pomona was circling the bench, looking behind the rose bushes as if she'd find a man there. How did Vertumnus appear to her? What gown or kirtle did the 'old woman' wear? Titania's enchantment did not change his form, but only his appearance to a mortal; he could not even seek a mirror to tell whether his face bore its lines well as a woman, or how he dressed his hair.

Pomona picked up the book. His book.

"Such a beautiful cover. I have never seen its like."

She opened it.

"'But love unexplained is clearer,'" she read aloud in the Persian, as if to herself. "My ghost reads Rumi."

She read Persian! Who was this curiosity? Could she be some new trap of Titania's making? She seemed, all in all, very unlikely.

Mab flitted through the air, her team of atomies like a swarm of midges. She circled Pomona's head, and teased, "Did Cupid's arrow knock you from that tree? I regret to say you have fallen into a phantasmagorical sort of love, madam. There is no husband for you here."

Pomona coloured. "I know you fairies like to trick us, to show us things that are not and to hide the things that are. I saw a man. Whether he was real or counterfeit I cannot say, but I did see him here."

"And so if you had seen this man, what of it?" squeaked Mab. "Why seek him with such ferocity? Whenever you think you glimpse a man, you charge toward the place he was last sighted and seek him behind any bush or tree? I advise you as a woman of some years myself: your fond chase will only make your quarry despise you more. Chase cattle, not men. You are, by your looks, not wealthy enough to atone for your wrinkles in the eyes of any man worth the hunting."

The woman set her lips together but said nothing. If she were a trap, sent here by Titania, she must have no awareness of it— or else she could play a part better than any mummer. She had wandered into this garden only to be taunted, to be called ugly and foolish by a bitter old gad-fly.

By Jove, he would *prove* the little harridan wrong if he were wearing his own appearance.

"You rere-mouse," he scoffed to Mab. "You speak of love as you would speak of farthest India, knowing nothing of either."

In response, she flew at him, her ghastly team stamping toward his nose. Without thinking, he caught her between his cupped palms for just a moment, but it was long enough for Mab to work her magic on him. He screamed as pain spread from his feet upwards, all over his skin, and in his mind flashed a strange vision, so that for a moment he thought his prison was not a beautiful garden but a dank stone cell, smelling not of blossoms but of mould.

He opened his hands and Mab flew away, and the sunlight returned.

Pomona put the book down on the bench and a hand on her hip. "Do not trouble the fairy, madam. She speaks the truth. I know full well I am no beauty. I do not seek a husband, here or anywhere. Show me the way out, then, I will trouble you no more. Where is the gate? I see none."

Vertumnus' gaze fell on his beloved Rumi. The book was his—his name was written on its first leaf, in the inscription from Oberon who'd given him the book. In the early days, when Oberon was still not sure of his loyalty.

Surely, all Illyria must be buzzing with speculation about his disappearance. Surely, if this Pomona saw the words *Given to Vertumnus to delight those hours when Oberon needs him not*, she would put the puzzle together? But she must come to that knowledge privily, outside the garden. Would she have the wit to get a message to Oberon? She must; a woman who read Rumi—in Persian!—would need little coaxing or coaching, once the facts were before her.

He stepped closer to her. This would be a delicate affair; he must seem to have some reason to give her the book. Let Mab think him enamoured of the woman, or at least pretending to it out of chivalry after Mab's cruel gibing.

"The book is mine," he said, picking it up and then turning to face Pomona. He took her arm and led her down the white path, knowing Mab hovered behind his shoulder. "I think perhaps you saw me, reading it, and some trick of the light or the gods fooled your vision. I am sorry to have disappointed you, and sorry to have subjected you to the little fairy's scorn. I will not keep you from your road any longer, for the day is growing old. But from one old woman to another, let me lend you this copy of Rumi, since it delights you so."

Pomona shook her head. "When it comes to books, I am neither a borrower nor a lender, by long practice."

"And a wise practice it is, but this would be a great favour to me, for if you take it, I know you will return it, and therefore I know I will see you again. Therefore you are not borrowing anything but agreeing to take my book as a kind of surety for friendship yet to come."

"You argue by the book," she said with a laugh. She took it from him, opened it idly.

"No, no, do not read it now," he urged, putting his hands over hers to close it gently. "The day is waning."

They stood, his hands over hers, over the closed book. Her hands were warm and rough, with dirt bordering each fingernail.

"The day is waning indeed, and you must also be going to your home," she whispered, glancing about.

"I am a kind of lazy anchorite," he said, loudly, merrily. "I do not leave my garden. I have forsworn the affairs of men but not all company, not the best sort of company. I would like you to read the book and bring it back, but make it soon. Oh, I know you have read Rumi before—but this book has much front matter of interest, and illustrations like nothing you have seen. Read it quickly but read it thoroughly, and return to me."

She took the book from his hands and looked up into his face. What did she see there? Could she read the truth in his eyes?

Pomona turned from him to face the unbroken garden wall. Titania's wall, carved out of what looked to be a single expanse of feldspar, fine-grained, twinkling a little in direct light. Comfortable, warm, friendly stone, save where a thick vein sparkled like milky ice.

Along the top, Titania's wand had carved skulls, so close together they almost touched. Human-sized. Waxy, dark-green vines wound through every orifice, thrusting out the eye sockets, curling into nose cavities, bursting through broken-tooth grins.

A reminder to Vertumnus that this wall would burn him if he touched it.

"I cannot help you over the wall," he said. "But perhaps, I might help you find a stronger branch in that tree by which you entered."

Pomona shook her head.

"No need," she said.

She walked to a mallow plant that climbed the wall, and plucked the biggest flower. She looked back at him over her shoulder, and smiled, and put the purple flower to her lips. It began to spin, and at first he thought she spun it in her fingers, but then he saw it was some kind of magic—and yet she was a mortal, not a fairy. Witchcraft, then. The petals stretched as they spun, until the flower was as big as a parasol, and Pomona turned from him again and lifted it over her head.

She stepped up on the broad dark leaves of the mallow that strained like a living thing to hold her weight, until she reached the level of the top of the wall with its grinning skulls. Without stinting or looking back, she leaped.

Vertumnus ran to the wall and leaned against it without thinking, then pulled back with a yelp as smoke rose from his burning hands. On the strand below, Pomona was landing gently on her feet, her flower-parasol shrinking and folding.

Who was this woman, and what her history?

Oh, look back, look back, to see him as he was!

Mab gibbered in his ear. "What a lovely pair of old women you'll make in your dreams tonight!"

He shook his head like a dog with fleas, and watched Pomona cross the river. She never once looked back to see him at the wall, watching her.

He would wait—how long?—he had no choice but to wait, and to hope that tonight as he dreamed whatever dreams Mab chose to plague him with, Pomona would read the book, and start from the very first page.

Act II

POMONA REACHED HER house just after sundown. Friar Lawrence was hanging about the threshold, wringing his hands.

"I'm all right, dear heart," she said, laughing. "I took a shorter way."

"Too swift arrives as tardy as too slow," he mumbled, running his hand through his overgrown tonsure. "I have need of a mandrake. One of the Duke's men, a certain William, is troubled with memories."

"Well, I have one growing in a pot of agate stones. It isn't full-grown yet, but let me see if I can coax it along. They're stubborn plants, though, and it may take an hour. Come inside, and you can have a cup of wine while you wait. You look as though you could use it."

Pomona whispered to the little mandrake plant, which groaned but set about growing. While the friar busied himself with cups and bottle, she went to her trunk to put away the old woman's book.

Old woman, indeed. She had seen a man, and then she had seen a woman. She had seen the man while she was spying, unseen. She had seen the woman only after she, Pomona, had made her presence known.

She would bet a ducat they were one and the same. If the woman had been a fairy or a powerful witch, and had changed her looks when Pomona fell—why? Was the little Mab right? Did the man think Pomona was pursuing him, and scorn her glances so much he hid himself in a disguise? Bah. What did it matter? It did not—and yet she was curious.

"I have heard," she called to the friar while she opened her trunk padlock, "that there is an ointment that, when touched upon the lids of the eye, shows the wearer the forms of fairies and other sights that would be hidden."

"Oh, if such an ointment exists it would be too perilous to use," said the friar, coming to the back of Pomona's little house with two wooden cups in his hands. "To see the true nature of any of God's creatures, mortal or fairy, is more than we are made for."

The dear old coward. She knew a little of his history, of the reasons he had left Verona and taken up residence as a kind of country apothecary in the quietest part of Illyria. What would he say if she asked him to make her a love-potion? To distill the juice of love-in-idleness, so she could drip it on the lids of—no. She was long past such folly. Lovers she had, but never love. It was as she wished it. When she admired beauty of form or of mind, it was at a remove.

Pomona shook her head to banish her thoughts, and lifted the lid of her trunk. There were all her treatises on plant-lore: battered old Theophrastus, and her crumbling *Vrksayurveda*, and the *Kitab al-Nurat*. She pulled them out, one by one, until she came to the bottom and her most precious book, her gramarye in its plain goat-skin cover.

The book written not in any language known to man or woman, but in the language of plants as near as it could be written: in diagrams and ciphers, in pictures of curling vines and cavorting ensorcelled figures, in signs and stories of all the magics that she and Sycorax had taught themselves in secret. She would keep her promise to long-dead Sycorax; she would find the boy Caliban, and give him the book, and bequeath his mother's knowledge to him. Soon, soon. The moment Pomona scraped together the ducats.

She put the borrowed Rumi on top of the gramarye. There let it lie in her trunk, until she had reason to be passing by that strange garden again.

The whole encounter seemed like a dream; and yet, there was the book. Into the trunk with it. On top went the treatises, one by one. She closed the lid of the trunk. Yes, there let it lie. Let it not distract her thoughts. She had promises to keep, and no time for fancies.

"Did Silenus pay you with a book?" said Friar Lawrence behind her, making her jump.

She stood and took one of the cups of wine from him. The friar knew about her gramarye; it was he who had told her about the drunkard of Milan who claimed to be Caliban, the son of the witch Sycorax.

"No, the satyr is not a bookish sort. I borrowed it, on my way. Tell me, good friar, how you found Orsino's court. Silenus tells me that Orsino is no longer content with sending ships to the war, but would bring it right to our shores by goading Oberon. I cannot believe it."

"Oh, it is so," sighed the friar. "Orsino might be more patient, were it not that Viola urges him on. She loves him so violently that she takes offence on behalf of his honour when Oberon suggests that Orsino has done away with the fairy ambassador."

"Fairy ambassador?"

"Have you not heard? Oberon's ambassador, a fairy named Vertumnus, has gone missing."

"Missing?"

"Dead, or so Oberon assumes. The ambassador arrived here safely enough from Venice, and sent his first dispatch, and then that was the last anyone has seen or heard of him. Oberon blames Duke Orsino, calls him murderer."

"What cause could the Duke have for killing the fairy king's ambassador?"

"All Oberon knows is he sent Vertumnus to Illyria and now Vertumnus is gone. And Viola suspects the hand of Don Pedro, goading Oberon into the fray. Orsino, bless him, is not yet sure. He has the look of a man being torn asunder by his advisers, as a piece of meat is torn apart by dogs. When I was there, I heard him cry out that any citizen of Illyria in possession of knowledge of the whereabouts of Vertumnus, who kept that knowledge from Orsino for even so much as a day, would hang."

Pomona shook her head. Orsino was a good man, but too easily swayed.

"Fortunate I am to have no business at his court for the time being."

"A storm is brewing and it must break before it passes. Orsino and Oberon, once so noble in their respect for one another, once so gentle in their courtesies, have each become so enraged they spit when they speak of each other. And yet I think neither of them knows what truly happened to Vertumnus. Perhaps he is playing some fairy trick of his own. It seems to me that if a fairy wished to hide himself, he would have no trouble in finding some out of the way spot, or some disguise."

Hiding! Some out of the way spot! A coldness washed over her skin. She set her cup of wine down. Her hand shook.

"What is it, my child? What makes you go so pale?"

"Oh, father, have you an ointment to show my eyes the plain truth before them? I have seen a strange sight today, friar. I fear it must be connected to this business."

"This business of the missing ambassador? Tell me!"

"The book I brought. I had it from a stranger, who insisted that I borrow it. A woman who lives in a garden on a rocky outcrop in a river canyon, away from all the world. I happened upon it on my way home."

"In the Pelting River? 'Twas strange, 'twas passing strange."

"As I said."

"Here," said the friar, putting his wine down on the one bare spot on Pomona's deal table all bestrewn with wax tablets, tally sticks and cuttings in little clay pots. "May I see this book?"

"Oh, it is mere poetry," Pomona said, and opened the trunk again, pulling out the treatises again until she reached the heavy

Rumi, its cover all whorled in gold and brindled in silver. Friar Lawrence wiped his hands on his habit and flipped it open.

"Here's the title, but I can't read it. What language is this? Ah, but here's an inscription in Venetian, in a rounded hand. 'Given to Vertumnus to delight those hours when Oberon needs him not.' Holy Saint Francis!"

"Let me see, friar," said Pomona, and looked over his shoulder. "Does it truly say 'Vertumnus'?"

"It does. Perhaps the woman who gave you this book got it in turn from him."

"Perhaps," said Pomona, taking the book back and running her fingertips over the page where the inscription lay in faint violet ink. "But I think the tale is more tangled yet. I could see no easy way into the garden, so I went up in a tree over the garden wall, and there all concealed I looked in and saw a man."

"A man? What sort of man?"

The image of him was still bright in her mind's eye.

"A gentleman, reading a book. But when I fell into the garden, the man had gone. In his place there was a woman, and a small fairy, like a pixie. The woman, I thought, bore some resemblance to the man. Her skin was the same colour, her hair the same curling brown streaked with white—here, at the temple. Some fairies, I have heard, can change their shapes, or make others appear to have changed theirs. But the question is, if this woman was in fact the ambassador Vertumnus, was he hiding, or being hid?"

"Whatever the truth of it, you must tell Orsino, and tonight. You can end this feud between the two courts. You can sow peace! Take my donkey and ride at dawn and take the message to his court. I will join you there as soon as I have mixed my potion for this William."

"And what of Vertumnus, in the meantime?"

"What of him? He gave you this book; he must have intended

for you to learn his name. Therefore, reason suggests, he is captive. And if he is captive there, let him remain so, until Orsino can get at the truth of the affair."

"Perhaps my coming will have startled his watchers, and when Orsino arrives at the garden there will be no fairy within—or no garden at all, if fairy edifices are as insubstantial as stories say. No, let me go back to the garden and make this fairy, be he man or woman, come with me to Orsino."

"You mean to capture a fairy, all on your own?"

"You could come with me."

"Oh, but I cannot delay my commission from Orsino to bring a potion for his servant. I promised to return in no more than two days' time, and it will take me a day to make the potion."

The old man had not a drop of courage in him.

She put a hand on his shoulder. "Go, then, take the mandrake and mix your medicines. I ask only that if you arrive at the duke's palace before I do, that you say nothing of this matter to Orsino."

He shook his head.

"And risk my neck, if he finds I have kept this knowledge from him?"

"We'll risk both our necks if we are wrong in our guess, or if the garden has vanished, and we make Orsino look a fool through false hope. Wait and watch for me. If this fairy is Vertumnus, I'll bring him to Orsino, and by Heaven I'll see his true face again. I knew I had not lost my wits!"

POMONA BEGAN WALKING before Lauds and arrived at the garden wall just as the sun was peeking over the canyon wall. The garden was still there. She had almost talked herself into believing it a dream.

The main trouble was Mab. If Vertumnus, a fairy himself, was an unwilling captive, the pixie must be powerful indeed.

Pomona had long ago made her peace with being a mere wyrtwitch, but a little battle magic would serve her well now, if only Hecate had seen fit to teach it to her. Plants had their uses, and there was always poison. But it surpassed her skill to guess the strength that would incapacitate Mab without killing her. And how to induce the fairy to take the poison in the first place? In the ear, sleeping? In her food, awake?

Pomona would prefer not to damn her soul if she could help it.

There was one spell Pomona could cast that might hold Mab long enough to get Vertumnus away and safe. It was never intended to be a weapon, never intended to do any violence at all. She and Sycorax had invented the dryad-spell together. They had dreamed of transforming themselves into lithe willows or strong oaks and bestriding their narrow corner of Algiers like Colossi, of so impressing their teacher Hecate that she would be bound to teach them the higher magics of flight, illusion and prophecy.

But Sycorax and Pomona had been young, brash and unready. They had tried to transform a cat and only succeeded in trapping the poor thing in a kind of half-existence, part cat and part tree. Its yowling face emerged from the trunk, and one paw scratched from behind the bark. Faced with the prospect of killing the thing or admitting their foolishness to Hecate, they chose the latter, and the great witch freed the poor creature and gave the girls the edge of her tongue.

It was then, perhaps, that the young Sycorax's attention to her magical studies began to wane. She was a few years older than Pomona, and began to speak of a lover, swearing Pomona to secrecy. They never had the chance to try the dryad-spell again before Sycorax fell pregnant. She insisted she would bear the child, and Hecate banished her to the island where she died.

In all the years since, Pomona had never dared try the spell. She would not succeed in making a dryad if she tried it today.

She was only a wyrtwitch, good for soothing a diseased vine or growing simples. She had settled into unremarkable haghood with some relief and years of long practice.

But she did not need the spell to succeed. She needed it to fail in the way it had before, to trap Mab for long enough to let Vertumnus go free, if he were truly captive. If Vertumnus were truly a fairy, and if his powers were only temporarily diminished, surely he could free Mab later if he chose, or send Oberon to do it. If it came to the worst, Pomona would ask Hecate for help just as she and Sycorax once had, although the very thought made her shudder.

If she was going to do it, best to do it quickly. She would lose the advantage of surprise with every moment she spent, revealed at the garden wall, searching for the tiny Mab.

Willows drooped at the edge of the canyon floor. There: a leaf, with a pale green canker-worm clinging to its shadow. Canker-worms were the only animals she could speak with, and only then with difficulty. They thought they were plants. She plucked the leaf and whispered to the worm, then blew the leaf up onto the air, blowing through her cupped hands until the leaf went up and over the garden wall.

The sky grew lighter while Pomona paced. At last, the leaf returned, the canker clinging this time to the top, terrified.

"Well?" Pomona whispered, catching the leaf in her hands. "Did you see the fairy? Not much bigger than you?"

Worms were poor spies. The thing could not speak but nodded, or shook its head, as Pomona asked question after question. It was a relief to both of them when at last Pomona determined that Mab was dozing in a lady's-slipper near the close edge of the garden. Pomona did not have the strength to ask about Vertumnus.

She pulled a little box-wood cutting out of her satchel and warmed it between her hands, a sturdy little twist of brown and green. It would bear her weight. Pomona thrust one end into a little wash of silt on the rocky shore, and sang to the plant under her breath, an old song.

Up and out the box-hedge grew, under Pomona's hands and words, until it formed a green stair rising to the edge of the garden wall. Pomona stopped her song and stilled her hands, and caught up her courage.

Seventeen soft steps up the boxwood stair, and she was crouching, peering through the gaps between the stone skulls that bounded Vertumnus' garden. There he was! Her disappearing man. Lying on the same bench where he had been reading. One wonderful arm flung over his face. And no sign of the woman.

And there was the lady-slipper. Pomona squinted and could just see Mab sleeping within, the flower like a blanket. A violet monkshood sleeping cap fluttered on her head with every snore.

Sycorax had composed the tune of their transformation spell. Pomona had spent many years trying to forget it, and finding all the same that it would circle in her mind when she was washing clothing or planting seeds. Sometimes she woke with it bellowing in her mind, as if she had been creating armies of dryads in her nightmares.

But today she had to think, for a long moment, before it came to her. And even then, the melody was a little her own, not quite the one written on the shores of Algiers by the long-dead witch. There was not so much menace in it, and a little more richness. But then she was older than Sycorax had been, and less angry.

From within the lady-slipper, a narrow shoot of barren pine grew, and then three pale green branches shrugged out of it, and held within the bark was the shape of a small, pinched face, screaming.

Pomona scrambled over the stone skulls and ran to the bench. She was right, she was right! There on the bench lay the woman. They were one and the same, the woman and the man, depending only on whether Pomona was inside the garden or outside it. And soon they would both be outside.

The shoulder beneath her touch felt as it looked: a woman's.

"Come, wake up," she hissed. "I have Mab trapped for now, but I can't say how long it will hold."

The woman blinked awake.

"You read the inscription," she said.

"We can discuss it," Pomona said. "Or we can get out of the garden."

"Are you alone?" the woman murmured, rising to her feet and throwing one end of her long, golden robe over one shoulder. "I had hoped you would send Oberon. How did you—"

"No time for questions. And no Oberon. You will have to make do with me. Come now, over the wall, before we are caught."

It would have been faster, safer, to take the woman's hand and run as if they were children, but Pomona contented herself with keeping the prisoner at the edge of her vision and the hideous Mab-tree in sight. She dared not turn her back on it.

As they passed an apple tree, Pomona could not resist whispering to two lovely gold-and-red apples hanging from a low branch and holding out her straw hat to catch them as they dropped.

They reached the wall and Pomona sang to the boxwood stair so it stretched over the wall and down into the garden. The woman stumbled just as she was stepping over—there was a trick to walking on hedges that came with practice—and the woman's shoe brushed the wall. She screamed in pain. Then she was on the boxwood stair, her foot smoking and bloody.

And she was a man.

There he was, just as she had seen him. Only now he was next to her. There was no time to wonder at his injury, or anything else.

"We must not stop," Pomona gasped, taking his elbow. This solid arm, knotted and warm, that had been a woman's a moment before! It was pure enchantment, and yet she could hardly fail to believe her own eyes.

"Do you see me?" he asked, still breathless from his injury.

She nodded, not knowing what to say, and helped him step down to the scree by the river. They walked side by side without speaking until they passed a bend in the river. Here they could cross without Mab seeing them even if she broke free from her tree.

Pomona called three vines down from the canyon wall and bid them stretch across the canyon. A bridge, of the simplest kind. One vine to walk on, and two to hold.

"Can you manage it, Vertumnus?" she asked, using the name as if it were nothing.

"I can," he said through gritted teeth.

So she had guessed right. Oberon's ambassador! Dangerous company indeed. But worth some reward, surely, when she delivered him to Orsino.

Vertumnus used the two rail-vines to lift himself and vault with each step, to put no weight on his hurt foot. Pomona followed behind him, coaxing the vines into strength, holding them as steady as she could over the rushing water below. How long did they have before Mab broke free? She must be powerful indeed to have kept Vertumnus captive.

They reached the far side, near where Pomona had left Silenus the day before.

Vertumnus bowed low, sweeping one arm before him, the other raised to the sky.

"I am forever in your debt," he said. "And I regret that I cannot stay even for an hour of a conversation I devoutly wish to have. But Oberon has need of me, and for desperate reasons of state I cannot tarry."

Ha! She had desperate reasons of her own. She shook her head.

"You are coming with me to Orsino."

He frowned. "I am Oberon's ambassador. I have been captive for weeks, with no word to him."

"I know. Oberon claims Orsino has killed you. But why should the Duke kill you? And come to that, how did you come to be imprisoned in that garden? It all seems very like a ruse, to justify Oberon joining the war against the Duke and his allies."

Vertumnus threw up his hands.

"It was no such thing."

"What was it, then?" Pomona put her hands on her hips. "How did a fairy of Oberon's court—an ambassador, no less, and a man of some strength if I judge aright—come to be at the mercy of a pixie behind a garden wall?"

He sighed, and ran a hand through his iron-coloured curls.

"Queen Titania bears an old grudge against me. She took my fairy powers and shut me up with Mab as my warden, and set the enchantment on me that changed my form in your eyes. And so I must return to Oberon, not only to put his mind at ease and prevent this strife from going any further, but also to regain my powers. If I encounter Titania abroad, in my current state, I can only imagine what she will do to me for escaping."

"A likely story," Pomona scoffed. "Are not Oberon and Titania married?"

"Theirs is an unusual marriage. I will tell you many tales about them one day. In the meantime, if you wish to halt the war between Oberon and Orsino, you can do no better than to bid me adieu so I can return to Oberon and soothe his rage."

"The enchantment must have addled your brain," Pomona retorted. "Oberon's court is in Venice, a long journey over land or water on your injured foot, while Orsino's palace is only a half-day's walk hence down the coast. By the time you find Oberon, you and I will be on either side of a vicious war."

"Oh, you must have more faith, Pomona. Oberon's anger flickers like a tallow lamp. I will send word ahead to him as soon as I can. Keep the book I gave you, as a reminder that we have conversations to finish. Come to Oberon's court in Venice, if you like. You may find me there, for the time being, as I doubt he will send me back to Orsino until this business is clear. Adieu!"

He turned and limped down the scree slope toward the dusty coast road. Orsino would have her head if he learned she had let him get away. She could not very likely hold a fairy against his will, but he said his fairy powers were gone. And if that were true, if he were no more than a man, she could hold him.

Pomona took up the end of a vine that had been part of the rope-bridge, pressed it into service again with a whisper. It shot out and snapped around Vertumnus' wrist. He cried out, but she yanked him closer and he had no choice but to stumble up the slope toward her.

"What satisfaction can I give you, witch?" he cried out. "I have told you the truth and done you no harm."

Another branch shot out of the vine and bound his other wrist to the first.

"It is Orsino's satisfaction, not mine, that matters," she replied. "You can tell him your tale, and if he is satisfied, he may put you on a ship to Oberon at his expense—or send Oberon a message. He is a fair man, and my patron. I have no choice but to bring you to him, will ye or nill ye."

"You freed me only to make me your captive?"

"I freed you so you could go to Orsino with me. How was I to know you would be so mulish?"

Act III

Vertumnus would have withered these biting vines to nothing, if he had his powers still. If this were a year ago, a month ago, if he were still Oberon's trusted lieutenant and not a ragged itinerant in need of rescue. Oh, if he were a true fairy, Titania would never have treated him thus.

Titania thought of his fairy powers as in her gift, because it was she who had given them to him; years before, when he was a mere human, a changeling child. She professed to love him for the sake of her beloved friend, the Indian lady who had died giving him life. She had, she said, purged his mortal grossness, made him better than he had been.

He had wanted to believe it, that he was a fairy through and through. He became such a bright and eager student, that Titania's fairies used to clap with delight to see him learn new tricks. They gave him the gift of language and he read them stories out of books, which they hated to do for themselves.

Oberon grew jealous and asked for Vertumnus to come spend some time at his court. Titania refused, until Oberon tricked her through enchantments into cuckolding him with a human in the shape of an ass, hoping to shame her so that she would hand over anything Oberon desired.

But Titania was not so easily shamed. She was angry instead, and well she might be, to have her affections so manipulated. If Oberon's anger flickered, Titania's anger burned like banked coals, most dangerous when they looked white as ash. She pretended to be mollified, to be tractable. She offered up Vertumnus like the Greeks offered their horse, while privily instructing him to act as her spy at Oberon's court.

"You shall be my eyes and ears," she told him. "And when I call for you, my child, you will return, and tell me all the names of Oberon's favourites, and all his mischiefs and follies."

But Titania did not call him back, not for a year, not for two. And by the time she did, Vertumnus was Oberon's man.

At Oberon's court, he was not called upon to perform as if he were some caged wonder in a menagerie. He was given every book he wanted and left to read it in peace. He was left to use his fairy powers as he thought fit, and no one laughed or clapped when he held debates with the squirrels or floated on his carpet high over the forest. He had thought himself a true fairy at last.

All the same, he was never privy to Oberon's laughing whispers with Puck and his other councillors, and never invited to join the Hunt with the other favourites. He was always more than human but less than spirit.

If he were a true fairy, he would be gone now, off on the air like a sylph, vanished like first love. If he were a true fairy, perhaps—probably—Titania would not have been able to take away the powers she had given him so long ago.

Instead he was bound, and hurt, and limping behind this witch like a pig being led to market.

"We have time, at last," said the witch, breaking in to his thoughts. "Time for you to tell me the story of how you came to be in that garden."

He laughed. "We would need a longer journey for the full story, I fear. It is a story centuries long, and that is only my part in it. The short version is: I was born in India, and taken as a changeling child to Titania's court. She lost me to Oberon when I was still a child. I thought she had forgotten her grudge, but Titania never forgets. When I arrived in Illyria at Orsino's court this summer, bearing Oberon's greetings, Titania chose to punish me for my insolence. She shut me in that garden."

Pomona slowed her gait so that they were walking next to each other now, although the vines still connected them, held in her right hand, wrapped around both of his. The world was so beautiful. How he would have soared over those hills, in his younger days, those domes of yew and minarets of cypress.

"Surely she must have known that an ambassador's disappearance, at a time of war, would cause great mischief," Pomona said.

"She has never cared too deeply about the affairs of humans, not in the way Oberon has. Each of them sees humanity as a game; only for Oberon it is Nine Men's Morris, and for Titania it is something more like bear-baiting. If humans tore themselves to pieces, that would only amuse her."

"And you? Are you human now, or fairy? I have never met a changeling before. One never thinks of them having lives, afterward."

All his life had been *afterward*. He was by nature and long practice the stolen child, even now when he was old enough to have had children of his own, and grandchildren a dozen times over, had he lived his natural life in India.

Every year Oberon had asked him if he wanted his body to stop aging, lest he become an immortal skeleton. Always Vertumnus said no, thinking that if he did not look like a child he would not be treated as one; thinking that if he did not look like a youth he would be respected; thinking that if he had a little white in his hair, Oberon would ask his advice.

But Oberon never did. Vertumnus' nature was too solid to be trusted. So he sought dissipation. He was more fairy than fairy, wreaking mischief on mortals that would have made Puck blush. He took lovers as easily as gathering flowers.

Until his fiftieth year, when Vertumnus drank a stoop of wine and then said yes, yes, I will stop here. Oberon pricked fifty marks on his back, each in the shape of a number in Malayalam, the language his mother had spoken. The pain of his mother tongue under his skin sent him to the wine again, for the last time, and then he returned to his books. He sought in contemplation and philosophy the answers that eluded him still.

"I am neither human nor fairy, I suppose," he answered. "All my life I have known how special, how unique I must be. Oh, you roll your eyes, you think me arrogant, I see. And yet I cannot help feeling I am not more than either, and not enough. I am not what I am. I have sought my true nature high and low, and not yet found it anywhere."

"Hmpf," said Pomona, and she pulled an apple out of her satchel. "Would you like one?"

Vertumnus held up his hands, bound together.

"I'll loose one hand if you'll be honour bound."

He shrugged. "Somehow I doubt I could free myself from one of your vines, even if I had a free hand."

She grinned. "I believe you're right."

One vine whipped around and around and shrank into nothing, and then only his right hand was bound. He shook his wrist, and then held out his hand for the apple. She took one for herself out of the satchel and they walked and ate, side by side. The apple tasted perfectly sweet, soft as river water, firm but not too tart. It could very well be the best apple he had ever tasted. Titania wrought well.

They walked in silence for a few moments. He could almost hear the whirr of her thoughts alongside his, her footfalls in time with his own on the dusty road.

"Plants change their natures with the seasons," Pomona said at last. "Paracelsus says that a plant may be poison or medicine; it is all in the dose. A plant's nature is in the uses it is put to, and the same may be said of a man, I've always thought."

"Then you subscribe to the view of Ibn Rushd, that existence and essence are the same?"

"Bah, I never had much time for the debates of scholastics.

Angels and pins, caves and chairs. What does it matter? A man's nature may be determined from his actions, so therefore his actions may be said to *be* his nature."

"Yes, but what is the truth beneath?"

"Truth is truth," she said. "Beneath, above, inward, outward."

"You say that, who saw me as a woman yesterday."

"And were you any different, when I saw you as something else than what you are? Would you have acted any differently than you had? You cannot seek your nature, you can only make it, moment by moment."

When had she realized who he was? Was it when she read the book, later, in whatever home she called her own?

"Then tell me," he said, "what is your nature, Pomona?"

"It is whatever I need it to be—or whatever the person paying me for my services needs it to be."

"So simple! But Rumi says the king knows not that he is a king when he sleeps, and the prisoner knows not that he is a prisoner. So what are we, then, when we are sleeping? When we are only ourselves, at night, naked and unoccupied?"

"Are you always unoccupied, then," she said, "when you are naked?"

He was startled into laughter. She kept her pace, looking not at him but off at the Adriatic shining in the sun, just past him. Still the sun shone on her face too, and she was smiling, a little twisted smile like a gnome's. She made as much mischief as a fairy, in her own ways, this witch who had broken him out of Titania's prison.

POMONA FELT A dangerous lightness in her step, a foreboding of joy, as if she were on the verge of some marvel.

The sun was very hot.

She heard the dogs before she saw them, before she realized that she and Vertumnus were approaching a fork where three roads joined. Fie on her wandering mind! All these years Pomona had been wary at such crossroads, preparing herself for Hecate; and today, of all days, the great witch chose to appear.

Hecate's dogs appeared one by one out of the air. The vine strained against her arm as Vertumnus stepped backward, but Pomona stood her ground. Bootless to avoid Hecate, once she had chosen to speak with you. Pomona had had cause to learn that, many times, long ago.

The dogs—a witch's dozen, Pomona knew without counting—yipped and snarled until Hecate appeared herself in their midst and they quieted.

The queen of witches had chosen one of the forms she used for strangers. Her body was one long, crooked stick, with another set across it for arms. Her head was completely covered in black cloth, tied at the neck, long enough that the four corners fell down almost to the ground.

Sycorax used to call it the Scarecrow.

Vertumnus was making a very good show of not being afraid, frowning at Hecate.

"What is this folly?" Hecate asked, gesturing at Vertumnus. No one knew the shape of that concealed head, but when Hecate spoke, a mouth seemed to move under the clinging cloth. The dogs grinned and slavered.

"A fairy," said Pomona. No point in lying if the truth lay within Hecate's sight; she had learned that, too.

"*A fairy*," sang Hecate, mocking. "*The* fairy, you mean. The wayward son angering Orsino. And here I find my own wayward beldam, dragging this very fairy off to Orsino, unless I miss my guess or my bearings. There was a wind, over Malfi, but I am no weathercock."

"I serve Orsino," Pomona protested. "I could not—"

"You serve *me*," Hecate hissed. "Albeit never very well. You have been secretive of late, Pomona. You have not told me all your doings."

The vines that bound Pomona's strongbox, where the gramarye lay concealed, would be as nothing to Hecate, and Pomona was often away from home. The cipher was not known to anyone but Pomona and Sycorax. Still, Hecate would doubtless guess the book's origin and purpose.

If that was Hecate's game, let her ask straight out. Pomona was too old to bandy words with anyone, least of all the queen of deception.

"My doings have been unworthy to tell," Pomona said. "A little work, here and there."

"I did not send you to Illyria to do a little work here and there."

"No, madam, you sent me here to punish me, to ensure that I would never be anything greater than a purveyor of simples. And so that is all I am and all I do."

Hecate's cloth-covered head moved from one side to the other. "Saucy!"

"If I have upset your plans, it was not my intent."

"Oh, it is never your intent," Hecate sneered, the cloth puffing and sucking at her mouth. "Lo these many years, you have done as you wished, and damn the consequence. When you whispered with Sycorax, and hid her secrets from me, were you thinking of me? No, I learned long ago that I cannot expect you to serve anyone but yourself. I had hoped, of course, that you would not interfere with my plans, as I do not interfere with yours. And yet here we are."

Pomona stared.

"I believe the lady refers to me," Vertumnus said drily.

"Oh, it speaks!" Hecate crowed. "Yes, I do wonder that a fairy places himself in the hands of a wyrtwitch."

It was Hecate who had made Pomona read Rumi, who had educated her in thirteen known languages and two unknown. Pomona had never liked it much; never liked any poetry, really. Pretty words were as much use to her as cobwebs.

"I place myself in the hands of my rescuer," Vertumnus said. "Is it Hecate I address?"

"It is she."

"I am astonished that one as great as you should care about the whereabouts of one fairy," Vertumnus said.

"One fairy who, when nicely misplaced, had Oberon preparing for war. Oberon interferes with my plans less when he is distracted. But I can see all things, Pomona, and I arrange the world to my purposes, with your help or without it. I am here now as a friend, to give you a friend's advice, if you will receive it."

Pomona bowed her head, to hide her flushed cheeks as much as to show respect. Could Hecate truly see all things? For two score years Pomona had hidden her gramarye. Did Hecate know of that, of the existence of Caliban, of Pomona's plans? But no, if Hecate knew of any of that, she would be more than peevish. If Hecate knew that Pomona sought the child born to Sycorax, to teach him secret knowledge, the earth would have bubbled up and drowned Pomona by now.

"Teach me, then, where my duty lies, for always the path seems to fork beneath my feet," Pomona said. "Do I follow love, or fear, or honour?"

"All three, and all redound to me," said Hecate. "But you never would be guided by my wisdom. In your youth I could forgive you being headstrong, but I cannot forgive disloyalty."

Disloyalty! Pomona had given her life to loyalty. She had tried to be loyal to the memory of Sycorax and to Hecate both, and to Orsino too. There was no disloyalty in anything she did, but rather a surfeit of loyalties that pulled her in all directions, and Hecate's supposed wisdom was no guidance but merely one more set of demands that Pomona could never fulfill.

"I am here in Illyria on your command!" Pomona said, looking up into Hecate's terrible face. "I forswore all study of the higher arts, because you wished it. I have no gift for prophecy. I cannot see the consequence of anything I do and yet you damn me for my blindness. I act as I deem best, and I am unacceptable to you, I am the seed you sowed yourself."

Sooty clouds gathered over the ocean. But Hecate laughed.

"Poor little Pomona," she said. "Would you hear my prophecy, then, to guide your feet?"

Pomona shook her head. "To me, it is no more use than to any mortal. I cannot read them."

"Here is my prophecy, will ye or nill ye," Hecate screamed, the four corners of the black cloth billowing.

A cell awaits at Orsino's court:
Wrath and war be your rewards.
Shackled be he that you would free,
And bound you both will ever be.

A wind blew up from the sea and even the dogs were quiet.

"A pretty verse," said Vertumnus. "But it cannot hold a candle to Rumi."

His voice banished the clouds. Pomona smiled, for Vertumnus, but also for Hecate, who could not be other than she was after all her years.

"I give you my thanks, teacher," she said. "But if I free him here and now, I will be breaking Orsino's law, and that I cannot do."

Hecate sighed, and the sticks came apart and clattered to the ground. A scrap of dark cloud floated on the air for a moment, and then all that was left was the distant baying of dogs.

How convenient such a mode of travel must be!

Pomona stepped carefully around the sticks on her sore feet, feeling the vine go taut, knowing Vertumnus must follow. And follow he did, saying nothing. Perhaps he was used to apparitions.

"Do all witches answer to Hecate?" he asked after a time.

She took a moment before answering. She owed him nothing. Yet he had answered Hecate too, and stood beside her bravely and without complaint. He could have asked to be freed. He could have complained of Pomona's treatment of him, made promises to Hecate to keep Oberon out of her way. He did none of that.

"All prudent witches show her respect," Pomona said. "But not all are her students. I was, once."

"When you were young?"

She laughed. "When the world was young, or so it seems sometimes. I was her student from a baby. I could do witchcraft before I could walk. She is in the habit of taking in orphan children. I was the unwanted child of a Barbary pirate and her lover. Hecate raised me at her school in Algiers, and taught me well."

"Until she found cause to punish you."

"Yes."

She said nothing further but listened to the uneven sound of his footsteps. She had forgotten his hurt foot. She slowed her pace, but only a little. They were not safe upon the road. Hecate had found them; Titania might be next, and who could say what she would do.

"We were both raised away from the human lives we should have had, you and I," he said.

She did not want to talk any more about the past, so she laughed.

"Like Romulus and Remus," she said. "Where shall we build our city?"

It was still hot when they arrived at Orsino's palace, but the sun was melting into the crucible of the Adriatic. Vertumnus, from his burned foot to his parched mouth, wanted nothing but cold wine, a soft couch, and a book.

At the gatehouse, a man in Orsino's livery came out to greet them.

"Madam, you are well met and welcome here, most well met,

and I will quarter your dog with the Duke's own," he said, glancing at Vertumnus.

"God's teeth, Joseph, your insults do your master no honour," Pomona retorted.

"I meant no insult, madam. It is a fine kennel, and the best meat. I would eat that meat myself, I swear upon my mother's grave, and I loved my mother dearly. It is very good meat."

"Let us in, for we have urgent business with the Duke," Vertumnus said.

"Your dog barks most viciously," said the man, mincing backwards.

Damn Pomona for binding his hands, and giving fools cause to joke at his expense.

"I'll show you my bite in a moment," said Vertumnus.

Pomona put her hand up.

"Hold, hold. Joseph, tell me truly, who do you see here beside me?"

"Why, no one, madam. Should I see someone?" He leaned forward on his pike and whispered to her as if Vertumnus were not there. "Are we being observed?"

"Not at the end of this vine?" she asked.

"Why, I see your dog at the end of its leash, of course. A most clean and well-mannered dog, I meant no insult to it. A handsome devil. A shame about the paw. Such an injury would make the sweetest dog growl, I know. I had a dog once, the sweetest orphan spaniel, a gift from the Duke himself, but one day she stepped upon a thorn and you would have thought her a dog to bait bears with, until we pulled it out."

Pomona took Vertumnus by the arm and stepped backward. She whispered to him, her breath on his cheek.

"Hecate. She must have enchanted you," she said. "Given you the appearance of a dog."

Vertumnus pulled back, looked up and down his body. It looked as it always did, but then it had under Titania's spell too.

"Do you see it?" he asked.

She shook her head. "To my eye, you're a man. But I know this Joseph. He lets his tongue run away with him, but he is kind, and not given to foolery. If the man says he sees a dog, he sees a dog."

In the name of Oberon, he was tired. Tired of being everyone but himself. Tired of the world seeing a face that was not his own.

"Can't you remove the spell?"

"If you were a leaf, I could change you. If you were a seed, I could coax you. As it is, you are beyond my influence. God's teeth, this is the last thing we need. But now we are here, it is our duty to tell the Duke."

"Always thinking of your duty," he said with a smile.

"Thinking of my life," she retorted. "If we delay, and he hears of it, I will answer for it."

"And if you stride into his hall with a barking, limping dog and say you have found a fairy ambassador? If I were to get a message to Oberon—"

"If, if. Fie on your hypotheticals. Do your best not to bark, then, and leave the rest to me. Orsino knows me. He has no cause to doubt my word."

She strode toward the doorkeeper, pulling Vertumnus after her. By Jove, he had had enough of being a prisoner.

"You believe that you see a dog, Joseph, but you are ensorcelled," she said to the gatekeeper. "What you see is Vertumnus, the fairy ambassador."

"Oh, no," said Joseph. "With the utmost respect, madam, and begging your pardon, I see a dog."

"If you tell the Duke that Pomona the witch is here, and that she says she has brought Vertumnus with her, I believe he will ask to see us both, directly."

Joseph frowned, but he went into the door of the gatehouse and then they saw him running across the courtyard on the other side.

Perhaps Pomona was right and Oberon would give him sea passage to Venice. Perhaps, even better, there would be a representative here from Oberon's court, who would send word to the fairy king—perhaps, if it were one of the more powerful fairies like Thistle or even Puck himself, they would make short work of removing Hecate's enchantment. Soon he would be himself again, whoever that might be, and if he was of little use to Oberon or anyone else, at least he would do no harm.

The man Joseph came hurrying back, puffing and waving at them as if he thought they would leave.

"Well?" Pomona asked.

"My master is in audience now with Esperanza Malchi," the man panted.

"Why is Esperanza Malchi here?" Vertumnus asked. Joseph ignored him. Of course, he had heard nothing but barking.

"Arf arf," Vertumnus said pointedly.

Pomona said, "My companion would like to know who Esperanza Malchi is. Isn't she an Ottoman?"

"I know who she is," Vertumnus growled. "I asked why."

"You may know, but I don't," Pomona whispered.

"Yes, she is the secretary of the Safiye Sultan, the chief consort of the Ottoman ruler," said Joseph. "It is the Safiye Sultan who truly rules the Empire, people say, but she does not leave her home. Malchi, being Jewish, is her public face, and speaks and acts for her at foreign courts, and tells her what she learns, and arranges presents and those sorts of things."

"An ambassador, to save words," said Vertumnus.

"I do not know what Madam Malchi thinks about dogs," said Joseph nervously, looking at Vertumnus. "Or any animal, to tell the truth of it. I have not asked her opinions on dogs or any animal. There was not time."

"Not time?"

"No, my master bade me rush back to you as fast as my feet could carry me."

"Rush back to tell us to wait?"

"Oh, no! The Duke bids you come, and present yourselves before him, and the Ottoman woman too, so she can see that the ambassador lives, that Orsino is not at fault for Oberon's bellicosity. He bids you come, and not to wait. I tried to tell him about the dog, but—"

"There wasn't time," Vertumnus said.

"Shush, Vertumnus," Pomona said. "Lead on, Joseph."

He limped along, his hands bound, trying and failing not to feel as if he were being led as a prisoner or a prize—although he had done nothing wrong. He must have done something, surely, or he would be in some other life, in some other skin. At some point there must have been a choice, and he had chosen awry.

"The Ottomans will be worried about the fragile peace with Venice," said Pomona as they walked.

"A fragile peace, you may call it, or a lazy war," Vertumnus said. "In diplomacy it matters very little which. The trick is to make sure no one gets any stronger—not Venice, and certainly not the Spanish, who are threatening England now. Malchi wishes to make sure that Oberon does not throw in his lot with Venice, as he is sure to do if he is angry with Orsino. She will be pleased to see me, then."

"Everyone will be pleased to see you," said Pomona. "Now stop barking, for the love of God, or we'll be asked to leave."

Act IV

VIOLA AND ORSINO were sitting on the dais in the palace's great hall, their chairs pulled so close together that their hands brushed, in a way that Pomona could not quite believe was accidental.

They were like two magnets, these two, even now, dressed like soldiers, their faces shining.

Pomona had chosen her lovers, over the years, by the book, and never felt much pang at parting. Some of that was prudence, having seen Sycorax banished into exile for the crime of bearing her lover's child, but Pomona knew how to prevent pregnancy. She had never truly had to work at preventing love—such love as Viola and Orsino had, at least.

"My lord Orsino," Vertumnus said, and swept a bow.

"What is this?" Orsino asked. "Pomona. You are most welcome here, if you bring news of Vertumnus. But where is he?"

"My lord, do you see a dog beside me here?" Pomona asked.

She stepped forward, Vertumnus limping at her side. He was bleeding through his burned shoe and left faint smudges on the blue-and-gold tiles of Orsino's floor. The blood of a fairy; that would make a fine addition to some witch's cauldron somewhere, some witch who had the training to do more than tend gardens.

Orsino laughed shortly, although he did not look amused.

A woman stepped forward, out of the crowd of courtiers. She was small and squat, but dressed in a fine golden jacket that buttoned to her neck, with silk the colour of oranges wrapped around her hair.

"This is Malchi," Vertumnus whispered. "She and Orsino and Viola should all know me, on sight, if I were myself."

"All the court sees your dog," said Orsino. "And hears it."

The courtiers tittered.

"Hush," Pomona said to Vertumnus. "My lord, the story I have to tell is strange, but I swear upon my life that it is true, and will be worth the hearing."

"Come closer, then, and tell it."

They walked forward. Malchi watched them with a little smile.

"Yesterday, I was walking home by an unaccustomed path, and I happened upon a walled garden where no walled garden ought to be. I entered and saw a woman of about my own age and a tiny fairy, no bigger than a butterfly. No one else. Before I left, the woman gave me a book. When I took the book home, I saw the inscription was made to one Vertumnus, from Oberon."

She pulled it out of the satchel and held it out, until a page darted forward and took it to Orsino.

A dozen courtiers whispered as the Duke opened the book and read.

"Did you question this woman? How did she come to have this book?"

"I guessed that she was none other than Vertumnus himself, under a spell. I released him from his prison, once I had dealt with his guard."

"The one no bigger than a butterfly," broke in Viola, and the court laughed again.

Pomona knew better than to answer Viola. She inclined her head.

"But where is this woman now?" Orsino asked, frowning. "Or rather, where is Vertumnus?"

Pomona gestured to him beside her. "On our way to see you, he was ensorcelled."

"What, again?" asked Viola. "Such misfortune! You would

have us believe that this ambassador, this trusted lieutenant of the fairy king, draws evil spells upon himself as a dead dog draws maggots."

Malchi approached them and walked around, looking at the two of them. She bent down whenever she looked at Vertumnus, as if she were seeing him only a few feet off the ground.

"The Vertumnus I knew could turn himself into any form he pleased, at will," said Malchi. "Why does he not transform, then, now?"

"Titania took my powers," Vertumnus growled.

Malchi stepped back.

"Curb your animal!" Orsino snapped. Then, more gently, he said, "Pomona, I know you are an honourable witch. But I fear you are much deceived."

"It is Titania's doing," said Pomona weakly. "She imprisoned him, and took his powers."

"Titania, Oberon's wife!" said Orsino. "And you expect me to believe Oberon did not know?"

"What do you see when you look at it, Pomona?" Malchi asked.

She looked at Vertumnus, his back straight, his strong arms clasped before him, his wrists still wrapped in her vines. She could have released those before now. She had not thought of it, and he had not complained.

"I see Vertumnus," she said. "In what I believe to be his customary form. The form of a man."

"Some trick of Oberon's," said Viola.

"What does he look like?" Malchi asked.

"A man. With dark curls gone grey just there, and golden skin, and a beard just coming in, flecked with gold and silver that catches the sun. He has kind eyes with crinkles at the edges when he smiles, and strong shoulders, and he stands a little taller than my lord Orsino."

Malchi quirked her brow in a way that brought heat to

Pomona's cheek. She had asked for a description, and Pomona had given it. There was nothing in that to quirk a brow over.

"I suppose you could have heard a description, or seen a painting. Perhaps you've met before."

"She has not, or I would have remembered," said Vertumnus. The crowd looked at him as though he had barked.

"Do you hear words when he barks?" Malchi asked, looking amused. "Then ask him for some proof of his identity. Some memory only he could have. Some question only he could answer."

Pomona turned to him.

POMONA'S EYES WERE distractingly clear, the irises golden pools ringed in brown. Waiting. What story could he tell, that was his alone? What would convince these people here?

"Tell them…" he whispered. "Say that when I arrived here, to present myself as ambassador, that Duke Orsino had a cold. He sneezed three times when I bowed before him."

Pomona smiled and turned to Orsino.

"He says that when he came and presented himself, my lord the Duke had a cold, and sneezed three times."

A murmur through the crowd. But Orsino raised his hand dismissively.

"Anyone who was here then could have seen that and spoken of it."

Pomona turned back to him with fire in her eyes and her jaw set, and said, "Tell me something of yourself. Something secret. Something that marks you out as you and no one else, but something they would recognize."

"Oh, is that all?" he whispered back. "What proof can I show them in this condition? I could show the world my skin paintings, but they would see only a dog's back."

"Your skin paintings?"

No, the world could not see them, but Pomona could, and she could read him to the world.

He shut his eyes and pulled his white shirt up and over his head. What did the people see when he moved? A dog scratching its fleas? Standing on its hind legs? But Pomona saw him. He turned his back to her and stood, naked from the waist to no one but her, alone to her, although they were surrounded.

Around him motes swirled in the sunbeams, as if all the lives he might have led were dancing a galliard around him, and everything might be possible.

He heard her breath stop. He felt—he could swear he felt—the inch of air between her fingers and his skin, as she moved her hand over the designs Oberon had burned into his body to preserve it. That inch of air had lightning caught in it. Then she touched him and he flinched.

"Pomona, if you have something to tell, tell it," said Orsino.

She said, her voice rough, "I see... signs. As if painted in indigo, but the paint is under the skin. All swirls and curves, as if circles and angles cavorted together."

Then she spoke to Vertumnus, whispered only to him. "What are they?"

"Numbers," he said. "Numbers written in Malayalam, a language of India. The language my mother spoke. She gave me this body, and Oberon stopped it in time."

Had he chosen, there could have been nine numbers, nine alone, and the pain would have been less—although, he suspected, more deeply felt in his child's flesh. Every year, Oberon had offered. And Vertumnus had delayed. One choice after another, or lack of choice.

"They preserve my body as it is, to match my now immortal spirit," he said. "There is one number for every year this flesh lived, before Oberon burnt the numbers into me, and stopped mortal decay."

"You waited," she whispered. "How many years? Forty? I cannot count them so quickly—I cannot read them."

"Fifty," he said. "I waited."

He shuddered, as her cool finger touched him again, just for a moment, tracing a curve, and then she snatched her hand back and stepped away.

"He bears a pattern of fifty numbers, in a language of farthest India. Surely no other person bears those marks. I can draw them for you, my lord."

"But who would know them to be his?" Orsino asked. "Do we know the true Vertumnus bore such marks?"

"He was a changeling, from India, and this man bears Indian marks made by a fairy hand. If you believe I am a woman of honour, if you believe I speak truly of what I see, then there can be no doubt."

"But has anyone else seen these marks?"

Vertumnus shook his head.

"Come now," Pomona said. "There must have been... someone."

He shook his head again. "Since I took these marks, I have lived a quiet life, and a solitary one. Not even I have seen them. The only one who has, other than you, Pomona, is he who made them. Oberon himself."

She dropped her head, closed her eyes, shook her head. What did she want of him? He had no maker's mark on his soul. He had only his body, and even that was unreliable proof.

"My lord, he says the only person who has seen these marks is Oberon himself," Pomona said, and her next words came all in a rush. "Even if you can have no certain proof, think, I beg you, of all the circumstances I have laid before this court, and of how your reason must read them. Of the book with the inscription. Of the enchantment and the garden. Of the marks upon his flesh. If it is not Vertumnus, who could it be?"

"Ha!" yelled Viola, standing, her sword glinting as it swung at her hip. "The fairy king mocks us, he thinks to make us stumble so he can catch us unready. First he hides away his ambassador so he can make false accusations against us, and then he sends a witch and her dog to make sport of us, to distract us, to make us doubt the need for war, to make us waver in our purpose. Do not tumble into this trap, my love."

Orsino rubbed his face with his gloved hand. "We cannot stand down, of course."

"And yet," said Malchi, circling like a cat with her hands clasped behind her, "If you do not make peace with Oberon, Venice gains an eldritch ally, and the world will change."

"If we crumble before Oberon, Illyria's enemies will only multiply," retorted Viola. "We have sorcerers and witches among our friends. A fairy may be captured, a fairy may be made to bleed. Let Oberon but once feel the edge of our blade, and then we will have peace in Illyria."

Orsino stood. "Enough. Pomona, I do not doubt you. And yet, even if you tell nothing but the truth, you might both have been deceived from the beginning. Titania could be an ally of Oberon's in this. She is, after all, his wife."

"I wonder," said Malchi, stepping back and looking at the two of them, "I have had dealings with Titania, and I wonder. She is no politician, but her grudges last an age."

Orsino bowed his head. "If you think me wrong to doubt, Madam Malchi, tell me so. Will the Sultan be satisfied by this tale told by a witch and her familiar?"

To be Pomona's familiar—to trot along at her heels. The thought nearly made him smile.

Malchi threw up her hands. "Oh, surely not. We must get to the bottom of this mystery. But in the meantime, we must ask these two to stay, until we know the truth of it."

Orsino banged his fist. "I'll ask nothing. They'll stay, all right, in my strongest cell. I cannot risk letting this fairy slip through my hands again, if indeed this cur is Vertumnus. William!

William, come forward, man. Put this woman and her dog in a cell, and see that they be given food and water."

A cell. A prison, again. Perhaps it was his nature to be taken from place to place, from life to life.

"I'll send a message to the Fairy Queen," said Malchi. "She will answer it, for the sake of old favours rendered, unless I miss my guess. And if this is Vertumnus, she'll come here in all anger."

"She will tell Oberon," Viola grumbled.

"So be it," said Orsino. "We lose nothing. We need not let down our guard or let our preparations lapse."

THE MAN WILLIAM walked them through narrow stone hallways, the walls so thick the air was mercifully cool, almost damp. Orsino's green and white livery fit him uneasily, the laces straining. Two of his teeth were missing and his eyes had a haunted look.

This must be the same dream-ridden William whom the friar had been bidden to tend. Was Pomona's mandrake cooperating?

By morning, the friar should be here. He would speak on her behalf, if his courage did not fail him. What good could that do? He had not seen the garden. He had read the inscription, but the existence of the inscription was in no doubt.

Still, it would be a comfort to have her friend here.

This William took them at last to a heavy door with a window no wider than a hand's breadth. He opened the door and gestured for them to go within.

"There's a pot at the back, just there. I'll be by with bread and wine later, and meat for the dog."

Pomona raised her eyebrow at Vertumnus, who merely shook his head.

"I have seen many wonders in this world," William said softly, "but never yet have I seen a dog imprisoned in a cell with its master. What sort of dog cannot be chained, or put to death? Is it the dog, or the owner, who merits such consideration?"

She said nothing but stepped over the threshold into the cool room. William took her elbow to stop her. Damn the man's impudent curiosity!

"Your satchel," he said.

Thank heaven she had left the gramarye behind. She passed over the satchel, empty save her waterskin, which William opened, sniffed, and handed back to her.

"And I'll take your knife."

They could try to overpower him—they were two, and Pomona a witch, and perhaps the illusion would give some advantage to Vertumnus—but could they get past all the guards? And then they would be fugitives, and Oberon and Venice would certainly join the war, and passage to Milan would be nigh-impossible, even once Orsino relented and freed them.

Oh, how she had hoped for some reward from Orsino to speed her on her way.

She pulled her little knife off her belt and handed it over. Vertumnus made no movement, though she could see the knife in its sheath on his own belt.

William examined her knife, holding it this way and that in the dim shafts of light that broke through the loopholes in one wall of the stone corridor.

"Is this all?" he asked, in a whisper. "You have no other knife for me?"

Pomona and Vertumnus furrowed their brows and shook their heads. Pomona turned her pocket inside out.

"No message?" he hissed.

What intrigues were here at Orsino's court?

"What message would you hear from us?" Vertumnus asked, voice low. He thought the man was fishing for a bribe, and indeed, perhaps he was.

But William heard only a growl. He stepped back, and shook

his head as if Mab herself were buzzing about him. He was pale, balding a bit on top, and behind his ear the brown hair curled where it was damp from sweat.

"In you go," he said.

When the door shut behind them, Pomona walked to the far wall of the dim cell. There was one tiny window in the door, and one tiny window in the outer wall. The stones were thick.

"If only I could have got word to Oberon," said Vertumnus. "If only you had let me go free."

"'If only' won't save us now."

"No. We may be here for days, while Oberon brings his sylphs to rain venom upon Illyria from the air and destroy all those orchards and vineyards you have nurtured, and while his nymphs race in their courses, poisoning all the waters of Illyria, and while his hunters trample the villages of Illyria under the feet of their strange steeds. And then the mortals will set nets of razor wire for the nymphs and the steams will run incarnadine, and then the Ottomans will send a wizard to blow the sylphs to bits and dash them upon the mountaintops, and then the English bowmen will land to fight the Spaniards and Oberon both and my friends, the great hunters, will fall from their steeds with shafts through their hearts. Will you stop pacing, Pomona? You are making my eyes blur."

She hadn't realized she had been. She put her hand out to the stone wall to steady herself.

"I do not want war, any more than you do," she said wearily.

"No, but it is not your failure that is about to condemn your friends to bloody deaths."

"My one true friend is long dead already," she snapped. "Such is life, Vertumnus! We fail each other. We fall down. I promised to care for the child of a friend whom Hecate sent to a rough exile and her death. I thought the child had died on that island too, but the friar says a man lives who has been claiming to be the son of Sycorax, that he has been seen in Milan. If the sea and land become impassable, it could be a year or more before I can make the journey and give Caliban his birthright, and by then he could be gone again somewhere else, or I could be dead."

He shook his head, smiling. "Your so-called failure is all to your honour. Not like mine. I may as well be a dog, I may as well trot along as someone's pet, as be a changeling, and be a traitor to both fairies and humans."

Fie, he was happy in his misery, and she had enough to occupy her thoughts. He was not her business.

"I think we shall be free within a day," she said. "Orsino must see reason."

"And if he does not?"

She bit her lip, and put her hand to the stones of the outer wall. She answered softly.

"I carry with me a small sack of seeds of all kinds. Some of them grow strong vines, and tough roots, and I could push apart these stones in an hour with them, if I wished."

"Where?"

"Hmm?"

She turned to look at him. He was lounging on the cold floor a few paces from her, his arm resting on his bent knee, smiling up at her. How the air had hummed between her hand and his scar-painted back! And then for a moment she had touched him, not an hour ago, unseen and yet in front of all the world, and yet here—shut in together, alone—she dared not.

"Where do you have these seeds? I saw you turn out your pocket when William asked."

"Oh!" she laughed. "In my bodice, of course. When I was young that would have been the least safe place to hide anything against a dungeon search, but at my age I knew it would be as safe as a worm under a rock."

He shook his head. "You do yourself an injustice, Pomona. If you could see yourself as I see you—"

"What?"

He cocked his head and looked at her. She would not divert her gaze. She would dare him to speak, if he had anything to the purpose to say. It might suit a fairy to be coy, but she had not much use for heart-flutter now.

"Say something, Vertumnus. Finish your sentence, pronounce sentence upon me."

"I was going to say—"

"What?"

"Which is the truer vision, do you think? We imagine that we know ourselves better than anyone else can, the inner eye looking outwards. And yet, perhaps—"

"Oh, will you stop philosophising!" she cried.

"What else is there?" he spread his arms wide.

"God's blood, the day will come when the world ends and the dead walk, and the seas will boil, and you'll think and you'll think and you'll think."

He laughed. "And you?"

"I'll do," she retorted, and crossed to him, three paces on the cold floor.

"I'll do," she said again. His eyebrows wriggled in puzzlement, or amusement.

She took his hands in hers and pulled him to his feet.

"And I'll do," she whispered, and took his rough chin in her hands, feeling the prickles of gold and silver on her skin, and stood on her tiptoes and kissed him.

He had his hands on her back, warm against her, and pulled her to his body. She ran her hands down the flesh of his back and pressed her palms against every inch of what she had hardly dared to touch.

"Let me see if I can find this concealed treasure of yours," he said, laughing against her teeth.

Act V

VERTUMNUS WOKE SHIVERING, with Pomona's head resting on his bare chest. He stretched his right arm out and pulled the thin blanket over both their bodies, trying not to wake her, but she lifted her head and looked, not at his face but at the bright window.

"Was that the lark?" she asked.

"Mmph," he answered, and put an arm around her. Their clothing was strewn about the floor: her green-stained petticoat held congress with his doublet; his shirt with her stockings. Her straw hat lay against the wall, like a cat waiting for its master.

"Never done that with a fairy before," she said, her voice muffled, echoing in his body.

"Never done it with a witch," he said, and laughed.

"I suppose it must often happen with prisoners."

"A night in prison is a small price to pay, then," he said.

She smiled, and sat up, and pulled her smock over her head. Then she rubbed her lip, looking at him.

"What is it? What's worrying you?"

"It is only... well, a prison dalliance is only that. A fleeting romance. It cannot last, Vertumnus."

He shivered, and to cover it, reached for his shirt. She was right, of course. He had his life and she had hers, and when hers was over he would live on, cruelly immortal. Perhaps—oh, he was wrong to wish, even for a moment, that Orsino would keep them in prison just one day more, for that would mean that the war would come one day closer.

"Both of us are long past the age of fooling ourselves about such matters," he said, as gruffly as he could.

The door opened and they both jumped. Vertumnus was still naked, save the blanket, which he pulled up around him. Pomona at least was covered in her smock, but her kirtle and apron were on the far side of the room.

But the man at the door looked the most startled of all. An ancient friar, thin and crooked as an old besom. Had Orsino sent him to take their confession?

"Father," Pomona gasped.

"What is this?" the friar gasped in return. "William told me only that I would find you here, Pomona. He said—he said nothing about a dog, but he was much distracted, poor soul. Where is the fairy, then?"

Vertumnus put his hand out, but the friar pulled back. He was not aghast at the naked man, no, but at the dog here sharing Pomona's blanket. Vertumnus laughed, and the friar backed up another step.

"We met Hecate on the road," Pomona said, pulling herself to her feet. "This is the fairy. This is Vertumnus, disguised."

"Then—" The friar pointed at Vertumnus, and then looked at the kirtle, at the hose, and the doublet.

"I'll leave you a moment," he said, and backed into the hall.

"That's for the best," said Pomona weakly. Then, aside to Vertumnus: "On my life, I feel fifteen again."

Vertumnus laughed, not caring if the world heard him baying.

"Dress yourself," Pomona hissed, thrusting his hose at him. "The friar is a good man, and the best friend we have here."

Any friend at all was more than they had yesterday. Perhaps this friar would carry a message to Oberon for him, if he could get the old man alone for a moment.

The friar waited for them each in turn to dress and use the pot, and then walked them through the chilly corridors.

"There are strange portents in the skies," said the friar, short of breath. "Streaks of red like blood. And in the rivers, sounds as of horrible laughter."

Sylphs were marking their battle plans, then; and nymphs were preparing their minds for war.

"Oberon's armies are amassing," Vertumnus said.

"Already!" Pomona cried.

"And Titania is come to Orsino's court, brought by Malchi's summons, and demands to see the witch who stole Vertumnus."

The great hall was full of people, although it was early morning still. Had they stood here only yesterday? The world outside their cell seemed like a dream. But last night was the dream, that was the interlude, and this bright confusion was life.

Titania stood in the middle of the hall with all her retinue. There were fairies he had not seen since he was a boy—there were Peaseblossom, Cobweb, Moth and Mustardseed, all floating a foot above the floor, trailing their gossamer trains and wringing their hands.

When Vertumnus had last seen Titania a month ago, she had been frenzied, black-haired, mop-capped, spilling out of a peasant's bodice. Today her hair was red as rubies and growing straight up in thick curls like a candle-flame. Her heavy gown was bedizened in gold. Had she made her neck a little longer? It was hard to say, but Vertumnus thought so: the better to show the silver ridge-backed amphisbaena that she wore as a ruff, each of its two heads trying to snatch the other, its horny feet scrabbling on her shoulders.

It seemed the fairy queen had chosen to take Orsino's court seriously, at least for as long as it amused her to do so.

Titania looked straight at Vertumnus and wrinkled her perfect nose.

"You have the stink of witch on you."

He glanced at Pomona, who did not look at him.

Titania floated toward him and then floated round and round him, sniffing, her train tracing a circle around his feet.

"Let us have you back in a form these assembled worthies

will understand," she said, and stretched out her hands. Her magic shivered on Vertumnus' skin, and the air shimmered. He looked to the crowd to see their awe at his transformation, but they only frowned and whispered. Titania scowled, and a satyr elbowed his way forward, his hoofs clicking on the tile floor.

"What witch laid this stubborn enchantment on you?" Titania grumbled. "Not this one, surely."

"A powerful witch indeed," said Pomona. "You are right. It is beyond my powers to transform a man."

"It is not beyond mine."

Titania spun around Vertumnus until she became a whirlwind of red and gold, and this time the shimmer brought tears to his eyes and all his skin was gooseflesh. He fell to his knees, his muscles and joints weakened.

Ah, there was the hush, the murmur. He lifted his head and saw the courtiers pointing at him. His body looked no different to him than it had a moment before.

"Woof," he said weakly, and all the courtiers laughed.

"Vertumnus, it is you," said Orsino, striding forward and taking his hand. "Or is this now some spell, some trick of yours, Titania?"

"What reason have I to trick you, Orsino?" she sniffed.

"To lull us into believing we had no cause to fear your husband's armies," said Viola.

"Oh, you have every cause to fear his armies. I expect blood and glory, and much amusement."

"But Vertumnus is safe!" Orsino cried, pointing at him. "So you admit that his abduction was all a ploy."

"Oberon knew nothing of it. I had my own business with this fairy. But I am pleased to see the armies gather. I shall goad my husband on to war, I think. I have a certain influence on him."

"It must be a strong influence indeed, to last despite the distance between your courts and the mischiefs you play," said Viola, with a glance at her husband.

"Not *despite*, you wet-eared wench; *because*. When you have been married a thousand years, come to me and tell me you play no games, that you make no wagers in your pillow-talk. You know what I mean, don't you, my Mab?"

Titania opened a pocket at her waist and out flew the little fairy in her chariot, swooping around Vertumnus and Pomona.

"They must be punished," Mab screamed.

"Oh, they will be," Titania said with a smile. "They will see Illyria suffer for their treachery. All my darling husband's tedious playing at diplomacy shall come to nothing, all his plans dashed and his favourites brought low. Then Oberon shall make his obeisance to me, and we begin again, as we have always done, and will always do."

Vertumnus glanced at Pomona but she did not look at him; her jaw was set. This was not her fight, and yet here she stood beside him. She had acted only out of loyalty to Orsino and the law, when she had worked for peace and her duty. All she wanted was to bring her book to her dead friend's son, wherever he might be, and Vertumnus would see to it that she could, if he had any choice in the matter.

"My queen, your quarrel was with me," said Vertumnus. "Let it end with me."

"Oh, but Vertumnus, you must learn your place. My little changeling boy, all grown into his old man's body, and pretending to be a diplomat! My pet, the fairy-king's confidant! You can dress an elephant in jewels, but that does not make it a prince."

His face burned. A peal of jackdaw laughter came from the crowd. He looked over and saw that the satyr was doubled over in mirth.

Pomona, beside him, said very quietly, "You are the one dressed in counterfeit jewels, Titania."

* * *

POMONA DID NOT even know what she meant by it. She was angry, because Silenus was laughing. And she had had enough of fairy politics.

But the queen's white face went as red as her hair. At Pomona's elbow, the friar hovered, then stepped back. The poor old dear.

"Insults from a wyrtwitch?" breathed Titania.

Soft footsteps on the tiles: Malchi walked toward them. She cocked her head, the ostrich plume in her headdress all a-quiver.

"My lady, I think perhaps there is something you do not know."

"And what is that?" Titania turned to her.

"If the witch insults you, she speaks not out of hatred for you. Pomona and Vertumnus are in love."

"In love!"

A murmur swept the hall. Silenus, thank God, was choked into silence, probably from an excess of laughter.

What could possess this woman to mock and shame them here? What had Pomona ever done to the Ottoman Empire?

Vertumnus opened his mouth as if to speak, but Malchi held up her hand to him and Pomona, quieting them.

"I know very well," the Ottoman ambassador continued, "how the court of Titania worships love above all else, how the Silk Road provides the sheets for your bowers and the perfumes for your shoulders. Surely you cannot harden your heart against these two who met by chance in such an unlikely place, cannot be aggrieved at a love that overleapt your garden walls?"

Titania put her long, red-painted fingernail to her lips.

"Is it true, Vertumnus?" she asked, frowning. "Is that why the witch meddled?"

"Pomona has only ever been guided by her duty as a subject of Illyria," he said.

Malchi, behind Titania, rolled her eyes and threw up her hands.

"It is true," said the friar, stepping beside Pomona. Him, too!

"God save my soul," the old man continued. "This morning I found them in their cell, intertwined as lovers are."

Pomona could barely hear the roaring from the courtiers over the pounding of angry blood in her ears. She took the old fool's arm and steered him a few steps away.

"Tell me what you are about, you meddlesome old man," she hissed.

"At Titania's court, love is the only sacrament," said the friar. "If we convince her, she might soothe her husband."

"Or it might send her into a rage. And, friar, it is a lie."

"It is true," said Vertumnus, loudly. "I love her."

His voice caught; perhaps he was not quite fairy enough to lie prettily. Pomona let the friar go, threw up her hands. She might as well talk to the walls as talk to anyone here, friend or foe.

"Hmm," said Titania. "I don't believe it. Prove it."

"Prove it? How may I prove I love?"

"Convince me," the fairy queen said, spreading her hands. "Tell me why you love her."

Vertumnus clasped his hands behind his back and paced. He loved an argument, above all else.

"If you wish to know why Cupid's arrow strikes when and where it strikes, that I cannot tell you, any more than I can tell you why it was my fate to be born to a mother who was the fairy queen's friend, or why it was my mother's fate to die."

"No, Vertumnus. I mean for you to rhapsodize. Speak to me of your love. Lay it out upon the table like a mercer and let me judge its weight."

He really meant to do it, the fool. He was walking into the trap. Malchi had some friendship with Titania. She must have set this up to mock them. Not enough that they should be drawn and quartered, but they must be the ones to spill their own guts upon the floor for the amusement of the court.

"I love her because—" Vertumnus said, and stopped.

"He does not love me," scoffed Pomona.

"I love her because she argues with me."

A roar of laughter from the courtiers.

Titania raised her eyebrows.

"Well spoken, sir, well spoken. Saying nothing about her appearance, yes, well that's for the best."

"I do love her appearance," said Vertumnus.

Oh, God.

"I love the line between her eyebrows, and I love the dirt around her fingernails, and I love the way her cheeks go round as apples when she laughs."

Now, the courtiers were silent. Waiting. Watching.

"And you, witch? Tell me, do you love my changeling?"

Pomona's smile dropped. She looked first at Malchi, whose expression was a blank. Then at Vertumnus. Oh, dear God, he meant it. He was being honest, or he thought he was. Pomona's stomach lurched as if she were flying, only this time there was no vine to tether her to the earth. There was nothing to save her if the wind carried her away.

She shook her head, and traitor tears welled in her eyes. She could not love him. She was not capable of such a thing. She was old, and tired, and bound on a quest that could take her far from Illyria. He was immortal, and she could only cause him grief.

He reached out and took her hand, and she grabbed on to it and found she did not want to let go.

"I do," she whispered softly.

"What?" Titania asked. "What's that, witch?"

"I do love him, God help me."

The lines around Vertumnus' eyes crinkled.

"Prove it."

"I love"—she looked at him, trying desperately to think—"his shoulders."

"Ha!" Titania laughed again. "My philosopher has found a lusty love. Good! Vertumnus, give us another."

"I love her because she loves my shoulders," he said without thinking.

"I love him because he put his hand to my cheek, when he thought I was sleeping, and traced the line of the bone as though he would study me."

"I love her because she is powerful, because the plants obey her as though she were Demeter herself. I love her because she is wise. Because she is loyal. Because she is honourable."

What could she say? What could she offer, that would not shrink and wither next to what he had offered her?

"I love him because he gave me a book. I love him because he walked on the stairs I made for him without hesitation or fear. I love him because his head is in the clouds."

"I love her because her feet are on the earth."

They stopped, and now they were looking at each other. Pomona was smiling at him, almost laughing. They had stumbled over the truth in trying to lie.

Titania clapped her hands.

"Now this is an unexpected delight! Why did you not tell me, Vertumnus? My Vertumnus, my dear one. In love. When shall we have the wedding? This very night? I shall ask Cobweb to play the harp."

Pomona looked at Titania, and then to Vertumnus. Surely they had done all that was required. They had declared their love, here in front of all the gawkers, and now could they not be alone? She did not want a fairy wedding.

"I am most grateful," she said. "But I have a promise to keep, and I cannot marry until I discharge it. I will be leaving Illyria, if the Duke permits, as soon as I may."

She turned away from Vertumnus. Of course he must know she could not stay with him. Love was all very well, but she had given Sycorax her word.

"Leaving!" Titania looked horrified. "Certainly not. What duty could you have? Is the coven gathering, and what is it gathering? Toads and eels? Leave behind such toil, and come and live with us! You can be a spirit of the air, or a dryad of the forest, or go like a canker upon a leaf—whatever you desire."

Pomona bowed her head. "I desire only the freedom to take ship to Milan, once I can pay my passage, and look for a man whose birthright is in my possession."

"And for that you'd leave your lover?"

"She will not have to," said Vertumnus. "If Oberon wants no further task from me, as I expect he will not, then I am free to travel with her. And if she will not be too vexed by my chatter, I will do so."

Pomona whirled to look at him. He was grinning.

"And I will pay your passage, as the reward for returning the ambassador and ending this war," said Orsino.

Viola frowned, and paced, but said nothing.

"Well," said Titania, sinking into a throne that was suddenly there behind her, all built of cobwebs and shadows. "Vertumnus, you are forgiven. I give you your fairy powers again. Fly where you will, and take whatever shape you like. Be an old woman, if that pleased you. Or a dog! What you will!"

A cloud of silver dust flew from Titania's fingertip and settled over Vertumnus' skin so that it sparkled in the shards of sunlight that broke through the hall's great windows.

"What form will you take, Vertumnus?" asked Malchi with a sly smile.

"Whichever best pleases Pomona," he said, and he took his lover's hand.

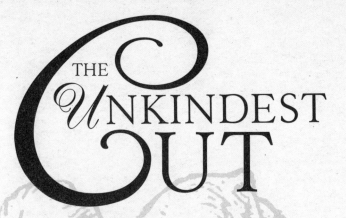

THE UNKINDEST CUT

BY EMMA NEWMAN

This was the most unkindest cut of all.
For when the noble Caesar saw him stab,
Ingratitude, more strong than traitors' arms,
Quite vanquished him. Then burst his mighty heart.
Julius Caesar, Act III, Scene ii.

Tuscany, 1601

"I SIMPLY CANNOT tell you what the future holds."

Lucia turned from her mother, chilled, and looked out of the carriage window. Why couldn't she tell her? She always knew.

There was nothing but her reflection to look at, the black night impenetrable on the other side of the glass, so she let the curtain fall closed again. It was cold and the furs wrapped around her shoulders did nothing to stop her shivering. Her mother *knew* what was to come, but was afraid to tell her. It was the only explanation.

"If you've seen something terrible, there's no need to keep it from me," she said. "I am old enough to face it."

Her mother's face was pale in the lantern light. She looked tired, and older than Lucia liked to think she was. The deep red velvet of her cloak made her look ill in contrast. "Dear heart, I have always told you the truth. I cannot tell you because I cannot see it."

"Have you lost your gift?"

"No."

"You can see the future for others, then, still?"

Her mother's sigh was one of a woman tired beyond words. "Sweet child, rest now."

"But where are we going?"

"To one who has answers to our questions. The one who taught me how to See. She will reveal the path ahead again and all will be well."

Her mother's eyes closed again and Lucia knew there was nothing more to learn from her.

So this was what it was like for everyone else. Their future was like the darkness outside of the carriage. How did they bear it? The uncertainty twisted Lucia's stomach into painful knots as she tried to hold on to what she knew—what she had always known—for surely that hadn't changed?

Her mother had never lied to her, not when it came to matters of the Sight. She had gifted the truth to her daughter in stories, now woven so deeply into her that Lucia could not think of herself without thinking of them.

The stories started with her birth and how her mother had taken the blood from the cord that had joined them in the womb and gone out into the moonlit night to smear it on her eyelids and lips to learn of her child's fate. She had seen her child's future so clearly it was like looking out of a window onto a pageant outside. Joy and celebration, drama and love, all were there for her to see; and her child at the centre of it, bringer of peace. She saw the tiny baby, crying even now for her breast, grow into a beautiful young woman, saw her marry the son of their enemy, saw her end the war. She saw the love she had to foster between the young couple and her duty was clear. She had to surmount the challenges of war and find a way for the boy and the girl to meet often, so that the gardens of their hearts could be planted with moments to bind them together. Such a handsome young man. So noble, despite his father. And her daughter, sweet as a pomegranate, so gifted in the arts of song and politics. She saw her grandchildren, the eldest ruling over Tuscany, the fields rich with bounty and the people happy and plump again. All springing from the blood on her lips and eyes, the blood in her baby, in her emptied womb.

Lucia de Medici had her future drawn out by her mother like a coastline beneath a cartographer's hand, and Lucia was all too happy to follow that map. Francesco de Medici didn't know his path, but he was happy to fall into step alongside her as the love between them deepened. Lucia reached beneath the furs to touch the locket, resting warm over her heart. She thought of the miniature of him inside it and the lock of his black hair that she longed to run her fingers through. They had kissed three times, when he thought her mother wasn't looking, not knowing that their chaperone was there to ensure the blossoming of lust rather than prevent it. His lips were like the petals of roses and just the thought of him sent a thrill through her body. Her moon's blood had come at last and her mother had prepared her as best she could. The mothers had met in secret, solving the problem of the war in a simple conversation over wine. So much more civilised that the breast-beating, sword-wielding men who couldn't get past their own pride to end the war they'd started. The betrothal was arranged, leaving only the fathers to be persuaded at the right time so that the formalities could be observed and the wedding arranged.

All had unfolded as her mother had Seen, some sixteen years before; and Lucia had found it nothing but comforting. Of course, there had been some trepidation before she met Francesco for the first time, but that was only natural. As her mother had explained, their love was inevitable. History and myth were riddled with stories of people doing all they could to escape their fate, only to meet it through their struggles. All it did was increase suffering on the way. There was nothing to do but sink into her destiny as she would let her head sink into a feather pillow. Francesco—handsome, noble Francesco—was all that she would want in a husband and there was no need to fear he would reject her attention. Attracting and winning him was as easy as breathing. And she fell in love with him the moment he kissed her hand, as if her heart had been waiting for it.

But this past week her mother had started to look tired in the mornings and the laughter that usually flowed from her dried up like a river in drought. She seemed uncertain when Lucia asked her how to reply to a secret letter from Francesco, and she wouldn't even talk about the wedding. Lucia had taken to avoiding her—it was too unsettling!—choosing instead to practise her dancing for the wedding whilst the rest of the household fretted about the war. Her brother had shouted at her, saying she was a silly child for being so happy as so many suffered, but she forgave him. He didn't have the comfort of knowing that it would all be over soon.

As she was brushing her hair before bed that night, her mother had come to her chamber and bid her dress for travel. That had been hours ago, surely? Whoever her mother's teacher was, she liked to live a long way away from the civilised. With nothing to keep her from worrying about her mother's behaviour, Lucia had finally confronted her, and the answer had been far from comforting. She couldn't decide if knowing what troubled her was worse than ignorance.

She wished she was still a child and could move to the seat next to her mother and curl up with her head on her lap, like she used to. But now she was a woman and soon she would be riding in carriages with her husband and a new entourage; and besides, she was too tall. This was simply practice—yes, that was it, practice for her married life when she wouldn't be able to consult her mother daily and would have only her own thoughts for counsel.

Just as she had settled into patience, the carriage tilted as the road climbed a hill. A mournful howl made Lucia pull her furs tighter around her. There was no footman, only the driver. The worst of the fighting was far from here, but in these times of war, violence spread like the plague. Had her mother not considered bandits or deserters? She shook her head at that; her mother wouldn't have set out if there was danger ahead. She would have Seen it. Lucia settled again, hoping above all else that her mother still had the Sight for her own safety, even if it had been lost when she tried to see her daughter's future.

The carriage tilted as the road got steeper, and she slid forwards in her seat, rousing her mother. Grasping Lucia's hand, she moved across to sit next to her, pushing their backs into the seat against the incline. Her mother didn't let go and Lucia wrapped her other hand around hers too, squeezing it affectionately. Her mother kissed her cheek and it felt better again, like it always had, the two of them together as they moved forwards.

"We're almost there," she said to Lucia's relief.

"Are we to stay the night?"

Her mother's smile suggested she'd said something ridiculous. "I think not." She kissed the top of Lucia's hand. "Now you must listen. I cannot go in with you, so you must remember everything I've taught you about respect for the craft. Speak only when you are invited to, and if you must ask a question, think carefully before you do."

"How should I introduce myself to the servant who answers the door?"

"Sweet one, my teacher waits for you in a cave near the base of Monte Prado."

Images of a fine mansion were swept from her imagination. "A cave?"

"One that is steeped in history. A place of power for those of the Sight. It may look humble, but you know better than to trust the lies your eyes tell you."

Lucia nodded, greedy for the information, preparing herself for whatever awaited her. "Is there anything I should not say or tell her?"

Her mother smiled again, this time filled with love and appreciation. "Her knowledge is vast and her interest in our politics is negligible. If she asks you a question, reply truthfully. Everything I have done is in accordance with her teachings and you have nothing to fear."

"Will I be tested in some way?"

"I think not. I have asked her to divine your future and see which force impedes my Sight. We are so close, dear heart, so close to ending this war and giving you your heart's desire. I cannot let anything endanger our plans or your happiness."

The carriage slowed and then stopped, Lucia's heart with it. She pulled the curtain aside to see the entrance to a cave lit from within by a flickering, orange glow. "What if she finds me wanting in some way?"

"My teacher will see your purity and your merit. They are as impossible to hide as these mountains."

Lucia pulled up the hood on her cloak, its midnight blue the colour of her eyes, something Francesco had commented on when they last met. She tried to remember the last time she'd done something important without knowing how it was supposed to go. She battled the impulse to stay safe in the carriage with her mother, and reached for the door handle as the driver climbed down.

Her mother rested her hand on her shoulder. "Lucia, you are the world to me. A mother could not hope for a more delightful daughter. Have courage."

She kissed her mother's cheek and let the driver help her down. Only when the door was shut behind her and she started towards the cave did she realise how warm it had been in the carriage. The wind howled and tugged at her furs and cloak, but she gripped them tightly in her gloved hands and made her way to the mouth of the cave. As much as she wanted to, she didn't look back, fearing that if she saw her mother's face pressed against the glass with worry, she might lose her resolve.

A few paces inside, away from the wind, Lucia relaxed her grip on the furs and pulled her hood down to shield her eyes and see better. The cave was lit by torches and huge candles set into natural recesses in the rock walls. Heaps and streams of tallow beneath each candle marked the years in their thickness and length. Towards the back of the cave the floor sloped downwards into darkness and she knew that was where she had to go.

Lucia lifted the hem of her dress and made her way deeper into the cave, taking care to avoid pits in the rock, deep enough to turn an ankle. The place smelled of smoke, animal fat in the tallow and damp stone. She had never been anywhere so primitive; she wondered if this was where her mother had learned her art. The slope was steeper than she'd appreciated, and as she moved away from the entrance, she could see that it fell to an area about the size of her bedchamber. It was darker, only one torch lit between her and something that caught the light right at the back... a puddle perhaps?

She paused, uncertain if anyone was there, and then remembered what her mother had said. She closed her eyes and stilled herself, becoming aware of another presence at the back of the cave, shrouded in shadow.

"Aaahh..."

The voice was that of an old woman, deep and rich with age and wisdom. Lucia curtsied deeply.

"Such beauty, such manners... Come, child, come."

Lucia straightened and walked towards the voice, into the darkness. She had no sense of a cave wall ahead of her. It felt as if she were in an alcove on the edge of a chasm so wide and so deep that all of the night-times of the earth could be contained within it at once.

Just as she lost sight of her feet in the dark, she saw a small pool of water, held within a natural stone bowl hollowed out of a stalagmite at waist height. It was lit by a single pale yellow flame that burned without a wick at the centre of the water. The sense of magic was so strong it made the tiny hairs on the back of her neck prickle.

"Are you afraid, child?"

"A little. I was taught that magic is like fire. If it's respected and one takes care, it can be of great benefit. But if one is ignorant or careless, it can destroy and disfigure. I don't know you and I'm not in control of the magic here. I respect you—and it—enough to be fearful."

"Your mother taught you well. Come to the pool. No harm will come to you here. There is no magic to be worked against you, little bird, and no nightmare that will manifest itself before the dawn."

As Lucia approached the pool, the woman did too. Lucia couldn't see her face, which was hidden beneath a veil of spun silver, but she could see some strands of hair it didn't cover and they were black as a crow's breast. She was wearing a white samite gown with a silver cord about her waist. Only her hands were visible, slender and elegant. Lucia wondered if she was beautiful beneath the veil, and then remembered that it hardly mattered. With a magic such as she could sense under her command, surely she could appear as she wished.

"Your mother was one of my favourite pupils. I could see she wanted a child, even when she was younger than you. For most, I would deny it, but she was a brilliant, bright thread in fate's weave and to deny her that would have been to deny a force greater than I. And now you stand before me, ripe yet unplucked, woman yet still child, innocent. You have beauty, yet it is of a budding rose, one yet to bloom; and when it does, the world will know it. Why did your mother bring you here?"

"She cannot see my future. She said a force impedes her Sight. With so much resting on my betrothal to my love, she wanted to be certain that nothing could interfere with our plans."

The woman walked around the bowl, moving to stand behind her. She eased the furs and then the cloak from her shoulders, letting them fall to the floor. Lucia still wore several layers of cotton, silk and wool, but she felt the cold nonetheless. "When did you last bleed?" The woman rested a remarkably warm hand over the space a child would grow. Lucia could feel the heat penetrating her dress and undergarments.

"Almost a moon ago."

The woman's hand pressed in, as she had seen a midwife press a pregnant woman at her friend's house once, and a murmur of satisfaction rumbled behind her. "Good. Yes. Good. Look into the flame."

Lucia did as she was told as the woman moved away and returned to her station on the far side of the bowl. The flame floated just above the water and she worked hard to accept it as it was. Disbelief and questioning would only get in the way. The flame was there, now; it didn't matter how.

"Draw in a breath, deep, and think of your love, your marriage and the destiny you believe is yours. Hold it in your breast until it burns and then breathe out, over the flame."

When Lucia drew in the breath, the flame guttered and she felt a quickening deep inside her, beneath where her hand had rested but moments before. She forced herself to think about Francesco and the marriage and ending the war, and her thoughts were pulled back to him: his body, the wedding night and the moment they would join.

She breathed out, a flush in her cheeks. Her fear that she would blow out the flame was short-lived. It spread outwards until the surface of the water was completely covered with fire. Instead of a pale yellow it burned a ferocious red, and the heat made her pull back for fear of singeing her hair.

"This pool was formed over thousands of years from the tears of the earth," the woman said. "There is power here that men cannot understand. There is power here that sorcerers cannot understand. There is power here that the fairies themselves cannot understand. But it speaks to me. Look at the fire you have made, rosebud. Are you willing to hear what it will tell me?"

"I am."

The woman lifted her hands until her palms were either side of the fire and tilted her head as if looking up in to the rock above them. "Lucia de Medici"—the flames turned a cold blue as her voice deepened—"you are destined to wed Francesco de Medici two moons from now, on a day that will see snow fall and the sun shine. This union will end the war and bring peace to this land. But the path to that day is beset with suffering. There is a man who intends to destroy your plans." The flames paled and rippled, as if bent by a sudden breeze that Lucia couldn't feel, yellowing at the tips. "Prospero, sorcerer Duke of Milan possesses a knife he intends to use against you and your love." The flames brightened again, taller than before, radiating a cold that she could feel as if she were leaning over a pool of ice. "The blade will shed blood that will worsen the war. The blade will kill the man you love. You will never bear his children."

The flames went out and they were plunged into darkness. Lucia fumbled for her cloak and furs, trying not to cry, trying to hold herself together. She couldn't take it in. A blade? The Duke of Milan? This was never the story her mother told her. This wasn't the way it was supposed to be!

The pale yellow flame returned and she pulled her cloak about herself, shivering, as the woman gripped the sides of the bowl. "This is why your mother cannot see," the woman said. "Prospero weaves a dark magic about you, thinking that no woman would be able to see his design. He does not know the extent of my power."

"He's going to kill Francesco? But why? It makes no sense. Unless..." She grasped the locket tight, as if it could somehow hold him close and safe too. "Does Prospero know that our marriage would end the war?"

"He is a powerful man, with many skills."

"He must want the war to continue. Father thought as much— else he would have allied himself to him, or my uncle. I heard tell of his foul disposition since the death of his daughter. Now I and the man I love are to suffer because of it? Can nothing be done? Am I not fated to marry Francesco? Are not destiny and love enough to prevent his foul scheme?"

The woman moved around the bowl again, cupping Lucia's face in her hand. This time it felt cold and Lucia's cheek burned against it. "Perhaps they are, if you have courage too."

A flicker of hope ignited in her chest. "What must I do?"

"You must steal this blade before he works his evil and you must take his life with it, to cut that evil from the world."

Lucia shook her head. "I can't even kick a dog or step on a spider! How can I kill a man? I haven't the stomach for murder!"

"Perhaps you have the stomach for grieving over your betrothed's coffin. Perhaps you have the stomach to live the rest of your life without him as your family is torn apart by war, and its sisters, famine and plague? Perhaps when everyone else you love is either dead or grieving, you will find solace in the purity of your conviction that you could never kill a man."

Lucia looked away, back to the pool, stealing her face from the woman's touch. "How could I possibly succeed? He is a sorcerer. I... I know nothing of use."

A finger beneath her chin made her face the veil again. "You are a woman and the one you love is in danger. You will find a way. And you will not be without help. Tell your mother what I have seen in the pool's flames. She will get you to Milan. But only you can enter Prospero's tower and only you can kill him, because you will have fate on your side. His actions pull you away from your true path, like a bow string pulled from rest. There is power to be used here. Kill him with the blade before he can kill your love, and fate's thread will draw you back into place, making you stronger than you may believe."

"And if I kill him? Will all be well?"

"Little rosebud, ask yourself this: if I do not kill him, will all be well?"

Lucia bit her lower lip to stop it from trembling. Could she find it within herself to do such a thing?

"And I will aid you," the woman said. She presented a tiny glass bottle, pulled out its cork, filled it with water from the pool, stoppered it and gave it to her. "Thrice you may drink from this, and thrice you will see your future. But have a care, there is always a price when such magic is employed."

Lucia took it and the yellow flame flickered again, a chill

spreading over her skin and seeping into her breast. She couldn't stop shivering as the woman kissed her through the veil, once on each cheek, and wished her well. She was still shaking when she got back to the carriage; and even in her mother's arms, with her hand stroking her hair and her gentle voice saying they would find a way back to her destiny, that chill did not lift from her heart.

AT THE END of it all, Prospero could summarise his decision so neatly it brought the first smile to his face for years. Better to let go of a life that had ultimately disappointed him, than to spin dark magics and prolong it. He had power—both political and magical—and yet the sense of dissatisfaction was immense. What use was power without desire? What use was life without love? What use was holding on to the present when there was no future anyway?

His daughter was dead these twenty years. Whilst the sharpness of the grief had faded, the misery it had left behind had only deepened. He could keep it at bay with study, and the occasional thrill of mastering a new technique but it always crept back. It was like a darkness had settled within him, one that he had to constantly battle to lift. Sometimes he couldn't even find it in himself to do that.

She had been unhappy in her marriage and he had ignored her plea for help. No matter how many times he told himself that her death after childbirth was no fault of his own, he couldn't help but think that if he'd freed her from that miserable union, she would still be alive today. Perhaps she would have found love elsewhere, had children. Heirs.

Perhaps he should have settled for one of the women who'd shown an interest over the years since and started a new family. But he'd known their interest was in being Duchess, not in him. And they were such gutless, vacuous things, all silks and no substance. He wanted a woman who had the courage to fight for what she wanted, who would light a fire in him to drive away the darkness. Such a woman did not exist in Milan, not one that wasn't already married. And he wasn't willing to settle for a glorified house cat just for the sake of having a son. What if they'd had a daughter? He'd lost his stomach for flighty, mercurial creatures who wanted something with all of their soul and then changed their mind as soon as they had it. No constancy. No depth of spirit. A pox on daughters everywhere!

He stood and stretched, feeling the creak in his joints from sitting in maudlin silence for so long. The candles were low and there was still correspondence to address before making his final journey. He poured himself another cup of wine and cut himself a hunk of cheese, taking a moment to look about his study.

It used to feel bigger, but over the years he'd brought in books and curios and never taken them out again. Now every shelf of every book case was stacked to the brim. Tables and chairs were simply differently-shaped shelves, and a film of dust covered them all. He hadn't seen the corners of the room in over two decades and was sure a family of mice had made their home in one. The rest of the ducal palace was pristine, because he didn't live in it. He didn't care about what was in those rooms. Here, where the most valuable things were, he preferred to let dust settle than let a servant in with a will to clean and disrupt.

Of course, arguably the most valuable thing in his possession wasn't in this room, but at the top of the turret two floors above him, where he kept the most dangerous artefacts he'd amassed over the years. The knife was wrapped in cloth and bound with golden thread, sealed in its own box. Soon he would return it to Scotland in accordance with his pact with the Scottish King and formally mark the last year of his life. The decision to return it wasn't reached easily—it was the acceptance of and the commitment to his death, after all—but it felt right. It sat well within him, like a good meal, satisfying and natural. The knife had served its purpose when he needed it and he wasn't prepared to go down the path of exploring its other uses. Unnatural thing! He would see his obligation through and return it to Macbeth by midwinter, knowing that he would be dead by St Stephen's Day. The return of the knife and his death were bound, and to put it off any longer was a folly. If he didn't return it by midwinter's day, Milan and its people would suffer. He might have been a relatively cold Duke, but he wasn't a monster. He would see the people under his care free from any suffering he could prevent.

The pile of correspondence on his desk drew him back. It was the final task before he could pack his last items for travel. Miranda's tomb had been swept and fresh flowers laid there that afternoon. His will was written and deposited with the appropriate parties. He couldn't leave months of letters for his successor to find, no matter how tempting it was. Half of it was from the damn Medicis, each family begging him to side with them for whatever spurious reason they could dream into existence, so those could be sifted out and burned quickly enough. Months of letters he'd resolutely ignored and still they came. He had no interest in taking sides, no matter how much his so-called advisors urged him to. He knew the truth of it; whichever side he chose would win and then he would be blamed for all of the consequences thereafter. War was not something easy to recover from and he wanted none of that burden upon his shoulders. Let the arrogant Medicis slaughter each other. As long as they did it within the borders of Tuscany, he was incapable of having a care.

A third cup of wine went down before the last of the Tuscan letters was burned in the fireplace. Prospero belched loudly with satisfaction at a task well executed. A noise outside of his door stayed his hand as he poured a fourth cup. He opened his door a crack. "Willem?" he called, thinking his errant servant was poking around again when he should be asleep. "Willem? Are you down there?"

No call came to him, but Prospero couldn't let go of the feeling that someone was in the tower with him. But if anyone other than one of his household were there, the wards would be sparkling now, and everything was as quiet as his daughter's tomb. He lit the candle in the holder he used when walking the house at night and stepped out. "Willem?"

He climbed the stairs, twisting as they rose up the tower, passing the door to his bedchamber—still locked—right up to the topmost room. The door was closed, but he heard a sound within. Had something escaped? He lifted the hoop of iron and twisted it to open the door. The moon's light streamed through the arrow-slit window, falling over a cloaked figure at the centre of the room, next to the box containing the knife. A thief? In his tower? Why had the wards not done their work? Were it not for the evidence before his eyes, Prospero would have thought it impossible. Anger swiftly followed the shock and he stormed in, thinking Macbeth had so little trust in him that he'd sent an agent to steal from him prematurely. Just two paces and then his hand was on the thief's shoulder, spinning him round. A girl? A glint of grey metal in the moonlight and then such a pain in his gut that he dropped the candle holder and staggered back.

His hands were wet with his own blood and the dying flame showed him the hilt of that foul blade—cursed thing!—lodged deep within him. His knees crumpled as the girl rushed towards him, wrapping her hands around the handle and whimpering with emotions he could not fathom. The hungry dagger drew his soul from him and there was nothing he could do to staunch the flow of his blood or the last moments of his life. He had time to think of Miranda, running along the beach on the island on one perfect day, laughing, then the sight of her coffin, until that too faded and he was left with the sure knowledge that whoever this wretched, murderous child was, she would suffer endlessly for this crime.

* * *

THE BLOOD FELT hot, spreading over Lucia's hands as she tried to pull out the blade. She could barely see it through her tears as she sobbed over the dying man. She couldn't understand how it had happened; she was unwrapping the knife one moment and in the next it was deep in his stomach. It was as if the blade had been pulled towards him, her hands with it, as if it had a will of its own—bloody, bold and resolute. She was only going to steal the knife to prevent Prospero's plan and then seek a way to turn him from his scheme, and yet she had done as her mother's teacher had asked. All that wrestling with what she'd been told, all the planning and debating and constant arguments with herself and her mother since the night at the cave, all came to nought. Perhaps fate had driven the blade into him and left her—

"Hell's teeth!"

The voice at the doorway snapped her head up and it felt like her heart was tumbling out of her. Francesco in Milan? Now? "My love—"

"Love? If there was any love for you in my breast it is dead now! How could I have thought you sweet and pure when you are capable of this?"

She abandoned the blade and struggled to her feet, blood all over her dress, her hands, her sleeves. "It wasn't my intention to—"

"I saw you strike him! With these own eyes! Murderer! Was not our marriage solution enough? Was the Duke about to support my father? Is that what this is?"

"Francesco! I—"

"No matter the reason, the end is clear enough. As surely as your soul is damned, so is our union."

He turned and fled, his footsteps loud on the flagstone steps. In moments he would be calling the militia and no matter how painful her breaking heart felt, the instinct to survive was still strong. She went back to the body, closed the lids over the

Duke's lifeless eyes and pulled out the blade as easily as one might pull straw from one's hair. Not stopping to wonder why, she wrapped it in the cloth she'd found it in, tied the golden cord around it again before slipping it into the small bag under her cloak.

The key her mother had made to get her into the room had crumbled into dust now its work was done, so she merely shut the door quietly and ran down the stairs, expecting to hear Francesco shouting the servants awake any moment. But the mansion was just as silent as it had been when she had crept in, and she couldn't even hear his footfalls any more. She ran through the rear servants' corridor that she'd used earlier, hoping that Francesco had done the same—it was the easiest route into the house, after all—but she couldn't see him anywhere.

It was many hours since sunset and there were still more before sunrise. She resolved to escape the grounds, get to her horse and see if she could intercept Francesco on the road to plead her case.

The wine cellar was just as silent and empty as before. She lit the lantern she'd hidden behind one of the barrels and hurried through the vast pillared hall, the length of most of the mansion, to the back door left unlocked by a bribed servant. She blew out the candle, hooked the lantern on her belt and then slipped out into the grounds.

She could hear the guard snoring in the gatehouse as she crept past it and the orchard at the far end of the garden was just as deserted as when she'd crept through before. Francesco was nowhere to be seen and hadn't raised the alarm either. She made it to the wall unhindered, climbed over it using the gardener's ladder and pushed it away to land softly in the long grass. It was simple enough to drop down the other side into bushes left overgrown by complacent guards.

Prospero's winter mansion was on the southern edge of the city and surrounded by vineyards. Hardly believing that she'd managed to get out of the house and its grounds without any hindrance, Lucia ran until her legs gave out from under her and she fell into the dirt. She picked herself up and pushed herself on as her throat clogged with tears and guilt rode her shoulders like a serf's yoke. Finally, she reached the shallow river at the edge of the vineyard and collapsed on its bank as the horizon blushed an ominous red. Every time she closed her eyes she saw the blood, and every breath brought with it the memory of Francesco's disgust. Safe for now, she let down her guard and sobbed into the dirt until her throat burned.

"Now there are tears? What sort of creature are you?"

She screamed and threw herself backwards until her arms were in the river. The sorcerer Duke of Milan stood before her, the blood staining his robes too, and he looked very much alive.

"Are you... but I..."

"Killed me, yes, I am aware of that. I was there."

"I swear to you, I only wished to take the blade before you could work your plan."

"Did he have so little faith I'd return it as agreed?"

"I know of no agreement, only of your desire to kill my betrothed."

The Duke's brow wrinkled and he looked genuinely confused. "I have no idea who you are, or who may have the misfortune to be betrothed to you. My plan was to return the blade to Scotland." He looked down at his robes and tried to touch the blood stain, but his fingers passed through the robes and body as if through mist. "God's piss, now I am dead and unable to rest. Were I corporeal, child, I would wring your neck."

"You have every right to haunt me."

"I have no need of your permission, you wretched boil, and don't think I will stop at this. Enjoy your last moments of freedom, for I intend them to end soon enough." He looked as if he were about to walk away, but he didn't go anywhere. He simply stared back towards the mansion as if willing it to lift itself from the ground and walk to him instead. Then after a muttered curse he shook his head. "The blade... of course. Well, this is a sorry affair. I cannot even go back to my body and condemn you, despite the precautions I took against assassination. Cursed blade... Tell me, who sent you, if it wasn't the Scottish King?"

The shock of a ghost berating her having eased, Lucia felt another emotion settle into place; worry. "One gifted with the Sight."

"A witch? I have been murdered by a witch's familiar? How I am brought low!"

"I am no familiar! And she is not a witch, how dare you call her that. I am Lucia de Medici, betrothed to Francesco de Medici, the one you intended to kill with that knife."

The Duke looked at her as if she were a madwoman. "Medici? Perhaps I should be flattered that my killer is no mere serf, but a daughter of a noble house? I have no knowledge of Francesco, other than a scrawl on a family tree that has never held my interest. Why should I wish him harm?"

"I... I was told you wanted the war to go on. Our marriage is supposed to end it." The tears stung again. "And now there will be no marriage. He saw what I did."

"He was the one at the door... I was somewhat distressed at that point. Oh, stop weeping, you pathetic creature! Who do you weep for? Not me! I'm the one you've murdered, and you weep because your betrothed has seen what a villain you are? Only the Medicis are capable of such self-interest!"

"I weep for you too! The knife... it was as if it flew into you, I swear upon my soul! And Francesco saw and thought I intended it, and I swear I did not! I was going to steal the knife, I admit to that, but not murder you, even though I was told to do so to save him and my family!"

"You are like a bottomless pit into which sense sinks and never returns. Why bring him with you if you didn't want him to see?"

"I had no idea he was in Milan! Why should he be? What reason could he have to be at the tower, this night of all nights? It makes no..." She squeezed her eyes shut. "Oh, who schemes against us? I have been tricked! And you are dead because of it. Oh, ground open and swallow me now!"

"Enough of this wailing and drama. There is a design behind all of this, and a solution, even though neither present themselves as yet. Now, it is in both of our interests to discover them, as we are bound to each other; as much as I would like to see you at the end of a noose, it would do nothing to improve my state. We will unravel this together, and then you will see me put to rest. Otherwise I will haunt you with such cruelty and ferocity that your hair will be white by the new moon and you will be mad by the new year."

There was sense in his words and it penetrated her misery. She nodded. "If we could find out how Francesco knew to be there, it would be a great help." Could the woman in the cave have told him? No, her mother's faith in her teacher was absolute. She'd said the warning her teacher had given could only be the truth, in such a sacred place. Someone else had to be involved. "I feared he would raise the alarm, but he hasn't. I don't know where he is now."

"Of course he stayed quiet," the Duke said, trying to fold his arms only to give up with a scowl as they kept passing through each other. "How could he explain his presence there without putting himself under suspicion? No doubt he will wait until he is in the bosom of his family before denouncing you. We have time. Wash yourself and follow this river upstream for an hour or so. There's a lodge up there that is empty at this time of year."

In the dawn light she could see the blood all too clearly. She plunged her hands beneath the icy water to scrub at them desperately. "I have a horse nearby, I'll get him and do as you say. But wouldn't it be better for me to try to find Francesco?

There are few roads he can take, and—"

"If you wish me to find him, I will," the Duke said with a bitter voice. "That is the way of things for now."

"Very well," Lucia dried her hands on her cloak, the blood still caught under her fingernails, making her shudder. "May I say, your Grace, you're coping with this turn of events so very well."

The Duke shrugged. "I had only a few weeks left. You just cast them into chaos. I would prefer things to be in order, but it seems I grew complacent. We will speak again soon and you will tell me how you got into my tower without my notice. Until then, stay out of sight. And don't smile at me as if I care about you. I simply care that you stay alive long enough to see me put to rest."

FINDING FRANCESCO DE Medici was far easier than the methods he'd had to employ to find someone as a living sorcerer. Now he was a ghost and the one who commanded his soul happened to be in love with the target, it was a simple matter. He followed a silver thread only he could see: from her heart, across the vineyard and along the road to the coast.

To move so swiftly without effort was a simple joy. The girl was only partly correct; he was not just coping well with Purgatory, he was enjoying it. Being furious with her had felt like opening the window of a room with stale air and having a gale blow though it. He could never have predicted that his death would make him feel alive for the first time in decades.

It wasn't just anger, though. It was the joy of being genuinely stirred into action. Only now did he appreciate how stagnant he had become. Without realising it, his life had become a study in turning things away, be they people or challenges or simply matters of the outside world. What he thought to be triumphs were merely insignificant details, made tremendous by the simple and tragic fact that he'd driven himself so poorly, and achieved so little since Miranda's death, that even the tiniest magical revelation seemed like a moment of genius.

Now he had a genuine question to answer. The Medici girl said she'd been sent by someone with the Sight. A witch, no doubt; and one of significant power, he'd wager. She must have gifted the girl with something to overcome his wards, for one thing, and no mere warty 'wise woman' could do such a thing. He'd have to question her more at the first opportunity.

The young man was in a room on the first floor of an inn that sold passable wine and excellent whores. Prospero followed the thread through the window to find him sitting on the edge of the bed, his head in his hands. He was white-lipped and still in shock, judging by the way his hands still trembled.

Prospero glided over to hover in front of him, his lip curling at the sound of the sniffling. "Can you see me?"

If the Medici could, he didn't react. Prospero went over to the table in the corner with a letter resting upon it.

> *Snr de Medici,*
>
> *To commit one's heart is no small matter. Be sure you give it to one who is worthy. If you wish to learn of your betrothed's true nature, be at the top of Prospero's tower in his winter mansion, south of Milan, on the night of the full moon. Ensure you are seen by no-one. Only then will you know if she deserves your heart.*
>
> *A friend*

The handwriting was familiar, but Prospero couldn't place it. A feminine hand, of that he was sure. He had expected to see the time of his murder—or something closer to it. There was a greater force at work here. Did this boy wait in the shadows all evening, all night, right into the small hours? No, he would have been discovered. He arrived at just the right time to witness the murder.

That, and the girl's immunity to the wards on his room, spoke of more than simple witchcraft. It spoke of the one the witches themselves worshipped.

Francesco went to the window and looked out, eyes bloodshot with weeping and lack of sleep, in the very direction Prospero had just come from.

"You're nothing more than a player on someone else's stage," Prospero said to him. "Fool! Do you hear me?"

There was no response and Prospero went over to wave his hand between him and the window, less than an inch from his face.

The first time he had ever *wanted* to actually speak to one of the Medicis and it was impossible. For such a long time, the only conversations he wanted to have were impossible. How many times had he ached to speak to his daughter, one last time? Death was a cruel separator.

The room took on a grey hue about him and then it felt like he was pulled from it by invisible hands. Prospero found himself on a road in the countryside, but unlike any rural idyll he'd ever travelled. It was too bright, too colourful, to be anything but Fairyland.

A young man was walking towards him and they noticed each other at the same moment. He was dressed in well-made clothes and had a neat, clipped beard and hair that brushed his collar in thick curls, brilliant white despite his youth. Prospero had never seen him before, but couldn't shake the intense sensation that he knew him well. The young man seemed to recognise him, though, stopping so fast he swayed forwards before leaning back, as if repelled by him.

"My eyes deceive me," the young man said. "How can you be here?"

"You can see me, then?"

The stranger's smile was wry. "And you cannot see me."

"But I can. Well met, young traveller. It is a day of wonders.

I am Prospero—"

"I know who you are. You were in my thoughts, but moments ago. You are rarely far from them."

Prospero paused. Something about the tilt of the head, the slant of the shoulders and the anger in the young man's eyes, warring with need... "You remind me of someone who was very dear to me... but forgive me, I don't recall having met."

"I remind you of someone? Of whom do you speak?" The stranger folded his arms. "An old servant, perhaps?"

"My daughter, my only child, who died many years ago."

The stranger looked as if he were about to say something cruel, but the sneer on his lip faded at the sight of Prospero's sadness. "Do you miss her?"

"Every day."

"Were you close?"

"When she was small. She married and we grew apart. It is the way of things. But I don't know your name, or why we are here. This has been a most unusual day."

The stranger looked away from him, choosing to attend to a flower by the side of the road instead of his face. "I'm no-one of importance. Just a traveller. Tell me, how did your daughter die?"

"A fever. She was too young. You remind me of her."

The stranger's eyes flashed a look at him and then he swept his hand up, as if to run it through his hair. Instead, his white hair grew as his hand passed through it and Prospero wondered if he had begun a conversation with a fairy and was about to see the glamour lifted. But then he saw the male shoulders narrow, the hips swell and the face soften and change to one he knew well.

"Miranda!" He moved forward to embrace her, but his reason returned to him before he humiliated himself. "What is this? Some cruel jest? Who are you, in truth?"

"Father... this is no jest. I am here, alive."

Age hadn't touched her. She looked just like she had the last time she came to him, miserable and disappointed by life away from the island. The petals of love's first bloom had curled and fallen and she hadn't been able to find any place in which she felt happy and wanted.

"I want to believe it is you, but we're in Fairyland; and I know that nothing here is as it seems."

"A... friend helped me to escape that life in Milan. I can be what I want now, go where I please, learn what I wish." She took a step closer. "I am Miranda, father."

The little island of joy that his daughter lived—as he had wished for so bitterly over the years—was swallowed by a tsunami of anger. "You let me mourn for you? You let me sink into despair and live a twilight life in the land of grief so you could play fairy games and do as you please? Did you not think for a moment of the man you married and left behind? Of your devoted father? Not once?"

The flicker of guilt on her face was swept away with an angry scowl. "What was there to go back to? Ferdinand and I could never be happy, and you were more interested in keeping Milan than my affection. How many times did I beg you to help me? You had no interest in my happiness when I was alive, and when you believed I was dead all you thought of was *your* lost happiness!"

"Such self-interest! I—"

"*Do not* condemn me for seeking my own life! If scolding me for what my decisions did to *you* is not self-interest, then pray, tell me what is! You think only of your own hurt and not once ask me if I have found some joy at last in these years apart. Is that not what love is? Wanting the other to be content and happy above all else?"

"And with your own words you prove you had no love for me," Prospero said. "How could I be content and happy thinking you were in that tomb instead of the fullness of motherhood?"

She held up a hand, her form changing back into the young man he'd met on the road. "I am more than what men believe to be the fulfilment of my sex. I am more than merely your daughter, who you would rather suffer than cause you shame."

"The evidence is before me," Prospero waved a hand at his— her?—new form. "Oh, how I ache for that island! You were far more thoughtful and obedient as my daughter."

"Perhaps you would have been kinder to a son. Perhaps you would have listened to me when we lived in Milan, or saw value in me, if I had been a male heir."

"Take no comfort in having a fairy glamour, *daughter*. You are still just as capricious and flighty as any woman, beneath that beard!"

"Enough!"

A flick of his child's hand and then Prospero was tumbling in a riot of colours and sounds that soon fell into the shape of his vineyard, stretching out beneath the late autumn sky. The lodge was in sight, a horse tethered outside of it, and he felt the pull of the Medici girl wanting him back, oblivious to the power she wielded over him with that blade.

So Miranda was still alive. And he was dead. The world had been turned on its head, and in so short a span, and unless he did something about the blade, it would soon be worse for far many more.

THERE WERE NO more tears left, only a hollow ache in her stomach; but Lucia couldn't bear the thought of eating the food in her pack. Her mother was leagues away and she had not Seen anything like this. After visiting the cave, her mother had been happy again, telling her each morning that she could see the wedding as clear as her own reflection in the looking glass. "All will be well," she'd said as she'd kissed her goodbye. "Do as my teacher asked and all will be well." Lucia hadn't had the heart to start the argument again and simply nodded obediently.

Even though her intentions had been to disobey, it had gone the way the woman in the cave had wanted. So how could it all feel so terribly wrong now? She didn't feel like she had been snapped back to her true destiny at all.

Then, like a sunbeam through a stormy sky, clarity of thought returned. Both her mother and the woman in the cave had told her she would marry Francesco and all would be well—and in the cave she had been told that if she dealt with the threat of Prospero, her destiny would remain intact. It could mean only one thing: there was nothing to fear. Francesco hadn't raised the alarm as he had no real intention of seeing her harmed. All she had to do was find him and explain, and love would smooth over the disrupted earth between them so they could plant trust anew. All she needed to do was ask Prospero to lead her to him as soon as he returned.

Even as she had the thought, the ghostly sorcerer appeared in the room, casting a disapproving eye over her.

"Good Prospero, at last! Tell me, where is my love? Has he ridden far? Is he travelling—"

"I found him," Prospero drifted closer to her, passing through the rough-hewn table and stools and making her shudder. "He's at an inn, greatly distressed. He was told in a letter to go to my tower last night by one claiming to be a friend, who was concerned he should know your true nature before committing to marriage. A female hand, I believe."

Lucia shook her head. "But the only women who knew of this are my mother and the woman in the cave."

"Is your mother cold enough to have worked such a plan?"

Lucia laughed. "It is as possible as my taking flight and crossing the ocean on wings. My mother has worked hard to let love blossom between Francesco and I. Why destroy that? She first told me we would marry when I was as tall as that table. If she didn't want the union to happen, she had ample opportunity to lie about what she had foreseen. Leave her out of your suspicions."

Prospero's eyebrows were high. "So there is a witch amongst the Medicis themselves? Divining political alliances with dark magic? Interesting."

Lucia's cheeks blazed. How careless she'd been! Not once had she betrayed her mother's secret. But at least she had committed the error only within earshot of the dead. "Did you speak to Francesco?"

"He couldn't hear me, nor see me."

"Only I can do that?"

She took his irritated grunt as agreement and the tension ebbed from her shoulders. Her mother's secret was safe still. "The only other woman who knew of this was the one who told me to do it."

"Then there is our adversary."

Lucia shook her head. "No, no, Your Grace, it cannot be her either. My mother trusts her absolutely, and there are very few people worthy of my mother's trust. And there can be no political motive; indeed, it would be impossible to explain why she would do such a thing. She told me of my destiny and then how to preserve it from your foul scheme—"

"Which did not exist."

Lucia pursed her lips. "I have only your word for that. You had the knife, after all."

"With no intention of doing anything other than return it whence it came! Foolish girl, it is clear you have been tricked. Tell me exactly what happened in that cave and what that witch said about me—precisely."

"It is of no matter now. I—"

"No matter? No matter! You murdered me and it is of *no matter*?"

Lucia shut her eyes, covering her mouth with cupped hands.

For shame, she was so thoughtless when upset. "Forgive me. I simply meant that this—" She stopped, realising she was about to tell the man she'd murdered that she'd realised all would be well. "I... I simply meant that it is done now and surely we cannot undo that harm."

"You cannot restore me to life, it's true, but I would dearly like to know which puppeteer pulls your strings. Surely you do too."

She nodded. The knowledge would help repair the rift between her and Francesco. After all, she still had to find a way to do that; as her mother had taught her, sitting back and doing nothing was a sure way to ensure that fate brought about its plan in the most tiresome way possible. Better to work with fate than do nothing at all.

"Now, tell me everything about this woman in the cave, with every detail, no matter how small." When she hesitated, he spread his hands. "I cannot tell anyone else. Come now, I'd wager this creature does not deserve your loyalty."

"But what about Francesco?"

"He isn't going anywhere yet; and besides, I can find him easily enough."

Slowly at first, she related her encounter in the cave. She remembered it all vividly, as if it had happened only hours before. Her mother had taught her to pay attention to detail. Prospero paced as she spoke, his silent footsteps horribly disconcerting. When she described the woman, he held up a finger.

"Her hands, tell me about them again."

"They were slender and soft."

"But not aged?"

Lucia paused. "No. But her voice sounded like that of an old woman."

Prospero nodded to himself. "Go on."

She told him the rest. By the end of it, he was still, staring at the floor. "Think back to the flames. Were they blue when she spoke of me? Think carefully now."

Lucia shook her head. "No. They were only tall and blue when she spoke of my marriage and what would happen if you succeeded. I thought the flames flickered yellow when she spoke of you because you threatened my fate."

"No! Ha! Here we have it. She used your ignorance against you and played upon what little knowledge you have to great effect. The pool was in a cave, I warrant this cave was near to Monte Prado."

"At its foot! But she said men had no idea that the pool was there or what it did."

Prospero snorted. "I've read about it, but until now, I thought it was mere myth. Now, the knife, where is it?"

She pulled in from her bag. He moved through the table again. "Wrap the cord about it more tightly and tie three knots as you do."

She followed his instructions and he seemed satisfied. "You know who that woman was, don't you?"

He nodded. "Not a witch, but the one they worship. The source of their power. Hecate."

"I was in the presence of a goddess?" Lucia felt her cheeks pale. Her mother was her student! "But... I don't understand."

"The flames in the pool are blue when true prophecy is spoken. Only she would dare speak a lie in its presence. And you said her hand felt hot when she touched you the first time, then cold the second."

"Yes, but my cheeks were hot, it is simple enough to understand."

"No, she placed a spell on you. Did you not feel cold afterwards? Did you think you had caught a chill for days, until you became accustomed to it?" When she nodded, he pointed a finger at her. "You were able to enter my house, my private tower and my most protected chamber without my knowledge. I have wards on that uppermost room that can keep *anything* out—be it a spider or a thief—so tell me, why could you go in so effortlessly?"

"The spell she placed on me?"

"Precisely. I warrant you feel warmer now." At her nod, he grinned. "I admire her efficiency. No need to continue to protect you, now you have done her bidding."

"But... no! This still makes no sense! Why would she tell me to do this? Are you her enemy?"

"Not in person, but witches cannot abide the scholarly order we men impose upon magic. I can only assume this grievance is cast upon me tenfold by a goddess of witchcraft. And there's the knife. I have long suspected a connection between it and her. It was hungry. That was why it pulled toward me."

"If I am to believe you," Lucia said, wrapping her arms about herself, "and accept that she merely used me to kill you, then what of the marriage?"

"Can you think of nothing else?"

"This is my fate!" Her voice filled the hut. "All of my life has been working towards this moment. And don't say that this is my inability to consider others, for it is the very opposite! This marriage will end the war that is destroying my family and so many others. Francesco and I must be reconciled! She may have had the will to end your life, but those flames were blue when she spoke of mine and Francesco's marriage!"

"But they were also blue when she spoke of the blade killing the man you love, and—"

"Only because of your plot against him and the knife..." she stopped. "But... I don't know what to believe now. My mother said she could see our marriage, the very morning I left. And the blade killed you, not Francesco. Oh, would that my mother could help me now!"

"This is what happens when magic is left in the hands of women," Prospero muttered. "Now you cannot think of anything other than what your mother placed between your ears."

"Have a care, Your Grace. My mother is wise and wants

nothing more than to end this war and see her daughter happy. Is that not true of all good parents? To seek peaceful times for their children to flourish and to give them happiness?"

He turned away. "There is a more pressing concern," he said after a few moments. "The knife must be returned to Scotland by midwinter. Otherwise my people will be cursed and their suffering will dwarf that of Tuscany." He faced her again. "You must return it for me."

"I cannot! I must go to Francesco and resolve this. Two prophecies that differ so much cannot both be true. This blade cannot kill Francesco *and* see us married. All I can imagine is that her interference has made both possible—she is a goddess, after all—therefore I must ensure my path leads back to my rightful destiny. I will marry Francesco."

"No. Take the blade to Scotland and do more good than simply fawning upon a man who hates you. He thinks you a monster! "

"I cannot let him think that of me!"

"How are you to turn his heart? Will you say, 'Love, you were mistaken, for the Duke and I were simply rehearsing a play'?"

"You mock me. I am not some lovestruck fool. I need to end this war! How can I do that by going to Scotland? You must have a servant you can send with it."

"I would not trust that blade in anyone's hands. At least, if you have it, I can see the job done and help you as far as I can."

Lucia folded her arms. "I will go to Francesco first."

"Think, you thick-headed child! Let us say you go to plead your defence to Francesco. What if it sours? What if he attacks you and you defend yourself? And with what? The knife! Going to find him could play into fate's hands and fulfil the prophecy you fear."

Lucia shivered. How many times had she read stories of people rushing off to do something to prevent a fate they were terrified of, only to make it come about? "I know! I shall leave the knife here, where it can do no harm."

"I forbid it! You cannot abandon it here, it's far too powerful and valuable. Besides, if you did manage to win him back, I doubt you would care about returning it to Scotland once you've left it behind. No, you must keep it close. It's the very least you can do for me."

The guilt struck her in the chest, as if he'd hit her, and she felt the sting of more tears. What use were they?

"Wait, I know what I have to do." She rummaged in her bag until she found the pouch containing the tiny bottle given to her in the cave. "She couldn't have done anything to the water in the pool, could she?"

"I have no idea."

"I have one draught left. The first I used to determine that yesterday was the best day to come to your house."

"Aah," Prospero nodded. "Half of my servants are away on various errands and I was distracted. And the second draught?"

"I used it to check if I would be discovered on my route into the house."

"But wait, does each draught show you all possibilities from a course of action?"

"No. I was just being cautious. I bribed a few people to find out about your servants and then I bribed two of them to gain entry into the house and passage through it to your tower. I used this to check what I had decided to do was correct."

"Bribed?" Prospero looked horrified. "My servants?" When she nodded, he tried to kick a stool. "And to think of all the kindnesses I've shown them!"

"Well, they couldn't have been very memorable; they forgot them soon enough at the sight of some gold." Lucia wondered if he even knew the meaning of the word *kindness*. No, she was being unfair. "I'm going to go and speak to Francesco and I am going to leave the knife here—and before you protest, I swear that if this is the right course of action, I will see it's returned to Scotland."

"You expect me to have faith in a girl stupid enough to be tricked into murdering me?"

Lucia stood and slapped her hand on the table. "You are like an old wasp, you cannot resist the opportunity to spread misery! I am so tired of your cruel words. I know what I did was terrible but, i'faith, it was not my intention. Now you know a goddess was behind this sorry affair and whilst I will feel this guilt for the rest of my days, I cannot think of a way to put things right with your constant stinging. Now be quiet or I will ignore you and drive *you* into madness instead!"

His mouth had fallen open and he blinked at her, once, twice, before nodding slowly. "I have lived an unhappy life too long. I have forgotten what it is to be civil."

"Well," Lucia said, sitting again. "I understand that this is a difficult time for you too, so let us draw a line and start afresh, otherwise neither of us will find any resolution to our woes." She closed her eyes, mostly to relieve herself of having to look at his face and the odd expressions crossing it, and breathed deeply. She thought clearly about going to find Francesco and what she would say to him. Then she pulled out the cork and drank the last drops.

The third time was less of a shock, but still an unsettling experience nonetheless. There was the sense of being pulled from her body, floating momentarily in pure darkness before spinning in a chaotic rush of colour and sound as if days and nights were playing out around her all at once. Then there was only one image, one sound. A room in an inn, Francesco's reddened eyes looking at her as if she were Satan himself.

"*The reason? Do you think that reason enters into this? You killed a man and there is nothing you can say that will make me forget the blood on your hands.*"

A ripple of panic shot through her and Lucia fought to keep the feeling of the Sight just a little longer, shifting her decision into finding Francesco in a day or so, when he'd had an opportunity to calm himself and recover from the shock. The chaos returned and then she saw him in the woods on the way to the coast, getting on his horse, the sound of her weeping loud and awful. *"You are dead to me!"*

No! This wasn't the way it was supposed to go. Later, then, just as he reaches the border of Tuscany and has had time to remember their love; she'll speak to him then.

"You disgust me, Lucia. Unhand my cloak! When my family know of your evil, we will notify Milan. Prospero's successor will be all too happy to fight with us against such corruption!"

His hatred and contempt lashed at her every time she made a new decision and tried a new way to persuade him. All the while she had the feeling that some distant part of herself was under terrible strain. She ran out of places to speak to him and things to say and then the course of future events carried on being played out in front of her, images running together in a blur. She saw him reach his father, the look on his face, the sight of messengers leaving the house, one bound for Milan and the rest to his father's troops and supporters. She saw Francesco, beautiful, gentle Francesco, dressed for war, riding out onto the field with his brothers, that happy, trusting glint gone from his eyes. She saw her own father, her brother, forces arrayed behind them and an almighty clash on a snowy day, the white ground stained with blood. She saw her father standing over Francesco, plunging his sword into her betrothed's chest, and then she was screaming, falling, until she landed on her back in the wooden lodge, the ghost standing over her.

Her face was wet and her throat raw. Everything seemed too dull, too slow to be real.

"Yours is not the face of love redeemed," Prospero said, not unkindly. "Take a moment to restore yourself. I fear you grasped that magic's nettle for longer than you should have. I would help you to your feet, were I able."

She rolled onto her side, her body feeling heavy and

uncooperative, and then struggled onto her feet. She moved slowly, righting the stool to sit in silence until her surroundings felt real again.

"All is lost," she whispered. "Neither prophecy has survived. I have condemned so many to death. Francesco is impossible to convince and will not marry me. He isn't killed by that knife but by my father's blade, on the battlefield. I have murdered an innocent man, damned my soul and cast my family's future into Hell itself."

"Not a *very* innocent man, but yes, it does seem bleak."

She looked up at Prospero, the levity in his tone jarring her. "Is this amusing for you?"

"No. I apologise. But whilst you were looking forwards, I was looking back. To the day I made the pact for that blade, in fact. It's capable of so much more than inflicting a premature death. I see a solution, one that prevents the war, but it won't be easy for you."

She wiped the tears from her cheeks and straightened her back. "Then tell me this plan, Your Grace. I will do whatever I can to prevent the war. No matter how hard it may be."

"OH, LUCIA." HER mother's eyes shone with tears. "You look so beautiful."

Lucia stared at her wedding gown in the looking glass, unable to look herself in the eye. It was midnight blue velvet with gold embroidery and tiny seed pearls on the bodice. It was just as she had always wanted it to look, and evidently what her mother had always seen.

"Why so sad?" Her mother came over and fussed with one of the jewels pinned into Lucia's hair. "Is it nerves? That's perfectly natural. But you have no need of fear today, dear heart. You are not the ignorant bride who has no idea whether she will be making her home in a house of happiness or misery. We both know this is the beginning of a wonderful marriage, many times blessed, just like you are. So smile and enjoy the day! It's not just a wedding, it's the end of the war!"

Lucia forced her lips to curve just enough to send her mother bustling away to the door to shout at one of the servants, as she liked to do when filled with an excess of excitement.

Tired of her reflection, Lucia went to the window and looked down onto the courtyard bathed in winter sunshine. It was filled with a frenzy of activity. Servants carried platters of food from the kitchens to the hall, cutting across the courtyard as the cloisters were full of people arranging flowers and banishing cobwebs. She watched the gates open to admit a band of musicians dressed in their finery, followed by more florists. Were there any flowers left outside of this house?

Her brother, Matteo, strode into the centre to look up at the clouds and noticed her looking down at him. He bowed with a flourish and sent a kiss up to her. He had narrowly avoided death several times over the past year. The news he would never have to ride out again made him run over to her, scoop her up in his arms and spin her around, kissing the top of her head as she squealed. "My life is mine again! I hope this union brings you more happiness than it costs you."

"Of course," she'd said. But only because everyone was looking at her. She had endured a fortnight of pretending to look happy. Everyone thought her early nights had been to ensure she looked her best for the wedding, but in truth, it was simply the fact that by the end of the day, she was sick of their endless cheeriness and banter. She was tired of aunts taking her to one side to impart their paste gems of wisdom, tired of her father boasting of how easily he'd brokered the peace, as if the entirety of her mother's work had played no part, and tired of her mother's quiet satisfaction.

But more than anything, she was tired of keeping silent about what happened in Milan.

"It's going to snow," her brother shouted towards one of the ground floor windows. "I'd wager one hundred florins on it." The doors behind him opened again and a footman went to her brother. "Groom ahoy!" he called out. When he saw she was still looking down at him he waved his hands at her, as if shooing away a cat. "Go, Lucia! Don't let him see you!"

She ducked behind the curtain, heart booming in her chest. This was it. The day she had been waiting for ever since she could speak. She should be happy. She should be skipping down the stairs and giggling as her train was arranged. She bit her lip and waited for the tearfulness to pass. Her mother was calling her name. It was time to meet her destiny.

A flurry of attendants, her mother's last emotional goodbye, her father's arm at the doorway to the great hall. Whispered assurances that she looked radiantly beautiful, messages of luck, health and happiness and smiles everywhere she looked. A rush of guests taking their seats, the scraping of their chairs and the gentle murmur of their anticipation. It felt unreal, impossible, as if all of it was happening to someone else and she was a few steps back, watching. And then the doors opened and the musicians began.

"FRANCESCO! I CAN call you brother at last!" Matteo clapped him on the back. "Much better than running you through!"

Francesco laughed. "Better to be brothers, indeed. War makes fools of us all and I would much rather the wine do that."

"Have a care, brother," Matteo grinned as he clinked his cup against Francesco's. "An excess of foolishness in the daytime can lead to misery in the night."

Lucia blushed and Francesco laughed at her, wrapping an arm about her waist and pulling her close to kiss her cheek. "There will be no misery now. I forbid it. And as your lord and husband, sweet wife, you must obey."

Lucia forced a smile and extricated herself from his grip. "Forgive me, there are so many more people to speak to."

She spent the rest of the afternoon smiling until her face ached, talking until she was almost hoarse and dancing until her feet throbbed. As with all things borne on the wings of dread, the call to let the married couple go to their conjugal bed came all too soon.

Francesco, laughing and rosy cheeked, let himself be pushed by his groomsmen to the centre of the hall and Lucia knew better than to resist her attendants. The cheer when he picked her up made her ears ring. They were followed out of the hall, across the courtyard covered in snow, through the doors into the other wing of the house; and then watched as Francesco carried her up the stairs. When they reached the top, he swung her around so she could wave and see her mother dabbing her eyes and then they carried on down the corridor as the guests returned to the party.

Francesco fumbled with the door latch and then they were inside their room. He stole a kiss before putting her down and closing the door.

The bed was laid with fresh linen and rose petals were strewn across the pillows. The candles had already been lit, as had the fire, and pomanders scented the air beautifully.

She moved away from him, putting the bed between them. "Hasn't this gone far enough?"

He ignored her, singing some bawdy song that Matteo had taught him as he began to loosen his doublet. It was only when all the buttons were undone that he looked at her and realised she was standing still with her arms crossed.

"Oh... you're afraid. Yes... I see. I can only assure you that I will do my best to be a kind and considerate husband." His smile didn't warm her. "After all, hasn't it been foretold that we will have a happy marriage?" He came round the side of the bed. "With many children?" He looked at her breasts as he said it and she feared she was going to be violently ill.

She darted out of his way as he came closer and put the bed between them once more. "But don't you have another obligation? The blade must be returned to Scotland by midwinter, and that's so very close."

The sorcerer smiled at her with Francesco's eyes. "Oh, I have given that considerable thought and I've concluded there is no longer any need. After all, I find myself in a healthy, young body, with a beating heart and many years of life left in it. I would be willing to argue that as my soul is housed within it, I couldn't possibly be considered dead. Therefore the terms of the agreement dictate that I may retain it."

Lucia looked away, unable to bear the sound of his voice without the echo of her lover's soul. She had cut it from him as he slept, the sorcerer instructing her as she had sobbed, her only pitiful comfort being that he showed her how to do it in such a way as to send her Francesco's soul on, rather than trapping him in purgatory. The ritual had been complex and exhausting, but it was the only way to bring peace.

She made herself look at him, tried to reconcile the beauty of her lover with the wily old man looking back at her, as if his face were a mask he had stolen from another. Would she be able to live with him? Was it enough to know there was no other way to end the war?

Everything spoken over the blue flames in the cave had come to pass. She had married Francesco de Medici on a day with both snow and sunshine and the union had brought peace to the land. She had indeed suffered. The blade had shed blood that would worsen the war. It had killed the man she loved before they could have children and now another was in his place. And now, seeing it all laid before her, she wondered whether her mother's assurances about it being a happy marriage were even true. Nothing had been said about that in the cave.

She had been a child that night, and then her innocence had been peeled from her, leaving her raw and weeping. The last sliver was about to be lost, all because she had listened when she had been told what was to happen to her and accepted it without question.

No more.

She had written to Edinburgh; would see the horrid weapon returned to its master. She'd had no reply, though she'd seen things in her dreams, just as the unseasonably bitter weather had settled in.

She would learn about politics. She would learn about gods and fairies. She would study.

She would give her new husband a turn of the moon. If Prospero's soul didn't learn kindness and the art of being gentle from his youthful form, she needn't suffer for the rest of her life. After all, she hadn't only learned not to trust to the whims of others.

She had also learned how to kill.

EVEN IN THE
CANNON'S
MOUTH

BY ADRIAN TCHAIKOVSKY

And then the lover,
Sighing like furnace, with a woeful ballad
Made to his mistress' eyebrow. Then a soldier,
Full of strange oaths and bearded like the pard,
Jealous in honor, sudden and quick in quarrel,
Seeking the bubble reputation
Even in the cannon's mouth. And then the justice,
In fair round belly with good capon lined,
With eyes severe and beard of formal cut,
Full of wise saws and modern instances;
And so he plays his part.

As You Like It, Act II, Scene vii.

Act I

Illyria, 1601

A desert shore, after a storm.

Spars and ropes and broken fragments of ship are strewn in abandoned disarray, along with sodden mounds of cloth. All is calm. Seabirds call out and their shadows cross the sand.

The closest heap of cloth twitches, shudders, coughs, vomiting forth the briny element, as Jacques would no doubt term it if he were here. As far as this survivor is concerned, though, the briny element can kiss his arse.

Enter PAROLLES.

HE WAS NOT a man well-made by nature, though he could feign it well enough when the sea had not been at him quite so much. The clothes that clung to his spare frame would have been, when dry, the grey of Rousillon, his post an ensign's. Again, it was a role he could play, but the beach was affording him no rank and file to bully and browbeat, no officers to toady to. With a final cough, Parolles rolled over onto his back, regretted it and ended up retching on his hands and knees again.

"I swear," he told the air, "not for gold, not for sack, not for a woman's breasts shall I go back to sea."

"Then, when you leave this shore, teach me to walk on water too!"

Parolles sat back heavily, fumbling for a sword the sea had swallowed. The newcomer was a man just as soaked as he, though he carried it better. He was a dark and handsome bearded fellow, his fine clothes mostly blues that the water had turned to near-black: one of the Aragonese contingent who had lately been Parolles' shipmates.

"Once was an alchemist taught the trick to me," Parolles offered. "And, were the stars and other bodies well-aligned, I'd jog from here to Milan and scorn the storms that chased my heels." He was looking the newcomer over, reading the assured way the man stood, and the fact he still had his sword without having been dragged to the depths. "Why, sir," he added, "do not think this is the worst of wrecks this body of mine has endured, for once was I—"

"'Twere better to save our tales 'til we had a fire and better company than we two," the Aragonese put in.

A hand went out, and Parolles was not too proud to refuse the help.

"We two are rats so vile even the sea won't have us," the man observed with a weak smile. "Benedick, I."

"Parolles of Rousillon."

"Of the doctor's retinue?"

"Her closest confidante and friend," Parolles averred, on the basis that those who might point out the exaggeration were most likely drowned. "Alas, the sea has taken all her pills and potions, and not even changed its colour."

"Well let us hope it has been sick with them, and hurled her forth," Benedick said without much optimism. "As I must hope the same about my prince."

They travelled down the beach, which had been lashed by the storm and carved by the wreckage, but yet not crossed with human tracks before their own. Parolles wrung out the damp from a few of the stories that were his stock in trade—bold tales of the military campaigns he had spent mostly hiding in the baggage train, the scars he had never really given, the victories he had barely had a hand in. His heart was scarcely in it, not for mourning lost comrades, but because he was cold and damp and this upright Spaniard was not going to let him just slope off and take shelter. Overhead, the sky was still dreary with clouds, though the sudden storm that had so dashed their mission and their ship to pieces had fled as swiftly as it had arrived.

Benedick, for his part, obviously weighed those threadbare boasts and politely declined to tug their holes any larger. At last, though, he put a hand up to silence his companion's prattle. Parolles felt almost relieved.

In the quiet, they both could hear a voice, sonorous and mournful, intoning something that at first had the ritual cadence of a spell.

"In first of all his years does man emerge," so went the words, "from breaking waters of his mother's womb into the air; then Mother Church's grace must dash another sprinkle on his head to wash away the garden's primal sin. And are we yet content or must we dance upon the very malice of the deep, which so oft seeks to take us to her breast—?"

"I think he's complaining about the sea," was Parolles' considered opinion.

"Then he's our bosom comrade. Let's go add our voices." Benedick broke into a sprint, leaving the Frenchman to stagger along behind him, but then coming up short when a high voice cried for him to halt.

"Peace, I am of Aragon!" the Spaniard called. "Your allies, last I looked."

Parolles caught him up to see a youth with a bent bow—no more than a slip of a boy, attired in the greenish garb of the Arden foresters, and behind him, seated on a rock with a dark robe puddling about him, a lean old bearded fellow.

"I see but a single shaft, and your quiver empty," Benedick remarked, "and we are both near-drowned already. Best to save your shots for where your work is not half-done."

The youth lowered his aim mistrustfully. "You are Signor Benedick, are you not? I saw you with your master at the high table aboard ship."

He was Ganymede, he said, and his elderly friend was a philosopher, Jacques. The old man had been one of the diplomats, along with Parolles' lost doctor. They were to have reached Milan to beg ancient Prospero his aid in the Tuscan wars.

Of late it seemed no battlefield in Europe was safe from magic. Only recently the very lords of Fairyland had been on the verge of bringing war to Illyria, before the war had suffered one of its customary reversals. Oberon's hosts had melted away, and Orsino of Illyria entered the fray, seeming overnight to find fresh fiends and witches. There was no part of the conflict safe from spells and enchantments, monsters and prodigies. And unexpected storms.

Parolles looked glumly up at the sky and wondered why anybody had expected this nonsense to work.

The Arden youth ventured into the woods that ran along the line of the beach and came back with the makings of a fire. "Do you think we're the only survivors, my lord?" he asked Benedick.

Parolles broke in: "Frail youth, hold off, for he has lost his prince to the hungry gulf. I have no doubt that, of all the multitudes within our barque, only we four were..."

He sought for the elegant term, and was considerably annoyed when Jacques furnished "vomited forth by the briny element." More so when the old man added, "and besides, here comes a fifth. A kinsman of yours, Signor Aragon?"

Benedick leapt up, but the hope lighting his face went out the next moment. "None of mine," he said flatly, "though of my lord's. And proof that honour sinks where villainy sits like a slick upon the waves. What now, my lord Don John?"

The newcomer was another darkly-bearded Aragonese, more slender than Benedick, with cold eyes that rested briefly on each of them, and discounted them all. "Signor Benedick, I give God thanks the sea has spared you. Alas, is my brother not among you? I had prayed he might be spared the abyss, you may be sure."

Parolles could hear Benedick's teeth grinding. Listening to John, he had to admire a man who could put so much insincerity into so few words.

Overhead, the thunder rumbled. The clouds seemed to be growing visibly thicker, so that a dull day was becoming, moment on moment, full night.

"The weather has its second wind," Benedick observed thoughtfully.

"No more naturally than its first," Ganymede stated. He had his arrow back on the string, as though he could shoot the tempest out of the sky.

"When all the sky is red at eventime," Jacques began, "the shepherds and the farmers smile, but yet it takes no worker of the land to cry and point when all the sky goes black at noon—"

"Yes," Parolles broke in. "Yes, it's dark. Yes it's obviously some black magic. Can we get under the trees before it...?" He trailed off. "God's own truth, what *is* it?"

Down the beach, passing over the furthest-flung spars and planks of the wreck, came something that drew in the gathering darkness like a cloak, so that the air swirled and seethed about it like night. Overheard, the clouds seemed to circle directly above it, and stabs and starts of lightning crackled from its hands. In form it was an old woman, a withered hag in tattered rags. The trailing edge of its ruined garment hung clear above the sand as it glided slowly towards them. It seemed blind, the eyes just a deeper crease in that wrinkled whorl of a face, and the lightning flecked and flashed like feelers, searching out the way, investigating every piece of flotsam.

"Something wicked this way comes," said Jacques with commendable brevity.

"Perhaps a retreat?" Parolles suggested, because they had one sword and one arrow between them and this thing was likely vulnerable to neither.

None of them wanted much to acknowledge his tactical guidance, but they were shuffling back despite themselves. Parolles decided they could shuffle all they liked, but his experience was that a bold tale tomorrow could cover up any amount of cowardice today. He turned and almost barrelled straight into a woman.

She was very beautiful, and her robe was plastered to her in a way that, under other circumstances, would have given him considerable delight and opportunity for comment. As it was, however, he knew her of old, and had no wish to be on the wrong side of either her tongue or her skills.

"Hello, Helena," he observed weakly.

"Down, all of you fools, and make no noise!" she hissed, shoving Parolles out of the way and striding into the midst of the bedraggled band. As the floating witch approached them, Helena wrested the bow from Ganymede's hand and drew a circle in the sand about them, then spoke swift words under her breath, looking at none of them. Parolles wished he'd run the moment he'd seen the approaching creature, because now he was between the mercy of *two* witches.

"No sound, no stirring, let not your eyes rest on the hag," Helena murmured. "Keep even your thoughts close in your head." She gripped Parolles' shoulder hard, and had her other hand on Don John's, as though identifying them as the most likely to breach her terms.

But they all held still, and the witch drifted past them down the beach in a swirl of rain-lashed air, darkness and the sour smell of rotting seaweed. The crone was a long way past them before even Helena dared to speak.

"Don't think that we are safe," she told them, "for we are in

Illyria, whence came the storm that sank us, and if the magic of their witches cannot find us then they shall send mortal agents for the task. We must flee inland while we still can."

NOT LONG AFTER the castaways fled, a band of cavalry picked its way down the beach, pausing at each humped snarl of sailcloth and rope to prod it with a lance, in case a live body was concealed beneath.

At their head rode a young officer who might have given Ganymede a contest for beardlessness. The soldiers used the name Cesario and were none the wiser, for their leader could sit a horse, fence, gamble and swear with the best of them. Only the old sergeant riding behind knew her by the name Viola.

This was not the first time the young wife of Duke Orsino had slipped from the palace to put on britches and show the men how it was done. The old lord indulged her; indeed, seemed to love his old page the more for it.

Now, Viola scanned the sand, turned over by the witch's stormy passage. She swore, in terms to make the regular soldiers blush. The rain, thoughtfully left behind after the witch had moved on, pattered down on the lot of them, and her sergeant tugged his dripping hood further down his face.

"Faith, tell me again why I went to play soldier a second time," he complained.

"Because you never yet passed up a chance to be a fool, Feste," Viola pointed out.

"Oh, so?" Feste leaned in and murmured. "Would I not be the greater fool if I let my lord's lady play soldier, and no man there to help her?"

Viola bristled from long force of habit. "If you think I need your help..." She shrugged and smiled. "Yet I'm grateful for it, while you have wit left in you. I see tracks here. Our doubtful allies have wiped most of them clean, but I guess some party made it to the woods. A half-dozen, perhaps."

Feste squinted at the sand. "In this light, what man can tell? Marry, we've had our share of midnight middays since these Scots graced us with their company."

Viola said nothing for a moment, then gave the troop leave to dismount and rest their horses. She goaded her own a few steps away, Feste's following obediently.

"I warned my lord against the Scot and his lot," she confided, glancing at the preternaturally gloomy sky.

"I well know it," Feste confirmed, "yet is there no honest battlefield left in Europe without this black magic to spoil it? You have the fairy king's temper to thank for that. And what general has more command of it than the Scot? A man who cannot be killed, who has three witches chained to his girdle and the favour of Hecate besides. When such a sword is offered, your lord would wear my old cap and bells before refusing."

Viola only shook her head. "And has it profited us? Or has it just made the slaughter on both sides the worse? Just as their magic fouls our tracking here, so it makes more costly every battle, win or lose."

"Faith, and you're more in your wits than most, to say so," Feste agreed. "But so long as the Scot darkens your husband's court, we are the fellow who rides the bear. Let him find it disagreeable, he'll like it even less when he gets down."

Act II

A campsite in a hollow in the woods.

The shadows of trees cast long stripes across the scene. At the centre, a fire made smokeless and so low that only the guttering reddish illumination escapes; no sign of flames all.

Helena, whose fire it is, tends it not with twigs but artful words and pinches of dust taken from her many pouches. The other castaways slouch, tired and slowly drying, about the hollow, saving only:

Enter BENEDICK, bearing more sticks.

BENEDICK HAD TAKEN it as his role to keep the company's spirits up. It had been a thankless task. Aside from Don John, with whom there was no love lost, only the youth Ganymede seemed capable of an honest smile. Parolles was a lackey wanting a master to flatter, Jacques could complain for a living and Helena was just... cold. That she had been spared the waves, Benedick was glad, for she was their most potent ambassador to go begging to the sorcerer-duke of Milan: one whose medical arts had, through tireless study, surpassed the purely natural and opened the book of the uncanny. Benedick reckoned she'd make more headway with old Prospero than having Jacques moan at the man in iambic pentameter. Still, she was a hard woman to get along with. Benedick was used to words sugar-coated by the demands of the court, and Helena would have none of that. On their first encounter he had greeted her as a lord of Aragon should a noble lady, and her frosty disdain had run his charm through like a rapier.

He briefly considered lapsing into his own sullen silence, but *noblesse oblige* spurred him on. "Well now," he announced. "See here, a lesser drink has escaped the greater," and he slipped from his ruined doublet a silver flask. "Usquebaugh from the Scot's own country. Glen Macduff, no less. Who'll join me in drinking it to spite him?"

That roused some interested even in the dolorous old philosopher, and Benedick lifted the flask up. "Those that have 'em, drink to the loves we left behind, who might be mourning soon, but shall be joyous once we find our way back home."

"I'd sooner hang myself than drink to the sharp tongue of *your* wife," Don John spat, predictably enough.

Benedick widened his smile for the man's sole benefit. "I drink to the finest of women, my wife, whose words are as keen as her wits, and whose only tragedy is the pitiful husband her whims have saddled her with." He took a swig and offered the flask about. "Ganymede, is there some young maid of Arden swoons for you?"

"I am wed, sir." The youth took the flask and sniffed it suspiciously. "My love I would wager against all others: noble, kind and just, a worser poet than any alive, but yet a better wrestler." He stopped abruptly, colouring, and Parolles laughed uproariously.

"It's a fine thing, lad, to love the wenches apt to wrestle," he snickered, despite Ganymede's warning glower. "I have one in every port and camp, and no doubt each will wear her widow's weeds when they hear our boat miscarried."

Don John reached for the flask, but Benedick broke in with, "My lord, did you marry yet?"

"How could I," the other Aragonese hissed, "when my fool

brother will not? Who'd wed the poor second son when the first still struts a bachelor? And we both know 'tis your wife he would have had, Benedick, if she'd have had him. Do you not think his eye hasn't roamed there since."

Benedick put another inch on his grin. "You think to wound me that I am the envy of princes? Ganymede, pass the flask on to the next of us who's wed."

"Just give it here." Helena plucked it from the youth's hand and took a long draught. "Let us just say," she told them when she'd done, "I mightily pursued a fair young man in younger days. And, because I had set my mind on it, I won him, and have regretted it ever since. Sir"—and here she addressed Don John—"do not wed. It makes you the front end of an ass, and your betrothed the rear."

Jacques stirred himself to defend this calumny against the male sex and the institute of matrimony, but a single stony look from Helena silenced him. Wordlessly she passed the flask to John, from whence it travelled to Parolles.

The soldier eyed Helena in silence for a moment before shaking himself and saying grandly, "I will confess I think too much of the greater run of womankind to chain myself to any one, and so deny the rest my charms. But if this is truly Illyria, I shall drink to something more desirable than love, more lasting than virtue. I shall drink to treasure, for a sot I met once told me I should find myself a wealthy man, should I e'er find myself on these shores."

"He's a disgraceful liar," Helena told them, as Parolles paused to drink. "Set no store in any word he says."

The flask found its way to Jacques, who discovered it to be mysteriously empty. Seeing the old man was on the point of raising a complaint to vex the very gods, Benedick jumped up again. "I'd rest here at your fire, Mistress Helena, but my conscience has a hook in me. My prince Don Pedro is somewhere on this shore, or else he's taken by the enemy already."

"Or drowned," Don John murmured darkly.

"You might well wish so."

"And if it is so, you might well wish you had shown more respect, for who then takes the throne of Aragon?" John demanded.

"Then I and all the people pray it is not so," was all Benedick would say to that. "And for that reason, I do not beg your aid, but I will go and search, and find the nearest town and ask, until all chance has been exhausted."

"There is the port of Apollonia," Jacques intoned, "which should lie south along the coast from here. There will you find the lucky who were spared the wave, yet who were by our foeman taken up—"

"Good, and thanks," Benedick broke in hurriedly.

"We'll go with you," Ganymede offered, pushing himself up from the fire. With sinking heart, Benedick realised the 'we' included Jacques.

"No need—" he started.

"Your face and speech and clothes mark you as Aragon," the youth put in, "who stand amongst the vanguard of Orsino's foes in the Tuscan war. In how many battles have the Illyrians crossed their swords with yours? But we of Arden have made little show so far. So let us be your mouth and ears, or you might only find your prince from the next cell."

Benedick nodded, conceding the point, then turned sharply as Helena hissed at the fire. "What is it?"

"The witch that sought us on the beach is coming back. Her immortal master is not satisfied with her lack of captives, I'll wager." The physician's eyes glinted in the firelight. "If you must go, go now and travel swiftly. She comes in from the sea; head south and I will send her from your course, even as I hide us."

Benedick grimaced and nodded at Ganymede. "Come on, then; but, I pray you, let philosophy wait on safety or we shall never reach this port at all."

"You know of Zeno then, whose paradox the ancient world did marvel at..." Jacques began, and continued and then continued further until distance hushed his voice.

HELENA TOOK A stick and began to mark a circle in the dirt about their fire, calculating in her head. The magic of Old Scotland was a very different matter to hers, a thing of fairies and diabolic pacts, chaining its practitioners to ruinous powers she had no intention of dealing with. Her magic was book magic, an outgrowth of the natural philosophy that had made her such a prodigy as a doctor, able to cure all ills and almost raise the dead. Hers was the magic of an age of reason: of alchemy and philosophy and the clear light of day, not the smoke and cobwebs of the past's dark night.

"Should I douse the fire?" Parolles asked nervously. She should, Helena mused, make him scared more often. His sense of self-preservation was probably his best quality, though that was a low bar.

"She does not search with eyes," Helena told him, relishing his expression. They had history, she and he.

The witch was near, now: the wind picking up about them and rattling the trees.

"Stay close within the circle," she warned the two men. "Say nothing. Do not look at her."

Overhead the clouds were racing, and she spared a thought for Benedick's search party, hoping her misdirection would cover them. The Aragonese seemed a decent sort, the philosopher might be needed, and Ganymede... Well, Helena could not deny a little affection for one who had been forced to go to such lengths to make a way in the world.

Then Don John seemed to stumble, tripping over a root and scuffing backwards until his heel had broken the circle.

"What are you doing, you fool?" Helena demanded. For a

moment there was a look of pure malevolent cunning on the nobleman's face, swiftly covered by almost theatrical contrition.

"Alas! My clumsiness has undone us!" he cried out, far louder than necessary. "Fear not, sweet maiden, I shall draw the enemy off and save you and your man." And he actually grinned at her, just before he ran towards the witch waving his arms. In that moment, horribly exposed before the magic of her enemies, Helena could not help but admire the sheer barefacedness of him. *Honesty in a villain is a rare thing.* She was turning to her circle, hoping to repair the damage, but Parolles bolted too, in the opposite direction, following after the search party, and she was left with nothing to repair, too many feet in too many places.

So she stood, gripping her stick as if it were a true magician's staff, and waited to see if the witch would be satisfied with John and, if not, whether Helena's new magic was a match for the sorcery of old gods.

The garrison at Apollonia.

Soldiers and servants alike in slovenly attire bustle about a great table groaning with meat and drink. Presiding over the general disarray, the duke's kinsman by marriage, Sir Toby, topples ever deeper into his cups as the day grows on, calling for more cakes and ale.

Enter MACBETH.

THE GENERAL SOUNDS—of drinking and wenching, of dice-rattle, of oaths and counter-oaths—fell silent, leaving only Sir Toby singing tunelessly to himself, his voice cracking and vanishing into the otherwise silent air as he saw the cause.

The Scot—whose name no man dared speak—cut a formidable figure in this latter age. Perhaps, centuries before, this had been a nobleman's customary attire: this dark mail, this hooded helm, within which the grey face could be glimpsed but darkly. He had come without darkening any doorway, his cloak trailing shadows and his hand about his dagger-hilt as though murder was never far from his mind. And what was he after all, but a murderer, a kingslayer, the consort of witches?

At least he had not brought any of his witches with him this time. He himself was a fearsome enough figure—the soldiers crossed themselves in his presence, but only behind his back. This current Pope had given up his crusade against magic, just as a predecessor had abandoned his prohibitions against the use of black powder. Back when the Scot had cast his lot in with his mistress, though, he had turned his back on God's grace as well as man's law. The air about him was cold, and smelled of musty graves and the iron tang of blood.

"What?" Sir Toby mumbled, squinting red-eyed at the warlord. "What, now?" Drunk enough to stare at that grim countenance and keep his ruddy colour, he waved at the table. "Has Orsino made you his messenger, or will you have a skin of sack?"

Abruptly the Scot was looming over him, and the drunkard cradled his mug protectively. When the warlord spoke, his voice was deep and hollow, a tomb-voice, ornate with the crumbling lilt of a Scotland five centuries dead.

"My hounds scared from the brush a curious deer," he intoned. "Your own dogs have taken it up."

Sir Toby nodded wisely, though actual understanding only came three heartbeats later. "New prisoner, you say? More sailors and servants to go on the prison ship with the rest?"

"A man of rank, or so he claims," the Scot confirmed. "No doubt you'll put him with the other."

Even then the sound of tramping feet heralded a new band of

soldiers, whose casual discipline shamed those of the garrison. At their head was the young officer known as Cesario and in their midst a dark Aragonese.

"What, now?" Toby stood suddenly, his belly jolting the table and spilling a tide of ale across its top. "Is this not the very fellow we took before? And did the villain escape, after giving us word for his conduct? I'll have him flogged!" He leant heavily on the table and glowered at Cesario with the full weight of his displeasure.

Viola stared into the blotchy, choleric face of her kinsman—the uncle of her sister-in-law, worse luck—and resisted the urge to march over there and slap him. Perhaps, if the walking mortuary that was the Scot had not been there, she would have given in to it. "This is not he," she said, "though the resemblance is plain. I trust you still have Don Pedro close until the Duke sends word?"

Toby goggled at her—perhaps perplexed by the young soldier's familiarity, perhaps just so drunk his wits were dissolving. At last he belched massively and sat back down, seemingly losing interest. She was about to have her new prisoner sent to the cells when he stepped forwards and spoke, practically elbowing her aside.

"Hold, brave sirs! Do I understand you have my brother, Pedro of Aragon, in chains?"

"In chains? What now, are we Dutchmen?" Toby growled. "No, he is held in comfort, but we have him. As we have you, so if you come to trade yourself for him, you've made a poor start."

"Trade myself?" the prisoner laughed. "Rather I come to warn you, good sir knight. I myself am John, a prince in my own right and one who regards my word as iron, ever one to respect the nobility of my foes even as I bear arms against them.

But know you, my brother Pedro has no such scruples. Chain him hard, or he will slip from the least crack and cut the throat of any who stand in his way. Rely not on any promises he gives, for he breaks them as swift as straws. Alas that I were not more a slave to fraternal loyalty, but my love of truth and justice forces me to give such a report of him."

What impressed Viola most was the matter-of-fact way the words were spoken. The Aragonese fixed his eyes on Toby and the Scot, and spoke his piece without the least attempt at passion and conviction. His skill, she saw, was in judging the interests of his audience. While the brooding warlord just stared thoughtfully at the prisoner, Toby was obviously won by the idea of having a prisoner he could bully, rather than one he had to respect.

"Warnings well heeded!" he exclaimed. "You, and you, go find that rascal Pedro and hold him close, if he has not already practised on our generosity and fled. It would not do for our great prize to vanish before the Duke pronounces on his fate. And you, sir?"

"I, good knight?" the Aragonese prisoner adopted a mummer's pose of humility. "I am Don John, poor second son, who has lamented the turn of events that ever brought our nations into dispute. For sure, had I been on the throne when this war had loomed, I would have found some other path than to make an enemy of bold Illyria."

Viola opened her mouth to object, but once again the words were plainly music to Sir Toby. "Find this fellow quarters, get him set," he ordered, "and then perhaps, Don John of Aragon, you'll join me at my table?"

"Nothing would please me more," and even in that, the man sounded mocking, but only Viola seemed to hear it.

Act III

The backstreets of Apollonia.

The echo of a hundred accents and languages sound here even in wartime. The voices of sailors and merchants, hurrying to their beds as night draws on, cries of street vendors, distant music from taverns, the ringing of the watchman's bell. The air throngs with the sounds of a hundred vices and depravities, such that only the vilest specimens of mankind would frequent such a place.

Enter PAROLLES.

ALL NATIONS HAVE their ports, but all ports in their way belong to one nation. Parolles had seen enough of them, now, to find his way in any of them. His Rousillon grey he'd disguised under a cloak donated by an incautious laundress.

About abandoning Helena, he felt no guilt. They had never been friends, and Parolles was only on this embassy in her company because her husband suspected her virtue. The idea that Helena might be unfaithful would be plausible to anyone, Parolles thought, who did not know her. She was comely enough, and she and her lord could barely stay in the same room as one another anymore. She was too cold to find a new love, though, Parolles guessed—and too unwilling to have another man meddle in her affairs. Even the King of France, whose life she had saved, had begun to fear her. The perfect emissary, therefore, to wizard Prospero.

There had been a time, back before she was either married, important or powerful, when she and Parolles had been able to exchange civil words. She'd had a keen wit on her, back then. The thought of that had almost given him pause as he fled. But then the witch-storm had been close, and his courage was a quality more boasted about than evidenced.

So let her fight it out with the Scot's witches. Parolles had other priorities. Ever since he had discovered the shore on which they had been cast up, his thoughts had been of treasure. Despite Helena's caveat, in this one thing he was truthful. A man—a man in a tavern, admittedly—had indeed prophesied he should find a treasure should he find himself on Illyrian soil.

He had certain particulars, vouchsafed by the same man—and he had read some books and heard some tales. The idea of Parolles engaged in research would no doubt have made Helena laugh him to scorn, but wealth and power were a strong goad. Parolles felt he had been hanger-on for long enough.

"And, when I am lord and others came to beg, I'll make them crawl and flatter," he swore to himself. He had just left his third tavern, buying drinks from another man's purloined purse and asking covert questions. So far, all word led the same way—a daunting way, truly, but Parolles felt himself nothing if not resourceful. "And those who mocked me—all those false friends who spurned me—well, they shall come to me and feign their friendship anew, and perhaps I shall not deign to recognise them, or I shall set them tests of loyalty." This was sounding good. "'Mercy, Great Parolles!' they'll cry. 'We always saw the star of greatness in you, but were misled!' and I'll say—" But just what Parolles would have said to those hypothetical supplicants was lost when someone stepped up behind him and thrust a bag over his head.

He squawked in fright, but there were arms about his, and a low voice whispered, "Quiet, or your next sound is your last," in a guttural accent. Obediently, imagining a world of knives beyond the darkness of the bag, Parolles went limp and let himself be led.

They took him some place enclosed, that reeked of animal—a stables was his guess—and there set him down on a barrel top. One man held his arms, and he tensed for a blow, but what he heard was a rapid foreign gabble, strongly accented and utterly unintelligible. His carefully constructed story about sympathy to the Illyrian cause fell apart in his mind. Some rogues of a country far further afield had apparently got hold of him.

"Gentle lords, please," he got out, his voice muffled by the bag. "Are you Turks? For I do hear the Sublime Porte is in alliance with Ilyrria—"

"Not Turkishmen," said the fierce voice that had spoken to him before. "Know you not the tones of Muscovy?"

Parolles racked his brains and failed to find any reason why a party of Russians should have swiped him off the streets of Apollonia. "Then, gentlemen of Muscovy, pray tell...?"

Again that babble, that now came to him on a cold wind all the way from the steppe—no doubt the magnate of these Tartars giving instructions to his interpreter.

"Pray tell you tell us, Sieur French, what cause you have to skulk about this town," the voice whispered in his ear. Parolles pictured sabres half-drawn, wanting only a mis-spoken word to find his flesh.

"Please, sirs, if you but spare me," he got out, "I can make you rich! There is a treasure here within this town, was promised me by a man—some gambling fellow, some drunken fellow, but very sage nonetheless; some *rosbif* braggart, Will of Stratford his name. Spare me slavery or death, and I shall lead you to it."

More gabble, and then the interpreter was at his elbow once again. "Why, Sieur French, you are so generous. What is this treasure of which you speak?"

"The treasure that divides the world, the knife that ransoms nations," Parolles trotted out. "So the fellow said. I thought him mad, but he assured me that there was a thing, a simple blade, that all the powers of Europe would empty their coffers for. Please, my friends, if wealth can move you, will you not be moved by wealth such as that?"

"A knife...?" And if the voice at his ear had somewhat less of an accent for a moment, Parolles failed to mark it.

"I know, I know, and I was wroth with him for playing me and trying to settle his stake with idle fancy, but he swore on it, and powerful convincing he was! A knife, a magic knife that can sway destinies, and here in Illyria waiting for me to claim it!"

"Stay put, Sieur French," the Muscovite told him, and then the three of them retired off and muttered together, a sinister buzz of conspiracy just past his ability to eavesdrop on. He might have reached up and taken off the bag, then, and bolted for the door—except perhaps there were another three Russians between him and freedom, and no doubt they'd be unamused with the attempt. He sat tight, and prayed that greed would quell even the legendary bloodthirstiness of Muscovy.

"Sieur French." The interpreter was at his ear once more. "You did not come alone, on this hunt of yours. We know others were spared from the wreck. What of them?"

"I cast them off!" Parolles assured them hurriedly. "An anchor to my ambitions, no more. What were they but a witch of a woman with a heart of stone, two haughty boasting Spaniards whose talk ever outstripped their skill, a beardless boy so rustic that he prizes his wife as a wrestler, and a dotard greybeard overflowing with bad simile. I left them in the woods to quibble with the witches and the Illyrians. Do you want them? I shall lead them to you, or you to them, only please"—and he felt the interpreter grip the bag as though about to twist the edge of it like a noose about his neck—"please spare me, spare poor Parolles and he shall be your servant always."

And then the bag was off, and Parolles' fear-wide eyes stared into the cheery face of Ganymede, and beyond him Benedick and Jacques. In that moment, his mind served him up a dozen different stories that might have cleared him of blame—how he had only been going along with his kidnappers to stall them, and would have tricked them or trapped them, or... But instead he hung his head in utter despair at himself.

"Not again," he got out. "How many times will I fall for this one trick?"

"No bold words, valiant Parolles?" Benedick asked him. "Perhaps you wish to slight my skill again?"

"No, sir," Parolles mumbled.

"Or will you lead us to ourselves? Betray us to ourselves, perhaps?" Ganymede put in.

"Or shall the knave cast the name of 'fool' upon the learned?" Jacques asked archly.

"For you, old man, I know only shame that you should disgrace your grey beard by playing bibble-babbler in this mummer's show," Parolles told him hotly.

"What ignorant men shall call a babble, learned men shall know as the most exquisite tongue of Muscovy," Jacques told him frostily.

"And have you now no boasts of how you abandoned Helena and John?" Benedick put in.

"Helena has no use for me or you or any mortal man anymore," Parolles said bitterly, "and as for your countryman, he abandoned us first into the very arms of the enemy. It was as though he wanted to be caught."

All Benedick's mockery vanished with the news. "Tell me everything," he said flatly.

"And tell us more about this magic knife," Ganymede added. He was plainly intrigued, and Parolles marked that. *I can use you, lad. I can always use a naïve boy who listens to stories.*

*   *   *

A tavern.

Raucous with the sound of merriment, the clink and slosh of tankards, the air hazy with smoke and fumes, the alcohol strong enough to make the eyes water. In the shadows, just out of sight, fortunes are being won and lost. In all, just the place where foreign visitors might come, if seeking news of a magical treasure.

Enter VIOLA and FESTE, disguised.

VIOLA CAST A sharp eye about the taproom. "I don't see them yet. But if they keep their course they'll end up here sure enough. Four foreigners, some say French and some say Russians, but asking curious questions—aye, of the garrison and prisoners there, but other matters too. And not of barkeeps or ship's masters, but of pox doctors and threadbare street magicians and wise women. So, let us be what they seek, and perhaps they'll tell us what they're after." She was attired as a man still, but had supplemented her doublet and hose with spectacles and a scholar's robe. Feste, for his part, had the hooks of a luxurious false beard over his ears and a divine's cassock over his uniform.

"I shall be Edward Kelly, alchemist and speaker with spirits," Viola decided.

"Father Topaz, I," Feste said, in a broad country accent.

Viola gave him a look. "Again with Father Topaz?"

"Why, and sure as the sun breeds worms in milk, those who dwelleth in the dark mire of ignorance seek only the light of the church cast to illuminate their problems." Feste chewed his beard and made a vague benediction, then, in a sharper voice, he said, "But attend: they're here."

Viola watched the quartet of foreigners duck in: an old man who could have been Father Topaz's close cousin in beard-chewing, a swaggerer, a well-made nobleman and a youth with a bow over his shoulder. The ancient was already heading for the fire to warm his bones, whilst the noble jostled his way towards the barkeep. The other two glanced around and, of course, bespied the learned-seeming pair at their corner table.

"Save you, masters," the foreign boy called out. "Pray, let youth and ignorance buy age and learning a drink."

"Why," Feste broke in before Viola could stop him, "the blessings of Saint Quinculencus upon you, generous swain! For all too oft we men of craft and lore, who hold within our hands the—"

"You are most kind," Viola spoke over him. "And pray, will you not join us, who has such respect for learning?"

They passed some moments exchanging compliments, then sent the noble Spaniard off for more mugs, consigning him to the seven-deep scrum about the tapster. Viola let Feste ramble, watching the two foreigners try to follow his baffling loops of logic. At last she said, "Aye, we two are belike the foremost men of learning in all Illyria, and yet you see how fortune treats us! I myself have converse with angels and airy spirits most nights, and have studied with no lesser man than Doctor Dee, while Father Topaz has honed his craft in the invisible college of Veruccoporcus and conjured the stone philosophical. It has been many a cold week since last a stranger showed kindness to two poor scholars such as we. So, tell us, how may we recompense you?"

The youth was about to say something cautious, no doubt, but his swaggering soldier friend broke in eagerly. "Well, if you'll pay us back the respect we give you, wise friends, perhaps you'll assist us in settling an argument of ours? For this young strip, he says—and it chimes well with your own words—that Illyria's no place for magician nor conjurer, for the place is barren as a desert for those of learning such as yours. But I, masters, have heard tales of marvels to be found in Illyria that all the world would envy. Why, amongst so many, let me name only a knife, which they say would sunder nations, a singular blade of potency unquestioned. Am I right to place faith in such rumours?"

"Faith, sir, 'tis clear as night you're a fellow with ears so open there's space b'tween them," Feste rambled hurriedly, for Viola had gone very still. *I came in with a fool and now I have found a whole pack of clowns. Is it* that *they're after, the madmen?* She cast a glance around for the other two. The Spaniard was still trying to purchase more drinks, and the old man seemed to have nodded off.

"I know the thing you speak of," she said softly, a touch to the elbow silencing Feste's incoherent exposition. "It is not of Illyria, but I know well it is *in* Illyria this very moment. But you are fools to seek it for, whilst it has wandered from time to time, you'll find it now back in the hands of its first master."

"Who might that master be?" the youth asked her, Viola's grim manner beginning to infect him.

"His name is not spoken; men call him only by the country he once ruled. And the blade you seek was the instrument of his ascent. With that knife, which came to him from who knows what infernal forge, he united murder and betrayal in a stroke. So that's your goal: the Scottish Blade?"

"You mean Macbeth?" the soldier drawled.

Swift as a serpent, Viola lashed out and rammed a knife into the tabletop, pinning the man's sleeve to the wood. She had another knife out in an instant, holding it before their faces, while Feste was out and around the table, boxing them in.

"In the name of Orsino, Duke of Illyria, I arrest you," Viola declared. "And if you have the wits you were born with, do not speak that name again!"

While the soldier cursed and scrabbled at the point that pinned him, the youth kicked backwards, ramming an elbow into Feste's chest and shouting, "Benedick!" Viola made to threaten the boy with the knife but, even as she did so, she registered how very dark the taproom had become. Dark and cold, and smelling of the tomb.

"You imbecile!" she spat into the face of the soldier, who stared at her, slack-jawed.

The revellers were abruptly clearing a space in the room's centre, for a figure stood there in armour of five centuries before, holding a great pitted blade two-handed before him. Sunken eyes beneath the lip of an antique helm searched the room.

"Who spoke my name?" demanded the Scot.

"Feck, i'faith," Feste muttered, ripping Topaz's beard off. "We are all the fool now."

Viola looked the foreign youth full in the face, mind racing. The Scot was approaching them, and what he might do to these two lackwits was anyone's guess. She had no particular regard for the soldier, but the boy... he was fair of face and very young, and reminded her of her brother, or herself.

With a quick levering motion she had the dagger out of the table, freeing the soldier's arm. "I'd have you for Illyrian justice, but not for antique Scottish execution. Run."

They bolted, and she turned to find her view all armour and grave dust and cobwebby darkness.

"You know me, Scot—I am Orsino's man, the servant of your ally," she tried.

"My name was uttered," the ancient warlord grated. "I am owed a death."

"There's none that is your lawful prey," Viola insisted. "Go back to where you came from."

Then she was skipping back hurriedly as the Scot lifted that sword, remembering how many times she had wished this dread apparition had never come to aid her husband's cause. Feste tried to get between them, but she slung him to one side. If this was going to end in tragedy, she'd make it hers alone.

Then a gleaming point appeared, lancing out through the Scot's broad chest between the links of his mail. With a bark of triumph the Spaniard had run his rapier into the small of the Scot's back.

"All steel and no substance within," he declared, merrily, then saw how everyone was looking at him.

"Go," Viola advised him. "Go, now."

The Scot shuddered, but more with exasperation than with any attempt at shuffling off the mortal coil. Instead he turned, the rapier sliding free of him, until he faced the Spaniard. The hollow laugh that issued from within his helm chilled every listener to the bone.

"Alas," the Scot informed them all, "I am bloody, bold and resolute, and fear no man, for none of woman born may harm Macbeth." He hefted his great sword. "One man thought he'd slain me once—aye, and I thought it too; but my mistress will not be denied on a lawyer's quibble. So the Thane of Fife met a most unnatural end and here I still stand, triumphant and invulnerable!"

"Ah, well, then," and the Spaniard waggled the bottle of spirits in his other hand. "Drink?"

The Scot growled like breaking metal and drew his blade back, but hesitated, his eyes fixed upon the bottle. Viola craned past him and saw the label, crudely printed: A woodcut of trees and the words, *Birnam Wood Special Reserve*. Something about it gave the Scot pause for just a heartbeat, and then the Spaniard smashed the bottle across the warlord's face and turned a very creditable pair of heels, racing out of the taproom. The Scot cursed foully, ancient Scottish words blistering the air as he rubbed the stinging liquid from his eyes. Feste was already tugging at Viola's elbow.

And their work had not been entirely spoiled by the Scot's intervention, for in the midst of their hurried exit they snagged the old foreigner from where he rested by the fire, forgotten by his fellows.

* * *

The Illyrian forest by night.

The moon's cold light gleaming through the branches' lattice throws a grid of shadows. The owl cries and the vixen screeches over the faint whickering of batwings. A night of ill omen, fit for dark deeds and wickedness.

Enter HELENA, fleeing.

THE STORM HAD gone. Eventually the witch had realized that carrying her own personal tempest about with her was a poor aid to hunting. Now the ancient hag glided silently between the trees, hook-nailed hands reaching out to find her way, her face a withered prune of wrinkles, eyes long lost amongst the lines.

Helena had been on the run ever since the witch had got the scent of her. For all her pride in her hard-learned abilities, the raw power of this ancient thing was a daunting prospect. *They had different ways, back then.* Five hundred years this crone had been chained to the Scot's coat-tails, and who knew how long she had practised her craft even before that. Helena had read accounts of how magic had worked, back in the days before Paracelsus, Roger Bacon and Prospero. In those old days it had been all deals with devils and powers of the ancient world; always being the slave and not the master. She saw before her precisely where that road to power truly led: withered and undying and the plaything of others.

But strong; she could not deny that. The creature had driven her in a wide circle about the wood, fumbling for her through the trees, smelling her out, reaching for her. Helena knew that if the hag had seized on her, or even had a plain idea of where she was, this would already have ended badly. And the Scot had *three* of these things at his beck and call, bedevilling the battlefields of Europe.

Yet Helena had stayed that one vital step ahead, and sometimes more than one. She had darted in and out of the witch's senses, led her on for what seemed half the night, making a broad arc through the forest.

She was almost back to her original campsite, the fire long since gone dark. There she would make her stand, pitting her young powers against the wickedness of ages.

"Come, then!" she called. "You've pursued me far enough. I grow tired. Come, bring your witchcraft and we'll see what powers I can raise against you."

The witch cackled as she drifted into view, her horn-nailed feet trailing with the hem of her dress, inches above the leaf litter.

"Well met, we two," she hissed through toothless gums. "A clever little child you are, to lead me such a dance. Why do you flee your older sister, girl? It's been a long time since our mistress Hecate had a new maidservant. We'll find a place for you at the fire, dear heart."

"Meaning hellfire, no doubt," Helena threw back at her. "The power I muster will not be squandered in the service of fairies or devils or antique gods. It's mine and mine alone."

The crone cackled again, claw-like hands spread as she floated closer. "They all say that, my dear," she whispered, and then she had crossed over the lines Helena had drawn in the dirt. With a single motion of her foot, the woman completed the circle and stepped back.

"Now, test yourself against my craft, will you?" In truth, Helena was tensed to flee: while she had practised these restraints against little spirits, ghosts and sprites, this creature was another order of being entirely. For a moment, the witch just hung there in the dark, muttering to herself and reaching out. Then the old woman touched the boundary of the circle and greenish fire exploded about her hands. She shrieked and cast herself backwards, only to meet the same boundary behind her. Helena watched as she rattled about the circle like a fly in a bottle, seemingly incapable of understanding that she was closed in on all sides.

"Sisters, aid me!" the old creature wailed. "Mistress Hecate, I am caught!"

Helena waited, listening with senses natural and unnatural, but answer came there none.

"You are caught indeed," she told the witch. "For you are strong, but I have studied, and my understanding of the world's secret ways is a science, whilst yours is mouldering superstition."

"My mistress shall strike you down for this impertinence!" the witch vowed.

Helena kicked about the campsite until she found Benedick's emptied flask. It had held spirits from Scotland, the man had boasted. The thought appealed to her. She smiled as she faced her spitting captive.

"If I had listened to those who told me that I *could* not, or I *should* not, or that I'd suffer if I did, I'd been nothing but a gentlewoman married off to some backwoods squire," she remarked pleasantly. "Lords, teachers, physicians, wise men— even he who would become my husband—all have told me what my place and station are, and I have heeded none of them. Nor will I now hold back for all your prophecies. So, 'older sister,' I have here a vessel of silver which I mark with the characters of your prison. I apologise for the smallness of the cell, but perhaps you shall have grander quarters later, if you please me. For now, I conjure you within the flask, and then you shall answer my every question."

Act IV

The garrison.

Viola's drunken kinsman still holds riotous sway. Little now has changed save that Don John sits at the inebriated knight's elbow, whispering poison into an already overflowing ear.

Enter VIOLA and FESTE with JACQUES, bound.

Sir Toby Belch stared blearily at the newcomers. "What's this? Have you brought your grandfather to work? Or has he chosen his dotage in which to trail the pike? We have enough stout fellows here have lost their teeth to fist and boot. No need for one who's lost 'em to nature!"

"Sir, this ancient is from the wreck of the Spanish ship," Viola announced, smoothing her false moustache a little as Toby's gaze fell on her.

"Is't so?" the bloated sot slurred.

"He is a very tedious old fellow," Don John confirmed, no doubt wondering where the rest of his former comrades were. "I well recall being confined upon the ship with him. For every word another man said, he had nine, and none to the purpose. Tell him the sun is high and he'd speak for twenty minutes on the Delphic Oracle."

"Not another to invite to my table, then?" Toby mused.

"Not unless you'd wish all mirth and good cheer driven from it," John confirmed. "He is a miserable ass."

"Still, he may know something of his friends—" Viola started, but Toby broke in.

"What else need we know since we have this sterling man of conscience with us?" He threw a meaty arm about Don John's slender shoulders, and Viola guessed the Aragonese had been flattering her kinsman assiduously since she had been gone. Then inspiration plainly struck the drunkard, for he gave a windy laugh and said, "Throw him in with that villain Pedro. If he's so intolerably dull, then let him practise his tedium on Prince Spaniard!"

Feste cocked an eye at Viola and she nodded. At least the two hapless prisoners would have some company.

Her sergeant was no sooner out of the door than a familiar and unwelcome darkness flooded into the hall and the Scot manifested himself, woven together from the shadows in the corners. Viola stepped back, but the Scot ignored her, practically elbowing her out of the way to stand before Sir Toby.

"What have you done with your prisoner, the Spaniard?" boomed the hollow voice.

Sir Toby waited for a servant to fill his mug, then drained it, obviously needing further fortification to deal with the apparition. "He moulders in the cells still, as befits a canting knave, or so this fellow names him."

"If he is such a knave, why is he not hung?" the Scot demanded.

"Wise counsel," Don John agreed. "Others before have thought they had him safe, but he is a very magician at escaping chains and bars, and at cutting the throats of his captors when he's free. His word means nothing."

"Hrm, well." Toby made an expansive gesture, almost slapping John in the face. "Some officious officer made sure word of his taking went post-haste to my cousin the Duke, so there's nothing for it but to wait his command."

Viola nodded to herself. It had been her thought, and her name upon the note.

"And how long before Orsino leaves off his music and his poetry to answer?" the dark warlord growled.

A new voice broke in, so that the Scot whirled round, reaching for his dagger hilt.

"He did not spare the time for a note or a couplet, nor even to instruct a scribe to pen a sonnet in reply." And Orsino himself was striding into the hall, a clutter of courtiers and hangers-on spilling into the room after him. "What news would move me more than to hear the prince of Aragon is in our hands?"

"My lord." Toby rose to his feet, swaying perilously. "This honest fellow beside me's one Don John of Aragon, the younger son, who's come to warn us of his brother's perfidy. He recommends we deal with his sibling sternly, or we'll regret it."

"A strange matter," Orsino said, eyeing John narrowly. "For popular report has it that Pedro's a man of honour, though no such words are said about John."

"Alas, how I am maligned!" John declared theatrically. "See how my brother's words go before me to poison the world against his poor sibling? Pedro's tongue is a very viper, sir."

Again, his protestations sounded patently false to Viola, and to her relief she saw Orsino plainly unconvinced. "I have determined already what his fate shall be," the Duke announced. "Even if nobility of spirit did not move me, necessity of state must. Illyria has not profited from our part in this war, which drags on season to season and ravages one nation after another. Our farmers and our artisans take up the sword in both hands and, like as not, return with only one, nor not at all. Our harvests go ungathered. Our women are made widows, our children orphans. Some small family feud of the Medicis over who is lawful heir to Tuscany has become a maelstrom that draws every crown of Europe to the fray. I think back on the blandishments and entreaties that moved me to enter Illyria in the lists, and I regret I let them move me."

"Duke Orsino," the Scot grated, "this is unmanly talk. Where is your soldier's courage?"

"Aye," Toby added, a man ever bold when no enemy was to be found. "If you find this war so ill-fitting that it rubs, then march and march until you mould it to your shape."

"You speak of war as if it were a shoe," Orsino addressed him. "And I fear who I'd have to trample to make it suit. I have word from the front. In a clash of ships off Salento, my-brother-in-law has been taken by these same Aragonese. It is my duty and my pleasure both to offer them their prince for his safe return."

Viola's gasp was lost in the general murmur. She felt a rush of emotions: a return of the fear she had felt when her brother sailed for the fighting, and a fierce pride in her husband who, in all this mob of sots and villains and monsters, would do the right thing.

Orsino went on, "Who knows if such a gesture may not bring about a more lasting understanding between us and the enemy? I am brought word of a union between Francesco's son and Ferdinand's daughter; can hate between brothers be stronger than such love? And I, for one, am full sick of this war."

"War is the only true game of princes," the Scot insisted. "Shall you be the runt of all the lords of Europe, womanly cowering from the fray? Have you no thought of how your countrymen shall be mocked, your borders threatened? In life there is but one path to advancement, and that's to seize it like the raptor."

Orsino stared at him levelly. "And if it is thorned, what then? I have seen hawks dead in briars when what they grasped could not be let go. You came to me and offered me your strength when this war came, and even now your witches fly o'er the battlefields of distant lands and blight the soldiers of the enemy and the souls of our own. And though you came with protestations of the rightness of our cause, I start to think you are not the noble eagle you claim, but the raven, that would have the whole world a charnel field so it could feed."

"Good Duke," John broke in. "Think not that my brother will keep any word he gives you. Free him, and he shall cut the throat of your kinsman the moment he sets foot on Aragonese soil. If you will make your amends with your foe, then you see before you the son of Aragon whose auspices can bring that about, if only my brother is not free to spite me."

Orsino turned a cold eye on him. "That Sir Toby has taken you as a drinking companion I shall not undo, for that is punishment and penalty enough, but do not think I cannot hear the serpent in your words, Don John. Now, have rooms prepared and well-cleaned so that they are, if not fit for a duke, then at least a Christian. I must compose some words for Don Pedro to take homewards with him."

AFTER ORSINO HAD retired, Don John found he could no longer even feign joy in Sir Toby's sodden company. For once, just once, he had been on the cusp of ridding the world of his brother and finding his way to the throne of Aragon, that dream which fortune had constantly dangled before him, yet never dropped in his lap.

He left the table, slipping out past the prodigious bulge of Sir Toby's gut, and stalked off into the garrison, seeking to be alone with his dark thoughts.

To be Don Pedro's brother was to live a blighted life. What chance had he ever had, growing up in the shadow of a man so universally admired, so crammed with good qualities? How could poor John aspire to honour or nobility or goodness of any sort, when his elder sibling held such a monopoly? John had nothing but the company of villains and the ability to tell them what they wanted to hear.

And it seemed this Orsino was proof against his mendacity. Popular repute had him as a clothes-horse, ruled by his mannish wife and given to verse and dreaming. That was not the man Don John had just seen, alas. Apparently Illyria was in better hands than he had thought. Which left that much less room for John's plots to prosper in.

He found a room far from the revelry to skulk in, and leant back against the wall, tilting his head to touch the cold, rough stones. He had not wanted to get on that doomed vessel to go speak to the Wizard-Duke of Milan. He would far rather have gnawed away at the foundations back home while his brother risked his life to the sea and the sorcerer. Don Pedro had insisted on leading the embassy to Prospero in person, as a mark of its import. The fairies, it seemed, were to stay their hands, but the armies lined up against Aragon and its allies—Illyria included—were fielding an impressive strength of magicians, astrologers and worse, not to mention the Scot and his cursed witches. If Prospero would commit Milan to the war on Aragon's side, even just to counter all their curses and spells, the entire course of the war would be changed. Everyone in Europe knew there was none to match him.

So they had gathered together all those who might sway the ageing wizard to their cause: the entreaties of a prince, the words of a philosopher, the remedies and spells of a woman physician. And John, because Pedro would not trust him to remain behind.

And if you had ever trusted me, brother, I might not be your enemy. But John was honest enough with himself to know that sentiment as sophistry. He was not a man to be satisfied with life in another's shadow.

As he slouched there, discontent and brooding, he heard a faint murmur, conveyed to him more through the stone than through his ears. He had burrowed deep into the back rooms of the garrison to find his solitude, and all the servants were out slaking the thirsts of their master and his cup-fellows. So who was this, growling to himself somewhere deeper in the building?

He crept out and followed the sound, piecing the words together until he recognised the voice of the Scot, which gave him pause. That grisly relic was hardly a creature to inspire much trust. But John was curious; he hunched closer, straining his ears to hear what the bloody-handed old monster was saying to himself in the quiet of a dark store-room.

"He is not the man," the grave voice grated out. "Orsino is a child, a weakling. There will be other armies to help, others who will keep on the war."

And then a new voice spoke—a woman's, redolent with haughty majesty and cold, cold anger. John could not listen to it without a shiver, and at the same time he felt a terrible attraction. He knew it was the evil in that voice, calling out to the evil in himself. In that moment all his illusions about how hard done by he was fell away. He knew himself to be no more than a villain, and this voice's slave.

"Did I gift you with life everlasting, proof against all the blades and arrows of men, so that you could tell me *can't?*" demanded the unseen woman. "Did I bind my witches to you so that you could shrug and spread your hands and make excuses?"

"Orsino has no love of war. I cannot make a warrior out of a poet." The Scot sighed, a surprisingly human sound of frustration. "If I push, it will be Denmark over again, all death without a purpose."

"Sometimes death is its own purpose," the woman stated darkly.

"And…" The Scot's voice faltered. "I cannot see what has become of your servant. She is lost to me."

There was a moment of silence, while John held his breath. Then the woman's voice spoke again, more slowly. "Also to me, and that is no small matter. But that is a question for my world. Yours is a world of swords and fire, and you fail me in it. If Pedro is returned to Aragon you shall know my fullest displeasure. If Illyria withdraws from the war also. Do your job, once-King of Scotland, for I would see all Europe in flames. I would have their thrones cast down, their churches burned, their glorious light of reason drowned in blood. We will bring back our time, Macbeth; a time of blood and rage, fear and murder. That is the purpose I saved you for; that is my will which you must carry out. Or you will know my most extreme displeasure."

Then the speaker was gone—John could not see, but he felt

her absence unmistakably, as if it were a kind of heartbreak. She had terrified him in every word, but had thrilled him, too. The world was full of bad men like Parolles or Sir Toby, who would go through their lives slighting and insulting, bullying and cheating. Some few there were, though, who chose not merely wealth or power or advantage, but *villainy*. Such a man was he, and such men were claimed by the Scot's mistress, Hecate.

So instead of backing away and returning to the vapid merriment of the main hall, he pressed on, until he came to a room so filled up with bitter darkness he could hardly see the armoured figure within it. There he was, though: the Scot, head bowed and brooding on the rebuke his mistress had given him.

He thought he had been stealthy, but the helmed head whipped up, and abruptly the Scot strode forwards and grasped him by the collar, lifting him to his toes. A knife-blade was cold against his throat, and he was sure he felt the metal of it throb with a rhythm like a pulse, independent of his own.

"You have eavesdropped on a secret communion," the Scot intoned. "I will have some blood of Aragon this day, even if it is not the prince's."

"Hold, do you not know me?" John got out hastily.

"I know you for a canting fool of a younger brother."

"Then know me as one who has a very deep interest in Don Pedro not returning to the throne of Aragon. Know me not as your foe, nor as one of Sir Toby's lackwit sots, but as a kinsman, a fellow admirer of your illustrious mistress."

He found himself lowered slightly, enough that the grip was not half-choking him.

"Speak," the Scot said.

"You are a man of great power, of magical protection," John whispered to him. "Why do you chafe under Orsino's commands?"

The Scot rumbled, deep in his armoured chest. "He is my host, and I am here at his invitation, for all he regrets it now."

"What matter such things to you?" John exclaimed.

Abruptly the Scot shoved him up against the wall. John stared at him, blood freezing in his veins.

"I first started on this path because I slew my guest," said the ancient king. "Yes, he was my king and my friend, and had shown me great favour, but my chiefest sin was that he was my guest, and I his host. Since then I have had children killed, cast down kingdoms, brought in the tide of war, that leaves starvation and ruin its only inheritors. I am so far in blood... but never yet have I been the guest who turned against his host." There was a faint tremor in the warlord's voice, an echo of a mortal man's fear. "So long as that one sin escapes me, perhaps the Devil shall not perfect his claim to me."

John stared into the dim, grey face within the helm and felt wonder and pity—and with pity, a little scorn, that even this monstrous creature should so lie to itself.

"But Orsino still frets over the wording of his orders," John pointed out. "Like any poet, he will word them and re-word them for a seven-night. Or at least for tonight. What if you were to slip into the dungeon and make an end to Pedro yourself?"

The Scot made a gravely, thoughtful sound, then shook his head. "It is only half a plan," he decided. "For Orsino will know full well what has happened. He will sue for peace all the sooner, for he never had the true love of war that befits a ruler. And he will cast me off—and my mistress—for the dishonour brought upon his house. But there is a remedy for that, O future lord of Aragon."

Don John flinched a little under that deathless gaze, but he bore up to it. "Go on, then, give your physic."

"Let not Don Pedro be found a corpse within his cell," the Scot pronounced. "Instead let him bear out the truth of your warnings: that he has slipped between the bars and gained his freedom. And what shall he do with that freedom but to take revenge against the chiefest of his captors?"

"I thought you were reluctant to harm your host."

"I? I speak nothing of what *I* shall do. I shall have taken your brother from his cell and found some lonely heath on which to make an end of him. I raise no hand against Orsino. But you..."

Don John felt something pressed into his hand: the grip of the same cold knife which had been pressed against his skin. Through the skin that wrapped its hilt, he felt that faint, terrible pulse.

"This blade was given to me by my dark mistress," the Scot told him reverently. "With this knife and one fell stroke I ended the life of my king and traded mortal judgment and reward for life eternal. The age is past when such dark deals were made, but you may yet win for yourself the throne of Aragon. Take up this knife and end Orsino's life. Be you the host-slayer, as I slew my guest. Leave by the body such signs of Aragon that, when they find he's vanished, none may doubt 'twas Pedro did the deed. So shall we whip to war the weary hosts of Illyria and Aragon. So shall you have your coronation. So shall I have my mistress's favour once again."

A street in Apollonia.

Hard against the garrison wall, the view is cluttered with barrels and crates. The muddy ground crunches with shards of broken glass, the broken corpses of Sir Toby's constant fare. The scent is of a midden. Here is cast all the wreckage of a drunkard's days and nights.

The garrison wall is high and smooth and windowless. Everything stands in its shadow.

Enter BENEDICK, PAROLLES and GANYMEDE.

THEY HAD BEEN more circumspect in their intelligence gathering since the incident with the Scot. Some dark hours in Apollonia had furnished them with more than enough rumour to know exactly how the land lay, though, and to drive them here to the very doorstep of the enemy.

"On a ship out at anchor is held the lion's share of the crew," Ganymede confirmed to Benedick. "But your lord is imprisoned within these walls, and also poor Jacques."

"Oh, by all means let's shed our blood for *his* few remaining years," Parolles said bitterly. "Would that he were here already. He could build us such a siege tower of his words, we could reach yon high opening and creep in."

"If all your wit leads to nothing but gall, be silent," Benedick told him.

Parolles lapsed into scowling. He was feeling hard done by, having been unable to shake his two companions. It was not so much the treasure that moved him now—not after witnessing just what manner of man held it. Instead, he was thinking of the myriad opportunities a port town offered to a fellow like him, not least escape back to France.

"They say the governor of this place is a drunkard," Ganymede noted, "and those men we've seen about the town were lax and slovenly; the servants will ever ape the master."

"The men on the gate looked keen enough," Parolles put in. "And don't think I would mistake Orsino's badge. If not he himself, some personage of note has come to call, and so you're out of luck. There's no slipping past the villains who have the watch now."

"Then what do you recommend? Abandon our comrade and the Spanish prince?" Ganymede demanded.

"Youth, I have seen more battles, kissed more women and stormed more cities than you've had sucks on your mother's teat," Parolles told the young forester. "There is no man bolder in the charge than I, but yet none reaches my age in a soldier's trade without learning wisdom. A prince is captive? Let his people ransom him. A philosopher? Let him use his solitude to hone his wits. We are but three, with one sword. We have no way to break into the garrison and, if by chance we might, the men within would make sure we'd have no way to leave it. At best we'd add to their store of captives, and at worst we put them to the trouble of digging three graves. And if we are taken up, whilst Sir Benedick here will likely bring a profitable sum to he who holds him, they will find a bumpkin of Arden not worth the cost of feeding. There's none will pay for the return of some raw stripling rustic. And as for me, whilst every maid in France will weep a bitter tear, I fear my credit is spent with those whose purses might have provided for my release."

"We could attempt disguise," Benedick considered.

"Oh, disguise!" Parolles exploded. "'Why, yes, good day to you, my fierce Illyrians. We are three travelling Russians desirous of an audience with your lord the Duke. Perhaps you have heard of the custom in our land, where those who donate spare prisoners to wandering Muscovites with unconvincing accents are guaranteed good luck for a year and a day? Especially royal Spaniards, oddly specific as our custom is!' What manner of fool would be taken in by such a story?" He caught their stares and spat. "Pah! There's no comparison! I was merely feigning compliance until I had you where I... Damn the pair of you, *and* your old man and your prince. I'll have none of you!"

"Then go," Benedick told him flatly. "Seek out what fortune remains to you amongst the dregs of this town and carry always the knowledge that you abandoned your comrades."

But it would hardly be the first time for that, and so Parolles took his chance and strolled away towards the alley mouth. He had a little coin in his purse and the town would be full of sots and sailors he could cozen for more. He had a hundred stories of deeds he had never done and places he had never been. They would be enough to hook him food and beer and perhaps a woman or two.

So involved was he in his petty plans, he almost ran into Helena.

His heart sank as he saw her, standing in his way as always. Her fine clothes were sea-drowned and briar-torn, her feet bare and filthy and her hair snarled. And she was beautiful, of course. Hers was a beauty that cared nothing for fashion, and that no ocean could wash from her.

He remembered when she had been a petitioner at the French court; the awkward, strange-mannered girl who had hung on every word of Parolles' rich friend Bertram. Then she had turned out to be some prodigy physician and cured the king, and tricked Bertram into marrying her because it was *something she wanted*. She had turned her lore of physic into magic for that same reason, because she was someone who saw the world in terms of what she wanted from it, and would not take no for an answer. That, Parolles decided, was the heart of what made her so unnerving. She was a woman who treated the world as a man ought.

He remembered bandying words with her, back before she had become the woman she was now. He had liked her then, for all she'd got the better of him. She had been someone he could cross wits with without his reputation hanging on every exchange. But then she had married and grown powerful, and then terrible. And he... he was the same fool he had always been, because when he tried to wrest what he wanted from the world, the world knocked him down and laughed at him. He felt as if she had grown up, and he remained a child.

"Let me by." He tried a tone of command, but it shrank and shrivelled in the face of her stare.

"Why, brave Parolles," she said, with a sly smile. "Surely you are not fleeing yet another battlefield?"

"Those two madmen have no use for one who speaks only sense," he told her. "So, let me past."

"The Turks say madness is the touch of God," Helena remarked. "Let us go speak with our inspired comrades. You may find there's method in them after all."

Parolles took hold of his courage, what little he could scrape together. "I will not be a spear-carrier in their princely rescue. I have seen too many carrion fields. I know what happens to the common lot when great men clash."

She put a hand to his chest. He felt a shock at the contact, a momentary yearning for a man he might have been—brave rather than boastful, steadfast rather than venal—who might have deserved that touch. Those bantering conversations came back to him then, with a piercing sense of sadness. *Innocent days. Can I believe I ever had more innocent days?*

"Must I press?" Helena asked him. "Must I make threats of what may befall your health, your fortunes and your manhood if you cross me...?"

"What spell have you cast on me?" he asked her hoarsely.

"Why, none, yet."

"What spell have you cast, that lays open all my life to me? That casts its light into every corner of the man I am?"

Helena stepped back, her hand lifting from him. "Such enchantments are beyond my power. You are the only magician who can so ensorcel yourself."

Parolles, liar and cheat and coward, felt sudden tears prick at the corners of his eyes. He waved Helena back, muttering some excuse, that he had not slept since the sea cast him forth, that he was weary, that there was a mote of dust beneath his lid that he could not dislodge.

By then, Benedick and Ganymede had made some cock-eyed plan and were coming out of the alley, stopping when they saw Helena.

"Lady," the Spaniard said, with an elegant bow, "I'm glad to see you well and safe. You come just in time to see us off, for Ganymede and I have devised a brave rescue—"

"No," Helena told him, not unpleasantly but firmly. "I have a rescue planned which shall make use of certain lore and powers I have of late acquired." And here, for reasons nobody then understood, she produced Benedick's silver flask and waved it at them. "With this, we shall gain access to the garrison without troubling the sentries at the gate."

Ganymede and Benedick exchanged glances, and the youth shrugged.

"Does it involve disguising ourselves as Russians?"

Helena stared blankly at him, wrong-footed for the first time in Parolles' acquaintance. "No..."

"Then it's going to be better than our plan," Ganymede decided, with an apologetic shrug to Benedick.

"Then it's decided," Helena stated. "You two shall travel with me into the garrison." And then she turned her sweet, fearsome smile on Parolles. "And for you, a special role, one that you are most well suited for. I will need you to be loud and raucous, Parolles. I shall have you lie and boast and spin grand stories of your time in harness. No spear carrier this, but a trumpeter, loud and clear."

Parolles took a deep breath, feeling his very nature balance on a knife edge. "The role suits me."

"Aye, it does. And this I swear: what care I give for the life of the prince we must rescue, no less shall I devote to ensuring your own survival. Now, gather close, and I shall explain just how it shall fall out."

Act V

The cells below the garrison.

The rooms were made for rowdy sailors or merchants who defaulted on their taxes, not for princes. Looking into them from the outside, they are small, formed from one large cellar partitioned up by bars.

One now has a little furnishing: a rug to soften the floor, a chair, a desk, some light; paper and ink. Since Orsino came, the comfort of Don Pedro has at least been looked at.

In the cell beside him, denied his rug and chair but permitted, by the space between the bars, to share his light, is Jacques, holding forth.

Enter DON JOHN.

WHEN JOHN CREPT down to the cells, the old fool was in full flow. Jacques sat on the hard stone flags with all appearance of comfort. After all, he had lived out in the forest of Arden for years; despite his years, he was plainly not a man who relished civilised comforts.

"The fifth degree of magic is but thus," he was intoning. "To conjure forth the spirits of the air and have them work great wonders through their gratitude. Whilst wicked conjurers might trick and catch and leave these hapless sprites in durance vile, a righteous sorcerer may set them free and thus command their service for a time. So Prospero or yet the Orient youth who freed the spirit from its prison lamp. And so, within our world, are men whose power derives from robbing others of their own, and other men with popular acclaim who free their fellows from the like oppression."

"Yet Machiavelli says within his tract," came Don Pedro's voice, "that fear's a mightier goad than love."

Don John rolled his eyes. *Can you not suffer even a little before the Scot makes an end to you?* But no, it appeared his brother was more than content to be lectured by this pedant.

"Alas, a base misreading of his text," Jacques droned on, and Don John decided to leave them to it. He had hoped, perhaps, to gloat a little before his brother, but now he was here he sensed too much risk and, besides, no doubt Pedro would find some new way to turn it all to his advantage.

"Let the Scot take him," he murmured. With his hand on the dagger's hilt he skulked off, heading upstairs towards the quarters given over to Orsino.

Bearing the Scottish Blade was a strange thing. The shadows rose to enfold him everywhere he went. He could step softly past guards and servants, seen by none, and doors seemed to open for him wherever he went. And when he took the hilt... Don John had never been a killer—he preferred the sort of plots a Machiavel might favour. When there was violence to be done, he had found men of violence to enact it. The idea of plunging a blade into Orsino was distasteful to him, not for the sin, but for the crudeness and the mess. He would rather tear holes in a man's reputation than his skin.

But when he held the dagger, his doubts faded. It was a tool of murder, given by Hecate to drive the Scot to regicide. When John held the weapon he was bloody, bold and resolute indeed.

And upstairs was Orsino, patiently labouring over the missive he would send with Pedro back to Aragon. A missive that would restore the prince to his country, rob John of his inheritance, rob the Scot of Illyria's part in the slaughter. However many strategems his mind revised, all narrowed to one when he gripped the dagger's hilt.

He paused at Orsino's door, seeing servants inside refilling their lord's glass. *Drink deep, Duke of Illyria. Blunt the pain before it comes to you.* John had already obtained Pedro's signet ring, that had been taken by his jailers back when he was being poorly hosted by Sir Toby. He would leave that beside the body and the Scot would ensure the convenience of the gesture was overlooked in the general outrage.

The servant went by about her work and Don John tensed, knowing his moment had come. His hand had left the knife for a moment and, as he stepped into the room unseen, he felt a cobweb touch of conscience. With Orsino's death he would have crossed a bloody Rubicon, wading in so far that it were easier to continue than turn back. He would not become some dread lord of myth like the Scot—as the warlord had said, that age was past—but this modern era's shadow of it, ruling by fear and suspicion, and destined for Hell.

And yet I would at least have ruled before I die. And that seemed to be enough, so he took the dagger out and drank deep of its well.

And then a riot broke out below. At first John thought it was just Toby Belch in a choleric moment, but then he heard voices raised in argument, and then at last just one dominating—a voice he felt he should know, waxing strong in strident account...

The idiot soldier... Parolles?

Orsino was on his feet, his poet's muse completely spoiled. With a frown he swept past Don John, unseeing, and was heading down the stairs to see what all the noise was, no doubt with every other occupant of the garrison who possessed ears.

Don John found himself trembling, now fate had prevented the fatal stroke. Carefully he slid the dagger back into his belt and padded back down the stairs. *I will have another chance.* But even his desire for power was giving ground to curiosity. *Just what is happening down there?*

He arrived back in the hall to see Parolles in the midst of some bizarre martial account. Skulking over to Sir Toby he murmured, "What is this?"

"This remarkable fellow," Toby told him, "has been a soldier of the enemy, now come to throw himself on Illyria's noted mercy like yourself. He has come hotfoot from Lepanto, where, he says, the Turkish fleet braved the sails of Venice."

Duke Orsino was plainly fascinated by the man's tale. He walked in circles about Parolles, questioning every bizarre particular, each question leading to some yet more unlikely exposition. All around them, the hall was steadily filling up as guards, courtiers and servants came to hear this prodigal story.

"Good sirs," Parolles insisted, "I was standing at the very left hand of Venice's great general, the Moor himself. Mighty wroth he was and, when he had disposed his foot and horse along the shore, he leapt into a barque no greater than a fisherman's scow, and me along with him. He bad me raise the sail and, even as the Venetian galleys were getting underway, he made of himself the vanguard, driving towards the warships of the Turk!"

"Where were the Turkish guns in this?" Orsino demanded. "Every soldier knows for range and aim they exceed all of our shipborne pieces."

"Why they made a very fearsome response!" Parolles swore. "Lead fell on us like the summer rains and full seven galleys sank in a single breath with all hands. But neither the Moor nor I were dismayed, and when a ball came square for us, red hot and hissing, bold Othello bad me slacken the sail so that its smooth front bellied out like the front of yon stout fellow's doublet."

Sir Toby bellowed his displeasure at that, but it was drowned out in the general laughter.

"Then!" Parolles raised his voice above it. "Then I twitched the rudder and the ball touched on our sails and rolled about the inside of their curve, so that it followed out and spat itself upon the Turk, and holed the very vessel that had sent it to us!"

Cheering at that. Even Orsino had apparently forgotten that the Turk was notionally an ally in the war.

"But what of the Turkish fire?" some academically-minded fellow called out. "It is well know the Turkish ships can breathe an inferno that even the sea cannot douse!"

"Indeed, and as we neared, so it came to us, a fire upon the waters so great..." And on went Parolles, seeming almost desperate in the ferocity of his confabulation, full of sound and fury and, no doubt, signifying nothing. And yet for the moments of the tale's telling, Don John found himself strangely captivated by it. Almost reluctantly he turfed a minor functionary out of the seat next to Sir Toby and sat down.

A bare stage.

Neutral lighting; no properties; no backdrop.

At the edge of hearing, a distant susurrus as of a multitude of players rehearsing their lines to themselves.

Enter HELENA, leading BENEDICK and GANYMEDE.

"What is this place?" Benedick demands. "I have seen desert shores and the barren places of the world, but a place like this, and but a step from that street in Apollonia..."

Helena sounds strained, holding the flask tight in her grip. "We are between the pages of the world's book. Each scene and moment of our lives is pieced together in this space before it's served to us. We are where none of us was meant to be."

"Then why bring us here?" Ganymede hisses, clutching his bow to him.

"Because this is not just one step from where we left, it is one step from everywhere—all the cities, all the forest glades, the blasted heaths, the desert islands and the wrecking shores." She shakes the flask and listened intently to whatever was inside. "If we were but to find the right exit, I could take you to Egypt to trouble Cleopatra, or to the forum to witness Caesar's death. I could bring you to Venice or Verona, London's fatal tower or Elsinore, if we but knew which path to go..."

"It seems to me just like a mummer's stage," the youth observes, sounding vaguely let down.

"Aye, and all the stage is yet a world," Helena declares. "And what most concerns us now is entrances and exits."

"Can this lead us to Milan?" Benedick puts in.

Helena laughs at him. "I tell you we can go to antique Rome, and you ask if I can take us to Milan? Yes, yes to Milan, and yet, and yet..." She stares into the wings and her face adopts a pensive look. "And yet I see the scenery of a different play laid out. A tower room laid for the death of Prospero."

"Old Prospero's been dying for a generation," Benedick scoffs, but Helena's raised hand silences him.

"And yet he has travelled to that undiscovered country swifter than we could come to Milan," she whispers.

"But then—!" the Aragonese nobleman makes a frustrated clutching gesture. "If you can step to Ancient Rome then why not yesterday's Milan?"

"For yesterday's Milan belongs to Hecate, and there I will not meddle. Milan tomorrow is the only Milan that we shall see, and that without a Prospero."

"What then, what then for all of us?" Benedick demands.

"Hst," she tells him. "Later turn our thoughts onto Milan; for now, just let us take a smaller step. Let us walk inside the garrison and save your prince."

Benedick nods emphatically. "So, which path?"

Helena joggles the flask once more, concentrating. "Let me work, for whilst it would be a fine thing to hear Mark Anthony sway the crowd, old Rome would be a poor place to visit by mistake. And there are other paths, that lead to nowhere in the world."

"What places?" Ganymede looks around himself, wonder overcoming fear.

Helena looks at you, out from the stage, out from the page. "Stranger places yet." She catches your eye and weighs your worth, the sum total of your words and deeds. "Perhaps I'll visit, when this business is done. I've always felt the walls of the world press on me. Am I not due a wider stage to play my part on, after all?"

Benedick coughs diplomatically. "Madam doctor, the garrison?"

She smiles at him, enough to make him take a step back, but then she says, "Of course," and chooses her exit, leading the others offstage. Perhaps she casts a final glance back at you before she goes.

The cells below the garrison.

From up above the murmur of the crowd as Parolles plies his lying trade.

Don Pedro is scratching away with the pen and ink the Illyrians gave him. In the adjourning cell, Jacques stands, one hand on the bars, pensive.

Enter MACBETH.

*   *   *

"My lord," Jacques said, "we have a visitor."

Not his tone but his brevity brought Pedro's head up. In a moment he was standing, stepping back for space, his hand moving to a swordless belt.

The Scot advanced until he was at the bars. "Do you know me, Don Pedro of Aragon?"

"I know you for my enemy, and the enemy of all the world," the prince confirmed. "It is for your sake that we ventured to Milan, to find a counter for your diabolic influence."

The warlord raised a mailed hand airily. "Ah, how many well-made plans have foundered when they went to sea? After all, there are no greater raisers of the tempest than my witches."

"Save for Prospero," Pedro said stubbornly.

The Scot chuckled, a deep, metallic sound. "Why, did you not hear? The wizard of Milan is dead, these two weeks, murdered in his own tower."

Pedro slumped, groaning. "No."

Macbeth's armoured shoulders shifted in a shrug. "It matters little either way. Your days end here, for I have come to take you off to execution. Your brother and I have already come to an agreement: he shall carry news of your demise back to your people, who shall fight the war all the fiercer for your death. And die on every field in Europe, with the rest."

His gauntlet closed upon the lock and clenched, crushing and twisting the metal until the cell door sprang open. In one smooth motion, he drew his rusted blade.

"Fight me, then," Pedro challenged. "But bring me a sword and I will face you like a soldier."

"I could bring you swords, knives, muskets, hatchets, cannon even," the Scot informed him. "They would not aid you. I am proof against any effort of yours. But you mistake me. Have you not heard my tale? Did your nurse not scare you with it when you were a child? What is left of he that was Macbeth in this shallow age? That he was a great murderer. And so I murder, and move on. The blood of one more man will barely shift the scales, should I ever come to judgment."

"But that is not what I have heard," Jacques broke in. "For well I know your story."

"You know nothing," the Scot growled.

"If only that were true, but I am yet on the cusp of man's last age, and my mind is sharp," the philosopher told him. "Do you truly think that history has picked the bones of you, until all that's left is 'murderer'? Then listen as I tell you of a man ambitious, of a warrior who fought his nation's foes. Another tale I have is of a man misled, who gave his trust to prophecies and powers and was sore betrayed. But yet of all the Scots that I heard of, the one that touched me most was of the husband, and the man who loved his wife."

"My wife...?" The Scot seemed frozen at the thought.

"How long is it, I wonder, since you last thought of her? And yet the stories tell of how in all the world you valued her, and how she was a strong, fierce woman worthy of you. And how she died."

"She died," the warlord echoed. "Yes, she died."

"There are a hundred men contained in you, and each one has a different tale to tell," Jacques told him softly. "You do not have to be the murderer."

The Scot paused in the doorway of the cell. It was impossible to know whether he was staring at Pedro, or at the sword between them. For a long, long time many things hung in the balance.

Then that helmed head shook and the warlord said, "No. I serve a harsh mistress. What am I, if I do not do her bidding?" And he stepped forwards, a hand reaching out to seize his prey.

With a sound like birds taking flight or ruffled pages, Helena, Benedick and Ganymede burst out of nowhere at all, stumbling over each other to land in a heap behind the Scot.

The warlord whirled, and Benedick saw and understood precisely what had been going on. He shouted a challenge and had his rapier from its scabbard just in time to turn aside the downstroke. With a flourish of his wrist he had his slender blade past the Scot's guard and drove it through the rings of his enemy's armour.

The Scot laughed. One mailed hand closed on Benedick's quillons and ripped the weapon from his hand. With the rapier still hanging from him he chopped at the Aragonese, but Pedro leapt on him from behind and spoiled his blow. Growling, the warlord threw the prince off him and shook himself.

"So, die elsewhere or die here, I shall have the blood of you all!"

Helena had a stone and was trying to scratch a circle into the stone of the floor, with little success. Ganymede stood away from her, bowstring drawn back and his sole arrow nocked.

"Hold off, monster," he warned. "Sheath your sword, or we'll see if my shaft fares better than his blade."

The Scot laughed him to scorn. "I laugh to scorn the power of man," he reminded the youth. "For—"

"None of woman born, yes," Ganymede agreed. "But it's ambiguous, is it not, your prophecy?"

"It has been plain enough to see me through five centuries and more," the Scot declared.

"'Laugh to scorn the power of man, for none of woman born may harm Macbeth,'" quoted the archer. "Does that mean none at all, or none of those who wield the power of man?"

"What difference does it make, stripling?" And the Scot took a menacing step towards the youth.

"Only that I have never owned to the power of man," explained Ganymede. "My name is Rosalind, in truth. I am a maid."

Macbeth paused, silent for a moment.

"Truly?" asked Benedick, and then he was stepping back with Helena as more company came down the stairs: the two Illyrians who had fooled them in the tavern.

Ganymede—or she who bore the name—kept her attention

on the Scot. "I am Rosalind du Bois, though not a one of my shipmates bar this old man knew it," she announced. "And I read your prophecy thus: that you are safe only from the power of men. If you dispute my interpretation then take one step more, and my arrow shall be the arbiter."

"And my blade also," and the younger guard had pushed forward to draw sword and stand by Rosalind. "For I am Viola, Duchess of Illyria, and I know full well my husband has spared these prisoners."

Three times the Scot tensed, ready to try the truth of his charmed life. Three times his mettle failed. Perhaps a man who had lived five centuries fearing nothing had never had to test his courage; and now he at last had cause to use it, the Scot found it rusted and brittle.

"And know this," Rosalind told him as he hesitated. "From this day forth each battlefield that falls beneath your shadow shall hold a maiden with a musket hunting for you. Your bloody reign I here consign to history!"

With a roar of thwarted rage the ancient warlord flung up his arms and gathered all the shadows in the room to him in a whirl of darkness. Ganymede's arrow zipped through the murky air where he had stood, but only shattered against the far wall. The Scot was gone.

In his absence, there was a moment of relief from all concerned, but then Benedick broke in, "There goes my sword. Madam Doctor, are you able to whisk us away as swiftly as yon Scot just left?"

"Not without some time for calculation," Helena informed him tightly.

Viola returned her blade to the scabbard and glanced across at Feste.

"It took a fool to see that clown above was naught but a distraction," her sergeant remarked. "But even this old fool did not think it was diversion for so many. Whose is he?"

"Mine," Helena confirmed. "So, may we ask, what is Illyria's pleasure now?" Her eyes were fixed on Viola.

The garrison hall.

The air riotous with laughter, shouts and cheers as all lean in to hear Parolles strut and fret his hour upon the stage. Sir Toby drools ale and spittle into his beard. Orsino is scratching at a scrap of parchment, trying to record the prodigy for posterity. Don John critiques.

Enter a company: VIOLA and FESTE, ROSALIND and JACQUES, BENEDICK and DON PEDRO, HELENA.

PAROLLES WAS STILL at his fictional Battle of Lepanto. Already he had travelled on a cannonball and hauled himself out of the water by his own hair. Each listener had tried to challenge the lie—Orsino, Don John and Sir Toby amongst them—and each challenge he slew, and then piled up the bodies to reach even greater heights of the absurd. Where his words might have taken him, when the newcomers broke in, was past all guessing. Some men, when given rope, refuse to hang themselves but instead weave a ladder to the moon.

He faltered only when he saw his comrades, and silence reigned as every ear there hung on the words he had not said.

Into that quiet Viola barked out, "Guards, arrest the Aragonese villain, Don John!"

The guards were slow to react, but John started at his name and turned. He saw his brother, free and with a knowledge in his eye that did not bode well. Perhaps, if he put on a bold front and denied all culpability, he might ooze his way into Don Pedro's good graces one again, but his nerve failed him. In a single motion he was over the table, kicking Sir Toby's cup to spatter Orsino with the dregs. In a flash he was down the other side and running for the door.

Parolles, finding at last an opponent who required no great courage to best, tripped him, sending Aragon's second son sprawling across the floor. As Don John spat and cursed, his assailant bent down and neatly relieved him of his purse and, to cover the larceny before so many eyes, of his knife. Thus drunken prophecy was proved true: the treasure that could shake the world had come into the hands of the world's most ardent liar.

By then, Illyria's soldiers were stirring, and enough of them piled on Don John to end his escape bid.

Orsino was staring at the young officer who had given the command. "What treason's this? Who has released my prisoners and who assaults my guests?"

"One whom you swore would ever rule you," Viola told him, stepping forward, and he went to greet her with a smile.

It was the matter of an hour before Orsino had listened to all that had happened—tales overlapping and sometimes contradictory, told by his wife, his fool and various of his prisoners. After that he sat in thought, banishing all save Viola, even the protesting Sir Toby, from the hall.

"HERE IS THE judgment of Illyria," Orsino proclaimed, when at last he had reassembled the unlikely company. He sat, stern as a judge, with Sir Toby slouched half-conscious at his left hand, and Viola on his right. She was attired as befitted a duchess now, her splendour and her beauty drawing all eyes. Only Rosalind looked on her and thought, *She is counting the minutes before she can throw all that off, and play the breeches part again.* She herself had resisted any suggestion that she should lace herself back into a dress. If she was offending the dignity of the family du Bois then, of all men, her husband would understand.

Parolles was merry—he had spent the hour in finishing his tale for Sir Toby and the wine-sops of the garrison, and had profited from it in gold and in ale. Benedick was glad he had his prince back, and Pedro plainly optimistic to be freed. Don John, under guard, stood hunched at the back, practising his black looks. Rosalind had heard something of his history from Benedick, and no doubt the elder brother would pardon the younger yet again. But then, as wife to a second son herself, she could hardly complain of it.

Jacques was pensive and self-involved. Had he been telling everyone exactly what degrees of cogitation afflicted him—in iambs and at length—she would have said he was his old self. It seemed he was thinking on the melancholy story of the Scot— not often a philosopher came face to face with such a shard of history. No doubt he would regale them with his thoughts upon the matter in due course, but for now he was sensibly silent.

And Helena, of course: but Rosalind could not categorise or anatomise her. Magician, physician, walker of worlds, she stood still and regal behind them as though she were king and queen both, and the rest of their party no more than pawns. Yes, she had got them where they needed to be, but she was a fearsome creature, a power in the ascendant. *Did we even need Prospero?*

"I free you all," Orsino pronounced, "but on condition that you, sir"—to Don Pedro—"go not about your task, but instead take ship for Aragon and there command the release of Sebastian, my wife's brother. For this, I give your own brother into your care. I do not judge him, for the chiefest witness of what he might or might not have done is fled to darker places."

"Though I had hoped to harbour in Milan," Don Pedro agreed, "it seems that errand was lost before e'er it was begun. I accept your terms with all thanks." He clapped Benedick on the shoulder. "So, you shall see your wife all the sooner. I hope you have replenished your store of wit."

"And take this message back to Aragon," Orsino added,

gesturing for a scroll to be taken over to Don Pedro. "Illyria is tired of war and offers terms for our withdrawal. Let the Tuscan throne be a Tuscan matter. Bring this to Aragon's alliance, and perhaps they will not fret that you never made Milan."

In the general celebration that followed that pronunciation, Parolles relaxed. Wintering in the sunny climes of Aragon was surely better than a stay in the shadow of a sorcerer's tower. The stories that came out of Milan turned the rumour-mills of all Europe: statues that spoke and moved, gusts of air with human faces; a city full of bodiless voices, lights and terrible wonders.

But, even as Pedro and Benedick drew apart to discuss their return home, Helena glided to his elbow, drawing Ganymede— no, Rosalind—and Jacques close.

"Let the Spanish run home to bicker about prisoners and war," she murmured. "Milan awaits us."

"You'll find no barque so bound out of this port," Jacques cautioned her. "Though all the winds—" And then he stopped at Helena's upraised hand.

"We need no ship, nor winds, to reach Milan."

"But what can we hope to achieve?" Rosalind ventured. "Prospero's dead, and far beyond joining the league."

"And would our journey ever have borne fruit?" Helena shrugged. "Old Prospero scorned the dealings of nations for many years; I do not think we could have moved him to meddle now. But there are surely books and things of magic still in his lonely tower; perhaps a student with power and knowledge will find much to reward her. Will you go with me?"

"To see the secret city of the magus," Jacques said swiftly, "of course!"

Rosalind was slower, but she nodded still. "The children and accounts can be my lord's burden for another season," she decided. "I have not had my fill of voyaging."

And then, of course, Helena turned that cool, clear gaze on Parolles. He remembered his moment of self-knowledge outside the garrison—a flash of a time long gone, for he had never been very innocent, and what she now was, he had no name for.

Yet at the same time, she was the closest thing he had to an old friend.

"My stock back in Rousillon was low, my debts high," he said, with unusual frankness. "And there are those in Milan who know neither my stories nor my vices. But may you bring me back to Illyria, after?"

"If your desire to travel is so meagre, than I shall," she confirmed. "I myself shall have grander ambitions by then, I have no doubt. Perhaps I shall go places even Prospero but dreamt of." And then she held a hand out to him—not to take his own, but to receive something. "If you would, keep Don John's purse, but I must have the knife."

"The knife?" Parolles frowned at her, then sudden revelation struck him. "The knife? This knife?" He had the thing in his hand, staring at its dull blade. "This is... the knife?" For a moment he felt a darkness coursing through him: a blade in his hand, and so many people within arm's length. But for all his many, many vices, that was one he never owned. He gave the thing to Helena, and—treasure or not—counted himself glad to be rid of it.

Helena regarded it in her hand. "I saw this, when we stepped between worlds. Do you know the source of its power? It is not from here. A poet—a mummer—sent it, bloodstained, from his world to this by means of his words. Drove it here out of mourning for a friend." She tucked it out of sight.

"Now stand close," she instructed them, and fished the silver flask from within her robe. "Today, Milan in our world," she tells you. "Tomorrow, perhaps, in yours."

ON THE
TWELFTH
NIGHT

BY JONATHAN BARNES

O spirit of love! how quick and fresh art thou,
That, notwithstanding thy capacity
Receiveth as the sea, nought enters there,
Of what validity and pitch soe'er,
But falls into abatement and low price,
Even in a minute: so full of shapes is fancy
That it alone is high fantastical.

Twelfth Night, Act I, Scene i.

On the First Night

25ᵗʰ of December, 1601

THE FIRST INTIMATION of the coming catastrophe arrives after nightfall on the feast day which commemorates the birth of your god.

You are woken from warm and fathomless dreams by the sound of a loud retort, like the inaugural drum-beat of thunder or of a clash of arms upon some distant battlefield. It pulls you back unmercifully to consciousness and brings with it that unwelcome clarity of the smallest hours, that invitation to unstinting self-examination which comes when all the world but you seems lost to slumber.

Your first thought is that the sound has been made by your husband, your spouse of almost twenty years, he who drowses beside you now, pot-bellied and damson-faced, unshaven and beer-breathed, whose sprawling posture speaks of purely animal pleasures and whose inveterate tendency to snore has been known to you (in what at the time was a gentle kind of scandal) for several long and energetic months before the church, before the aisle, before any public declaration of your love was made. Scarcely noticed at first, in the decades since you have become intimately accustomed to the sound of his slumber, to its noisy rhythms, its shattering crescendos and monotonous longeurs and its regrettable tendency to be affected by strong drink.

Yet on this occasion, the blame is unjust, for your man's sleep is, if not quite soundless, at least muted and sedate, no more than a rustle, a hedgerow snuffle, emerging from his lips. You sit up, you draw the blanket around you, for the night is chill and not kind, and you listen.

The sound comes again. Not from this room at all but from downstairs, from somewhere out of sight. It is, without question, a determined rap upon your front door, a knock, after midnight. Something which betokens in your mind only the worst—the very worst—of things.

For a moment you lie still, your head full of old tales about the nature of unexpected sounds, of fireside yarns of rapping spirits and purgatorial guests, of malevolent boggarts and of dread and nameless things walking, of strange prophets and of visitors from that which lies beyond death. And then, of course, being sensible—being renowned in fact, if not exactly celebrated, in this little fortress town, for your hard-headedness and stolid practicality—you put such foolishness aside, and, with affectionate determination, poke your husband in that soft, expansive realm which lies beneath his ribcage and hiss: "William? William?"

Your best friend, the father of your three children and (with decreasing but not especially disappointing frequency) your lover, groans once, stirs in his sleep and rolls away, his every movement groggily ursine. Being used from long experience to his admittedly modest frailties, you sigh, with a theatrical exasperation which you hope that some part of him will hear and which may also comfort you. There is a candle beside you which, although almost burned to the stub, flickers still. You must have neglected to snuff it out before sleep, almost as if you were expecting this visitation, as though you somehow already knew the truth.

You reach for the fitful light and, wincing against the cold, you rise from the bed, wrap your nightgown more tightly around you and step carefully from the room. The house is quiet, the children are all asleep and the night seems to possess that stark country stillness which always serves to remind you of your childhood, of the sombre silence of the forest, the ranks of watchful oak and ash.

The stairs creak as you descend, as if chiding you for being abroad at such an hour, for having the temerity to walk the earth upon this holy night. Chiding you and also, perhaps, you think in an echo of your earlier bout of superstition, warning you, urging you to turn back, to go to bed once more, to roll over and ignore this ominous and impertinent interruption. For an instant, you even hesitate. You pause upon the penultimate stair.

You consider retreat then, choosing cowardice over facing the unknown. But you are who you are and this hesitation is but a momentary thing. You go on, to the door itself, and you take the only choice which makes sense to you. In doing so, you set in motion a chain of events which will unstitch all that you have ever loved.

There is standing upon your threshold a stranger.

At least, so you imagine him at first to be. But then, peering closer... there is something familiar—something terribly, disquietingly familiar—in the lineaments of his face, in the unexpected intellect of his eyes, in the fervour (half-remembered from more than a decade past) in the resolute, bear-like set of his mouth.

He is a tall fellow, raggedly dressed and extravagantly bearded. There is about him a little of the wild man, a little of the beggar and much—you think, taking in this apparition with a single, cautious sweep of your gaze—much of the hierophant, of the prophet, the sage, of he who descends from the peaks with a tablet in each hand, of he who knows and understands.

"Anne?" he says and, to your surprise, at the simple speaking of your name, his eyes seem at once to grow moist with tears.

"Do I know you, sirrah?" you ask with that haughtiness which you reserve traditionally for hawkers, peddlers and wayfarers of every stripe, for those who are unwise enough to call at the Shakespeare residence without an invitation and at any inconvenient time. "Have we met?"

"Forgive me, my sweet Anne. Pray overlook the familiarity of my manner. I had not thought that the sight of you would in me evoke so great a tide of melancholy."

"Who are you?" you ask. "What do you want at such an hour? All of Stratford is abed and slumbering and so by rights ought you to be. From the look of *you*, sir, in some ditch or in some woodland bower. Somewhere safely out of sight of decent folks."

The stranger smiles sadly. "Oh, but your tongue is as sharp as ever it was. Your wit as pointed."

"You speak, sir, as though we share some old acquaintance. Yet, on the contrary, I fear that I possess of you not the slightest recollection."

"Oh, Anne, sweet Anne. This is the bitterest of meetings. I am not entirely as you knew me. For that I was prepared. But, surely, is there not something—something at least in me which your heart seems to know? Which calls to you from your past and from your future?"

You frown, considering the wisdom of giving even a splinter of yourself away to this outré stranger before, without quite understanding why, you say: "There is... perhaps... yes... there is, I think, something known, sir, in the angles, perhaps, of your countenance..."

The man upon the threshold nods as if obscurely gratified. "Then that shall have to suffice. There is comfort in it. But now, madam, I have a message for your husband. For Will."

"Is that true, sir? And what are you to him? I do perceive some small resemblance in you, though if you are a relative you must be distant indeed."

"No relative, I, madam. At least... not precisely so."

"I see."

"I think that you do not quite yet see."

"Oh? And is your message of such outstanding urgency that it must needs be communicated at the dead of night? Upon this day, of all days?"

"Tell him..." says the man and, as he speaks, something in his appearance seems to shift and alter. It takes you a few seconds to understand the sight. It is an odd transparency, a sudden quality of the insubstantial. "Tell him that the Guild is coming. Tell him that the void sweeps through the lattice of worlds and that he—Will Shakespeare—is at the very heart of it."

Bewildered by this torrent of language, by its florid inexplicability, you breathe in slowly. You try to take stock. "Your words are strange, sir. They are passing strange."

As you speak the man grows fainter still, vague and amorphous, like a ghost upon the battlements.

"Your message," you say, "what does it mean?"

The man blinks and the motion seems to rob him further of his presence, his heft. He flickers and shimmers as if he is not truly there at all. "It means," he murmurs, and his voice is becoming fainter now also, as if he moving further and further away, "that we are all in the worst kind of danger. That we are compassed and threatened by absolute disaster."

"Sir?" you ask urgently. "Sir, your form is growing faint. Your voice also. Tell me: what manner of visitation are you? Are you from Purgatory or from some darker place?"

"The Guild," he says, ignoring your question. "Tell him that the Guild have need of him. And that they shall be calling soon." He flickers again and he is reduced still further. Like a will-o'-wisp, you think, or, perhaps, more accurately, like an image reflected in a pool, a picture disrupted by a stone tossed into the heart of it.

"What are you?" you ask again. "Who has sent you? What is it that you truly want from me?"

The man bows his head and smiles wretchedly for the final time. "My answer to all three is the same," he says and pauses with a flourish, an unnecessary piece of drama which puts you in mind of some second-rate player. He meets your gaze and says, "your husband," and then, at the instant this final syllable is spoken, he disappears entirely, vanishing from the world as if he were never a part of it. And you are left upon the threshold, shivering in the night air, unsettled and afraid, and filled up with the most intense and palpable sensation of dread.

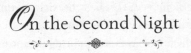

On the Second Night

26th of December, 1601

YOU WAKE, JUDGING from the quality of the light, towards the middle of the morning, hours later than you would by choice or custom rise. You are alone in your bed. William has gone.

You feel within you a rush of something very like panic. It is a sensation that you have not felt since the children were young: that this household, your little kingdom, is no longer entirely under your control. Some new element has entered the realm, you think, some rank, malignant humour.

At the moment when it occurs to you that you have absolutely no memory whatsoever of returning from the threshold to your bed last night you hear from somewhere below you the sounds of lively conversation. You listen and are able to distinguish three voices. The first—querulous; modestly argumentative; bemused—is recognisable at once as that of your husband, at the moment, experienced from time to time in any marriage, when he is confronted by some disagreeable truth. The second and third voices are not known to you, but they are riven with drama and alarm. The entire scene seems to you to be utterly wrong, an interruption in the way in which the world ought to work. It is as though your quiet and unvaried life has been by stealth and artfulness overrun by something rich and strange.

You rise swiftly, you wrap your gown about you once again and you hurry down to greet your uninvited guests.

As you approach the door that leads to the room in which the three conspirators are met—and how odd it is, you think, the speed and insistence with which that word, that description, has presented itself—you hear a phrase that serves only to exacerbate the rising unease in your breast, the sick certainty that some disaster lies just a little beyond the horizon.

"The knife which has no business being here is held now by the Scot."

The oddity of those words in that order, the icy casualness with which they are spoken, not by your husband but by one of these strangers, one of those interlopers, causes you to stop quite still, arresting your progress as fear and the knowledge of your own mortality and that of your children, surges to the forefront of your imagination.

You breathe quietly, trying to recover your equilibrium. The conversation in the chamber falls silent.

Swift footsteps, and the door is opened.

Standing before you, dishevelled and afraid, no longer the plump picture of contentment that he was mere hours ago, stands the figure of your husband.

Behind him, you see standing upon either side of the fire like sentries, the two visitors, both unknown to you but both curiously familiar also. Both are bearded, both well dressed. One has the quality of a clown, the other that of a sage. Yet you are afforded but the briefest of glimpses. Your husband closes the door hurriedly behind him, runs a hand through his thinning hair, a gesture of anxiety which you have not witnessed in him since Hamnet's long illness the year before last, and says: "My love, I fear I have grave tidings."

He always speaks in this heightened manner when he is afraid, as though he is seeking consolation in the floridness of his expression.

"There are momentous events afoot, my love. Events which shake us all to the very core."

"What do you mean?" you ask, a little exasperated. "What is happening, William? Who are these men and what do they want with us?"

"They are…" He stops, breathes in, collects himself, wipes sweat from his brow. "They are allies."

You ask him what he means by this, but your husband merely shakes his head. "More than that I cannot say. They have sworn me to secrecy. I have given my oath."

"Do you know them, darling? Have you some bond with them?"

"We are acquainted, yes. We are linked. And we are linked profoundly. Although I had not seen them before today."

"Then what is it… What is it that they want? Do they have some manner of hold over you?"

"My love, I must away."

"What? You have to leave? Why? With them?"

"I do."

"With these strangers?"

"They are not quite strangers. As I say. Not quite."

"Wherever are you going? And when shall you return?"

"I cannot say. I have no answer to either of those questions."

"But you must… No… You cannot be abandoning us in so sudden a manner."

"This is no abandonment, my love. I pray you to accept my word. On the contrary, what I do now is to be done in your name, dear Anne, and in our children's name, in Susanna's and Judith's and Hamnet's. There is a great battle to be fought and I have… well, I have been enlisted."

At this hideous and unexpected news you feel your eyes sting with tears.

"But you are no soldier, my darling. You cannot wield a blade. You would survive a moment in the killing ground."

"There are other kinds of battlefields. Other sorts of wars."

"You have to go? Truly?"

"I must. For the security of all that we have built together I have to go. Please. Please, will you not trust me? Have I ever given you cause not to do so?"

"No," you say. "No. Of course you have not. I have always been the most fortunate of women."

"Thank you."

"But... your clothes... I must get you some vittles for the journey..."

"No time, my love. There is no time left." William leans forward and he kisses you full upon the lips with a quiet, sincere passion that he has not exhibited for years and, at this action, you feel, once again, the unquestionable force of his love.

When he draws away you do your utmost to understand.

"There was a man," you say. "Last night upon the threshold. He spoke of some disaster. Something dreadful approaching. He... he was a part of this design, was he not?"

Your husband looks surprised at this—surprised, you realised, but not shocked. He understands, you think; he knows at least something of these strange events and far more, for sure, than he is telling you.

"William, what are these storm clouds? What crisis is upon us?"

"Hush," your husband says. "Hush now." And he kisses you again, in part to silence you, in part, you think, to seek succour and encouragement for his enigmatic quest.

Afterwards, he locks his gaze upon yours. "Everything will yet be well," he says. "The Guild shall be victorious. The battle will be won. And the catastrophe which threatens us all, it shall be averted."

And as he speaks you see the rising panic in his eyes and you understand, without the least uncertainty, that he is surely lying to you.

On the Third Night

27th of December, 1601

YOU ARE AWOKEN from dreams of carnage and disaster by a soft hand upon your face and by a familiar voice in the darkness.

You are woken, yes—undeniably—but the dream lingers, and it clings to you like mist, lending your every moment a quality of odd detachment, an enduring sense of the oneiric.

"Mother?"

You push yourself upright in bed, and you blink hard and you force yourself into wakefulness. In the doorway stands a dark-haired young woman, full-lipped and determined, a certain wildness in her eyes, one hand upon her hips. She is flanked by two others, the twins, a little younger than she, but just as wilful and idiosyncratic in their manner.

Susanna, Judith, Hamnet: the greatest achievements of your life, the best of you, the hope for the future.

"Where is Father?" Susanna asks. "And when is he coming back?"

"Your father has been called away," you say with as much authority as you can summon under circumstances, "on some very urgent business. He will be with us once more presently."

"Presently?" This is Hamnet, sixteen now, but still looking a good deal younger, soft-skinned and smooth-faced and boyish. "When exactly is 'presently'?"

"I cannot be sure, Hamnet, dear. I cannot be certain."

"But mother—" There is an uncharacteristic plaintiveness to Judith's voice, a forceful sort of distress. "Please. Why can't you say more precisely?"

"I've told you," you reply, regretting the snap the moment it emerges. "I have told you all that I know."

Hamnet sniffs. "He's never been away before. Not once. He's always been with us."

"A lot of people's fathers go away," you say. "Many go to town or to the fields. Some to the army or into service. Some even go to London. And once they are lost to that particular stew then they never return. Or, at least, they do not return entirely the same as they were before."

"But Father..." continues Susanna. "He is—has always been—different. Not like other men. He has always been here. His place—don't you think?—is with us."

"And he will be again," you say, striving to reassure her, filling your voice with a warm certainty that you most assuredly do not feel. "He will be back and all shall be again as it was. Mark my words. Everything will be restored."

As you speak you hear from outside the first, faint clatter of thunder, its *basso profundo* growl, the start of a storm which you feel sure, without quite understanding why, will be far worse than any you have known.

On the Fourth Night

28th of December, 1601

IT IS RAINING, as it has been raining for the past fifteen hours, hard and unmercifully and without respite. The downpour hurls itself at the windows, hammering at the glass, clawing at the walls of your home as if trying to gain entry, as if it wishes to tear down all that you have with such careful love built up.

You are sitting in the parlour, the room a little smoky from the fire, watching the dark water pound the sodden earth. Your son is with you, his demeanour on the border between watchfulness and sullenness, his head angled away from you, his attention (although you suspect his true thoughts to be far away, in some other place, with the man who sired him) seemingly riveted upon the intersection of the elements, the conjoining of sky with earth. His twin is upstairs, at work upon her embroidery; and his elder sister is elsewhere—sheltering, supposedly, from the deluge at the home of a friend.

You find that you do not wish to think too hard about her true whereabouts or of the identity of that acquaintance, or of how she might be engaged, for all that her sweetheart—a polite enough fellow named John—strikes you as being a just and decent man. You have spoken often to Susanna of the perils of maturity, of the lure of menfolk, of their musk and rigidities, their unexpected tenderness, but you have understood also that your words may not have carried as much weight as they ought to have done, coming from you, at one time the epicentre of gossip, your belly already swollen with your first-born on the day that you signed the parish register. And so you sit and you say nothing and you listen to the unrelenting rhythm of the rain.

It is, in the end, the boy who breaks the silence between you, interrupting your own bleak thoughts about the future, with words that are oddly—and, you tell yourself, surely coincidentally—pertinent to your strange, shifting state of mind in these last, curious few days.

"Mother? Do you dream?"

You are slightly startled by the question, seeing perhaps a perspicacity, even a cunning, of which there has been no previous symptom in the guileless, open-hearted boy.

"Of course," you say. "Well, naturally, I dream."

"Oh." At this announcement, Hamnet seems momentarily disconsolate. "I thought... I wondered..."

"Whatever do you mean?"

"I have almost forgotten what it is like."

"Why do you say such a thing?"

"For I have not dreamed in years. Not since I was... eleven, I think. Yes. Eleven."

He smiles crookedly, but it is a melancholic and too adult a smile, at which you feel a surge of instinctive sadness.

"My sweet one?" you say, speaking to him in softer terms than any you have used for many years, speaking as you have not spoken to him since his infancy. "They will come back to you. I have heard of similar instances. It is very common, I think, with boys. Your father was no different."

The white lie leaves you easily with only a trace of guilt.

"Darkness," he says. "Every night now, for so long. Only emptiness and darkness and quiet."

"Oh, Hamnet..." you begin. Then, stopping yourself, not wanting to alarm him any further in this time of profound uncertainty, you say, as conversationally as you are able, "Your last... that is, your most recent dream... Do you remember? What it was you dreamed of then?"

He seems puzzled for a moment and withdrawn, then, speaking carefully like some old divine bringing together the threads of a complicated argument, your beautiful, fragile boy says: "I dreamed of the people who dwell in the forest. Those people who are not people. The fair ones who have, it is said, upon our souls... designs."

He stops then and he looks at you with a gravity and candour which makes him seem again like a very much older man. No reply that you can summon seems adequate to this and so, for a long minute, nothing at all is said, and there is to be heard only the rough, insistent beating of the rain.

Something jolts you out of this weird lull, fraught as it is with inexplicable significance. Something forces you to confront the real world.

A hand hits the windowpane, a forceful interruption and, through the seething curtain of rain, segmented by the leading, you spy a face and a figure which are familiar to you.

Your first thought? William. It is William who has returned.

But that hope is almost immediately dispelled. For this is the lumpen, pox-ridden face of a beggarman, one who is well known in this place, a wayfarer whose comings and goings have become as predictable and inevitable as the seasons.

He bangs once more upon the window, this man, wild-eyed, exhausted and with something theatrical in his evidently drunken lunacy as if he learnt well long ago the part that life had written for him and so had decided to play it to the hilt.

"Turn away," you say to your boy, whose face looks drawn and drained of blood. "You know it's only old Tom again. And you know that he's too fond—too fond by far—of wine and ale. You know that he is fallen."

"He seems distracted, mother. He seems unwell."

"That is only his manner. That is only his way. We have all in our time tried our best to offer aid, but always he has spurned our charity. Always has he bitten the hand that feeds. Often with unnecessary violence and spite."

The vagabond strikes the glass again—for, you think, the last time, your attention having now been achieved—and he brings his face close to the pane.

He shouts above the storm and although you cannot make out every word of it, you hear a good deal of the rant. You understand its structure and its theme even if the rain necessitates certain ellipses.

"I have seen it... yes... between worlds... the blankness approaching... insatiate... unswerving... appetite... and without mercy..."

"Mother?"

"Don't be afraid," you say. "You know that he is quite harmless."

He peers in at the both of you, mad knowledge dancing in his eyes, and then, wordless now, his message delivered, he turns and he flees, back into the bosom of the tempest. He capers into the rain, lost to the world. You and your doomed child watch his departing figure, poor mad Tom, as it dwindles, fades and is, at last, swallowed by the storm.

On the Fifth Night

29th of December, 1601

"MY DEAR? MIGHT we come in?"

What is meant, you think, by this sudden rush of visitors to your door? What significance is there in this strange profusion of thresholds, of arrivals and departures, of the interruptions of one little world by another? And what is there also in the question of the progress of time which seems to you to be no longer smoothly continuous, no longer a ceaseless procession of incident, but rather to have taken on some more discriminating quality; as if you are experiencing only particular elements and individual scenes, as though your life is like the sea, your experience a pebble that skims upon the surface of it and that you are present—truly present— only at those moments when stone brushes against water.

Had you not been born several hundred years before the invention of the movie camera, the effect would almost certainly have struck you as cinematic. Existing as you do, however, at the tip of the seventeenth century, your nearest point of reference belongs to another of life's threads, one which has also come lately to preoccupy your thoughts. This, you realise—all of this— is somehow very like a dream.

"My dear? I am so sorry. This is, I hope, no serious interruption?"

Standing upon your doorstep are two women, both of about your age, both dressed with a sombre propriety which is perhaps just a trifle overstated. The rain having stopped, there persists all the same the sense that the respectable pair have been washed up by the storm.

You have known them for a long time, the span of your acquaintanceship equalling the duration of your marriage, and there exists between the three of you that particular brand of envy, competitiveness and mild despondency which often characterises relationships that are not themselves selected but which are rather brought about by your choice of spouse.

"Mistress Quincey," you say, "and Mistress Lock."

Your tone is studiedly polite, but just sufficiently frosty to make plain your true feelings at this unexpected visit. "How delightful to see you both."

Quincey who is, by some months, the elder of the two, stouter and more matronly in aspect, has with her a wicker basket, covered over with white cloth. Lock, still a little girlish in her manner, gestures in mock-excitement to this receptacle and, with wide-eyed faux-naivety, declares: "Eggs! We've brought you eggs, Mistress Shakespeare. Eggs for our dear Anne and for her beautiful family."

"Or, at least," interjects the other woman, "at least, for whatever is left of it."

Your smile grows more brittle and your eyes turn colder still. "How kind," you say. "How very kind of you both. But 'tis all, of course, quite unnecessary."

You consider whether it might be possible to simply take their sorry basket from them and despatch the smiling harridans straightaway without having to invite either of them in. You even start to reach out one hand to facilitate the gambit. Before you can succeed, however, Quincey steps unbidden into your home, Lock upon her heels.

"Is William not here?" says one.

"My dear," confides the other. "We've heard the most disquieting rumours. And we have both been so very concerned. Oh my, yes; yes, we have."

You set your face in an expression of grim courtesy. "Ladies," you say as if their arrival had been your idea from the start.

"Please, won't you tarry? I should, after all, like little more than to sit awhile and talk to you." You pause, allowing just a little of your real feelings to inflect the final line. "To sit and *gossip*."

A SMALLER SHIFT this time, mere minutes, the change discernible but not so dislocating.

You are in the parlour, with your guests, the chairs arranged in a triangle. Upon a table before you is the basket, now unveiled, in which six creamy eggs lie exposed, positioned as though at the outset of a magic trick, the centrepiece of some illusion, conjured by some mountebank or street sorcerer. Indeed, it will shortly emerge that this apparently fanciful assessment does not lie so very far from the truth.

"We were so worried," one of the women—the elder—is saying.

Lock nods in delighted agreement. "For four days. Four days! In which he has not been seen at all."

"And William. Our own dear William. Normally so industrious."

"Usually so visible."

"And... forever... such a devoted man to his family."

Mistress Quincey pouts, and arches her eyebrows. There is something feline in the pose. "Although, of course, we say *forever*... We lay such stress upon his eternal fidelity. And yet. And yet... Dear me, but my memory isn't at all what it used to be. But wasn't there something once... long ago... when the children were oh, so very young? A brief period, the tiniest of sojourns when, I suppose, the best and most proper word would be, would it not, he enjoyed a... flirtation?"

You breathe in slowly and your try to think of other things, telling yourself that your cage is being rattled with such sly art only out of boredom on their part, and frustration and spite, because these women's lives are stale and repetitive and, from all that you know of them, largely without love. Although, of course, within you are thinking what you have thought from the moment of his abrupt and unheralded exit—"William, oh, William, where are you, William, and when are you coming home?"—you manage to smile at their words, as if perceiving some innocent confusion or perplexity upon their part.

"Oh, but my husband has always been faithful."

"But of course," sighs Mistress Lock.

"There have been no stolen kisses for William," you say. "No wandering eyes. No unfaithful caresses. There has been, ladies, pray take my word on this, no need for him to spill his seed in anyone but me."

"Naturally," croons Mistress Quincey, unshocked. "That was not for a moment what was intended. That was not what was meant. No, my only implication... My sole allusion was to that rather ticklish, though faraway and now all but forgotten episode in which your beloved seemed to allow himself to venture into temptation in matters of... the theatre."

"Oh," you say, the memory long-buried, the mention of it bringing an unexpected surge and tang. "But that was a very long time ago. He made his choice. And he made the right choice."

"But as I remember he was tempted, my dear. Was he not? By the players. The glamour of them. By their vulgar artistry."

You try your best to appear wholly noncommittal. "A young man's folly. Nothing more. The most transient and passing of fancies."

Mistress Quincey bares her teeth. "Oh, but as I recall, the temptation was a deal more serious than that. He wanted to act, did he not? To write, too. Even, perhaps, one day, to go to London."

"He may have said so," you allow, "when at his dreamiest or when in his cups. But he could never truly have done so. He would always have chosen his family."

"I wonder about that, dear. I really do..."

"So you understand," says Mistress Lock, "when we first heard rumours of your husband's absence now, why we became concerned that... the old temptation might just have come back."

At last, you let your irritation show. "You believe him to have run away, then? To the players? To the playhouses? Is that what you mean? For shame, mistress. For shame!"

One or other of the women seems about to reply—one or other or both, perhaps, in some squawking, echoing chorus of self-importance—when, in the gap between your speech, you all hear something unexpected.

A slender cracking. A brittle tremor.

The eggs, you realise. The sound is coming from one of the eggs.

"Oh, my," says Mistress Lock. "Oh, by the saints."

And you all lean forwards and you watch with a queasy sort of incredulity as the shell is pushed open from within and something small and dark and bloody pushes its way into the world and looses a shrill, pathetic cry, full of anguish and foreboding.

It breaks free, this pitiful thing, its feathers slick with slime. There is something about it that seems utterly wrong, something freakish and broken. It stumbles on tiny, viscous legs. It totters, it rights itself, it stumbles again before it falls forward and gives up its tiny life. It jerks once before it lies still. Only then does your mind accept the truth of what it is that you are seeing— that this little creature possesses some grotesque deformity, that it has come here not whole but disastrously and horrifyingly warped.

The other women yelp and cry, but your thoughts are far away, far even from this nightmarish intervention—from this, the worst of all possible omens, out in the dark spaces of the universe, in the gaps between the stars, searching and searching for your lost love.

On the Sixth Night

30th of December, 1601

AND THEN, LATER, after another night, after another unrestful sleep and another morning, you are back once again in that place which seems, more than any other, to symbolise your childhood and to encapsulate your life before children, before William and maturity.

The forest was ever to you a changeless place, a land which defied the endless and indefatigable ambitions of time. Yet today it seems, impossibly, a little different from before. It seems darker, somehow, and more crowded. The trees seem closer together, more tangled, more ancient. The sky is blotted out by branches, the undergrowth climbs higher around you and the atmosphere is altogether more glowering and minatory than the sylvan idyll of your early years, a realm now more shadowed and malign.

You are still only at its borders and at first you fancy yourself to be alone as you cross over towards the heart of the wood. You are unclear in your mind as to quite what it is that has brought you here in this time of crisis. It is predominantly sentiment, you suppose; that and the desire for sanctuary, the urge to find solace in the past when your present and your future both seem so very uncertain.

Then, as you walk, something in the undergrowth stirs: some small creature, startled, no doubt, by your approach. Naturally, you take no heed and you walk on, deeper through the trees. The thing that is hidden, however, now seems to follow in your wake.

You hear it scuttling, pushing through leaves and snapping twigs, keeping eerie pace with your progress. A fox, you wonder? A badger, or perhaps a skittish deer?

Yet whatever it may be it is surely not so large as that, for it is never in the least danger of becoming visible; taking pains, perhaps, not to be seen and to skulk out of sight.

You pause and it pauses with you. You walk on and, evidently, it remains by your side. These things you know not only through the scuttling sounds of it, but also because of what can be sensed. You feel its proximity, its odd intensity of purpose, its unexpected slyness.

Then with a jolt of understanding which arrives from no particular quarter, you realise that you are being tracked not by any animal or by any human but rather by one of the beings that were always said by wise women and cunning men to dwell in these woods, beings both more and less than Man, the subject of poor Hamnet's last dream.

You call out, "Who's there?" and as you do so, you feel foolish and exposed and gullible. "Who's watching me?"

You do not see it—indeed, you never shall—but you hear its voice, high and sly and fluting, full of guile and intelligence.

"Oh, mistress mine," it says and you realise that you are quite unable to discern the gender of the speaker, whether it is male or female or else some indeterminate hermaphroditic being which lies beyond all known laws of life. "Your husband is already lost to you."

"What—" you begin, startled. "What do you know of my husband?"

"Even now your William is at war. His counterparts have been at work here for months labouring in secret. As envoys and spies and sneaks. Yet all their backroom diplomacy and cutthroat guile have availed them nothing. The knife remains at large and it is cracking the world. And so a battle is waged for the future of the lattice."

"Who are you? What do you want?" Your aim in these words is to project fearlessness and pugnacity. The reality, you suspect, is that you sound weak and ill-prepared and beyond the limits of your experience and skill. "Of what do you speak?"

Laughter, then. A glissando of casual wickedness. "You shall see for yourself soon enough, Mistress Shakespeare. Little Miss Hathaway as was. That was what they called you once. Was it not? Before you were plucked and uprooted from this place with such gauche enthusiasm."

"Tell me," you say stoutly. "When will I see my husband again?"

"Soon. Soon enough. But before then..."

"Yes? What do you mean?" Although you know that such creatures lie as easily as breathing, such is your desperation to know that you press this invisible being for answers.

"Oh, but before then... the Lover is on his way. Yes, the swain is to come a-calling and his eyes, oh, his flashing eyes. And by his side strolls... destruction."

"You speak, I think, in riddles."

"Then permit me to be clear. Destruction is coming, mistress. The undoing, the erasure of all that you have ever held dear."

And this thing in the undergrowth, the creature of the woods begins once more to laugh, shriller than before, higher now and madder. And so you turn and you run from that place, back towards civilisation, back to your home and your son and your daughters and you flee in clammy terror from that speaker of secrets, from the prophet of the darkness, from the treacherous spirit of Arden.

$\mathscr{O}$n the Seventh Night

31ˢᵗ of December, 1601

THE FIRE IS smoking a little once again and the night is now velvety and quiet. This ought by rights to be the happiest of times, with the family all gathered together, enfolded with care and love, everything illuminated by the soft and comforting aura of the known. Instead, as this old year dies, you sit a little apart from your children, your head full of William (still missing; still missed) and of all those troubling and uncanny portents which, since Christmas, have come to punctuate your life.

It is late and much wine has been drunk. The twins sit side by side, dozing. Once eager to see the birth of the new year, they are now both close to submitting to sleep. Susanna is sitting closer than propriety might allow to her betrothed and—you are almost certain—already her lover, John; a man of indifferent looks and no discernible intellect who seems, nonetheless, to have embarked upon a path that will lead eventually to his becoming a physician. William always thought it a good match, whilst you were always less certain, wondering whether his patient affection will ever prove equal to that passion and fire which you know resides within your daughter and which (how Mistress Quincey and Mistress Lock might have arched their eyebrows in delighted scandal at the admission) reminds you so much of yourself, your own reckless heart, your happy lusts, your willingness to be unabashed.

Such thoughts, tinged with a kind of fond and tender melancholy, are banished as the doctor-in-waiting, the square-faced swain, wriggles upright in his chair and reaches for his glass.

Wearily, it occurs to you that in the absence of your husband, this pup thinks himself to have become the *de facto* man of the house and believes, with that stolid self-importance which is amongst his defining characteristics, that it behoves him now to make a toast. Inwardly, you sigh.

"I do believe," says John, not quite managing to hide his pleasure, "that in the regrettable absence of dear Master Shakespeare, it behoves me now to propose a toast."

You smile without the slightest enthusiasm. The twins stir, blink, sit to attention and try to pretend that they have been nothing less than fully conscious since supper.

Susanna squeezes her lover's arm in a gesture of encouragement which, you suspect, she shall often have cause to deploy in the years of dutiful marriage that lie in wait for her.

John lifts his glass higher. "To the absent Master Shakespeare," he says. "To his speedy return and to all the good things that the year to come will surely bring."

You murmur some polite agreement and there follows clinking of glasses and many expressions of optimism and good cheer. Susanna seems happy enough and the twins are at least momentarily distracted by the lack of their father, although you cannot hide that disquiet which still is rising in your chest like bile, like a black and evil thing which yearns to be let loose.

And as the scene unfolds you are become a mere spectator, your every imagining filled up with fears of disaster.

You think of William, of that strange voice in the forest, of the men who took your husband away, of that half-imagined prophet whose arrival and disappearance seemed to herald these events. And as you watch your daughter plant a kiss upon the face of her unworthy beau and as you see the twins embrace, each seeking comfort in the other, you seem to hear within yourself these words, spoken by your husband, as clearly as if he is with you now by your side and not lost in some other, faraway place.

"*The lattice.*"

This is what you hear, understanding without any need for evidence at all that this is a message—perhaps the most important of your life.

"*The lattice, my sweet.*" It is him! It is surely him! "*The lattice is burning. The knife has splintered the world. And the void is even now approaching.*"

On the Eighth Night

1ˢᵗ of January, 1602

THE NEXT VISITOR, in this long season of unsolicited guests, arrives without fanfare or announcement. He is, all of a sudden and without the slightest warning, simply *there*, as if he has flickered, shimmered into existence like a playhouse illusion, a spectre conjured by trickery and misdirection. He comes not with the storm or after nightfall, but rather in the still of early afternoon.

The children are away and you are in the garden, standing amongst plants that slumber and grasses which await renewal. You are, so far as you are concerned, alone. You breathe deeply, everything that is in you still adjusting to this long, scarce-endurable absence.

You close your eyes, seeking the quiet comfort of self-inflicted darkness, and you start to summon up a prayer for your poor lost husband. Yet something in you halts the words of your catechism before they are even half-spoken. You open your eyes once more and there he is, standing, smiling, before you on the shabby green.

He is a young man, strikingly handsome with a full head of hair and a beard of raffish elegance. He is dressed expensively and with considerable élan and he seems almost to shine with possibility.

"Hello," he says. "Greetings to you, Anne."

You stand your ground and you do your best to ignore that troubling combination of disquiet and desire which this stranger— who is, somehow, not quite a stranger—has in you evoked.

"Who are you, sir?" you ask. "What is your business here?"

He makes a moue, a flirtatious pout which comes to him, it is clear, without the slightest effort.

"Anne? Please don't say that you do not recognise me? I'm not sure that my heart could stand it."

"Sir," you say. "I am quite certain"—and your certainty is feigned—"that I have never in my life seen you before this day."

Infuriatingly, his smile grows only broader and more charming still. "Please," he says and the sureness in his voice, its assumption of knowledge, causes your skin to prickle warmly, despite the gravity of recent days, and your heart to lurch in unintended excitement. "Please, my love. You know who I am. I know it."

The truth is unfolding itself in your mind, slowly and with stealthy inevitability, but you are not yet ready to face it. A thousand objections present themselves, but in the face of this young man's easy beauty all you can manage is a stuttering sequence of denial.

"No, I have never... it doesn't... it can't... Surely... entirely without sense..."

He steps closer towards you, close enough now that, if either one of you set the thing in motion, you might be able to touch, to hold, to be again in each other's arms. You are close enough to smell his maddeningly familiar scent, sweet yet manly, redolent of the English countryside yet spiced also with the darkly beguiling tang of city experience.

"You know me," he says again.

"But you cannot... No, you cannot be him."

"And yet, my love...? You see it now, I think. The truth... the truth is being shown to you."

You think again of the man who came at Christmas, of the men glimpsed in the shadows behind your husband, and so a pattern—fantastic, unbelievable, miraculous—begins to emerge. And so, at last, you simply decide to say it. You say his name.

"William..."

He smiles, but more sombrely now, as if in priestly benediction. "Not quite..." he says. "At least, I am not quite *your* William."

"Tell me," you say, suddenly greedy. "Tell me everything."

"'Tis easier," he says, "to show you."

And he moves closer still and he is all but upon you now and his lips are upon your lips and all at once you see in him something like a vision, in something like a waking dream, an infinity of possibilities, a plethora of worlds, each formed by a different decision or an alternative choice. And in every one of these realities, you spy a different version of your husband—the hierophant, the plotter, the lover, your own round-bellied spouse, thousands upon thousands more. These alternatives spread themselves before you, a chain of might-have-beens.

The man who is not quite the man you married pulls away from you. "Do you see?" he asks. "Do you understand now?"

"But a glimmering," you reply, your mind, a seventeenth-century thing, struggling to acclimatise and comprehend a system of knowledge far beyond you own. "A glimmering in the darkness. All of these possibilities, all of these worlds—"

"The lattice," says the man insistently. "It is called the lattice of worlds. And in all of them—in every last one—there is a William. But in only one world—in this one—did he (did I, did we) never leave Stratford."

"I don't..." You wince as if stung. "No, I do not understand your words." This protestation is, of course, only partly true.

"In every other realm," says the handsome iteration, "William left this town. He went travelling with the players and came to London and wrote and was famous and conjured whole universes. I did myself. I went to our capital and, I fear to have to tell you this, I fell in love there. Many times. Only here, in this volume of reality, did he stay. And it is, I fear, because of what has happened here that this is where it will finish. It has been chosen. The knife, after all, selected it."

"Chosen?" you ask. "Chosen for what?"

"To finish the fight. To make our final stand. For it is here that the war will end, here that we face the truth of things and make our final sacrifice."

"Your words," you say, "are full of portent. They prefigure no good."

"I fear that is so, Mistress Shakespeare."

William reaches out and takes your left hand in his. He raises it to his lips and kisses it once.

"For the lattice," he says, "the lattice is being burned away. It is being reduced to nothing. The blankness is swallowing it whole."

"Tell me what I can do," you say.

"Oh, Anne. My courageous Anne. Whatever makes you think that you can do a thing? For the void is coming now. And nothing, nothing at all, can stand in its path."

And then, in a twinkling, in the time that it takes to turn a page, he is gone.

On the Ninth Night

2nd of January, 1602

EARLY IN THE morning, as in every other morning of Creation, dawn creeps across the horizon, but in no other morning in all the numberless days of this earth has there come any dawn like this. Its rays are not golden or white, not the glow of a summer's day or the sickly paleness of a winter one, but rather something alien and new.

When the sunlight comes it is dark red; crimson. It is the colour of hopelessness and hate. It casts a scarlet shadow upon the land, rendering everything hellish, painting the world in the colours of Hades.

You wake into an eerie dream-state, the room illuminated by this strange, savage light and you rise at once, stricken by panic and by the worst of suspicions. You find the house already up, abuzz with the sounds of fear, of alarm at the arrival of this new state of being.

You call for your children and they all three come to you and somehow you find yourselves outside, looking up into the suddenly unfamiliar sky, wondering and much afeared. You hold them close to you.

"Father's coming home," says Hamnet, with unshakeable conviction. "He is coming home with many others. They who are like him and yet different."

"How can you be certain of that? Hamnet? How do you know?"

"Because," he says, the boy oddly proud, despite the nature

of this emergency. "Because I saw it in a dream. Last night. My first since..."

You look at him curiously, knowing that what he says next will possess some terrible, although as yet unguessed at, significance.

He shrugs, with a child's dreadful insouciance. "Since the day," he says, "when I ought to have died."

On the Tenth Night

3rd of January, 1602

As SOON AS you enter the church you understand that you should
not have come here. The place is filled to the very limits of its
capacity, and the packing together of so many human bodies in
so small a space is all but intolerable. Were it not for fear for the
immortal souls of those whom you love, then you should never
have set out at all; but Susanna insisted, and the twins agreed,
and so you acquiesced and you left the house and you made the
necessary pilgrimage, your every step illuminated by the blazing
scarlet of the sky.

Panic has seized the people of Stratford and, you assume with
some certainty, with years of knowledge and observation of the
human race, that the same is true of every town in every part of
England—yes, even in London—of anywhere, in fact, upon this
wide earth which languishes beneath this merciless crimson.
Panic is in the streets and in the ale-houses. It crackles around
every dinner table, from the highest to the low. Animals go unfed
and fields untended. Panic, then—in the eyes of everyone you
pass. Panic in the lunatic actions of a few. Panic in the restrained
despair of the rest. Panic in the faces of your children and, you
have no doubt though you have not dared to look, panic also in
you, in every fibre of you; and written, surely, for all that you
endeavour to disguise it, quite plainly upon your face.

As you push your way past the mass of huddled bodies at the
vestry (some imploring, others clasping their hands to their heads
in postures of exaggerated supplication) and into the house of

God itself, with your children by your side, you catch sight, high up in the pulpit, of the rector, Master Stilwell, stout and perspiring, gesticulating, clutching at the air. Always rubicund, today he is more florid-faced than ever and there is some weird combination of horror and elation upon his features. Decorum, that surface emblem of civilisation, is breaking down, and although much of his address is drowned by the clatter and lamentation of the swollen congregation, you recognise above the babble words of Revelation, words of Job—and too little, you think, too little by far, of any words of reconciliation or healing or hope. Too much brimstone; insufficient mercy.

The twins cleave close to you, a warm hand in each of yours, but Susanna pulls away quickly, greeting, with an unmannered shout, her lover. John is wading now towards you, against the tide of the faithful. He calls your name and shows appropriate concern for you all, although his eyes remain fixed throughout upon your elder daughter.

"Come," he says, "I've got us a pew."

You allow yourself to be led to where the doctor-to-be has reserved a place, crammed beside two other families and two rows in front of Mistress Lock and Mistress Quincey, who sit together, holding hands, eyes upraised, mouthing silently along with the plaintive zealotry of the padre. You pass by them without a word and you sit where you have been told to sit and, in spite of that new knowledge which lately has been gifted to you, the growing certainty that the universe is not arranged as you have always believed it to be, you draw out what comfort you can. Falling back into the old rhythms, you join with all of those around you and pray.

Outside the sky grows more vivid still, wilder and more pregnant with disaster and from some invisible realm. Somehow, in some conspiracy of heat and fatigue and the endless sleepless worry of the days since Christmas, perhaps because of some deliberate, unseen intervention, you contrive, even against the din of the temple, the shrieking of the flock and the bellows of the preacher, to fall into a light, fitful and distracted slumber. And as you sleep, you dream; and as you dream, you see it all, and you are granted understanding.

You see a legion of them—an army of Williams—all the same yet incrementally different. Some fat, some thin, some famous, some obscure. Here a swaggering braggart, perpetually drunk and swollen with his own self-importance. There a pinched, doleful scholar, pallid, every word that he sets upon the page a painful sacrifice. Here is a lecher, his tastes indiscriminate, his face pink with dirty appetite. There is a prematurely aged man, half-crazed and determined to tell his truth no matter the personal cost. Here a businessman, there a prophet. Here a genius, there a fortunate fool. A troubadour, an actor, a librarian, a traveller, a taskmaster, a wastrel, and many, many more. All life is in one man. All experience spread across a thousand thousand versions of the same.

You catch glimpses of those whom you have already met in person—the sleek, beautiful William who appeared in your garden, the hierophant who arrived first upon your threshold. They are both, you realise—they are *all*—members of the Guild.

And the nature of their battle? Not any literal conflict. No army, no swords, but rather something else, amorphous and indefinable.

There. There it is. The enemy.

A great, rolling bank of whiteness. The void. A bare, empty page which consumes all that is within its path. It rolls like an avalanche though world after would, devouring and obscuring, wiping away as though there were never anything there at all.

Amongst the throng of Shakespeares you search for your own—for the tubby family man, who, until now, stayed at home. But of him there is no sign at all. Is he lost, you wonder, shuddering? Is he lost to the void?

And then you are woken by the sounds of screaming, by your

children's hands in yours, by uproar and the sounds of new despair.

Your eyes flick open, you reach instinctively for those you love and you see at once what has changed.

The light. The quality of the light.

What was once deep red has now been changed.

For all around is now not crimson but something else—a bright, unflinching white, fierce and relentless and, somehow, unmistakably, hungry.

"It is here," you murmur, as much to yourself as to anyone around you. "It is here. And now the void has come amongst us."

On the Eleventh Night

4th of January, 1602

YOU HAVE BEEN running now for hours, running to the edges of your endurance, running to the limits of your sanity.

You ran from the church and through the streets of Stratford. You ran past home; you ran with your children by your side. You ran as behind you the world was eaten up, as all that you have ever known was dissolved and erased, swept away by that implacable, pitiless bank of sheer white, that wave of bright death which even now is hard upon your heels, the void which dogs your every desperate footfall.

If you are exhausted, then the children must be near surrender, though all three of them—Judith and Hamnet, stoical and determined; Susanna, tearful since her dull lover was swallowed by the hungry nullity a yard or two from the glovemaker's door—keep going, grim and uncomplaining.

You are all four of you running for your lives, until at last, panting and exhausted, you see, perhaps inevitably, the forest hove into view; you realise with a queasy certainty that it is here, in Arden, where everything has to end.

At the very moment when this thought presents itself, you hear a voice—familiar and much-missed—echo from behind you; from, it seems, the void itself, calling as if from the underworld.

"Anne! Anne, my love!"

It is a voice which you had all but lost hope of ever hearing again and at the sound of it, despite your determination to go on, despite your grit and rigour, you stumble. The past days and hours have taught you fearfulness and suspicion and so, as you force yourself onwards, your first thought is that this is a trap, a means by which to gull you and make you hesitate. But, that voice—unmistakeable and heartfelt—is heard once again.

"*Anne, please!*"

And so you relent. You let yourself believe and you stop and you turn around. At the second that you do so, you understand that your children have gone, that they have been erased from the world. And when you face your husband again, it is with a shrill peal of despair upon your lips.

Impossibly, the void has stopped moving, not gone but waiting, a great unmoving monolithic wall of white, pure absence made manifest.

And yet, standing before it, outlined, silhouetted by the unforgiving glare, like an inky pictogram upon blank parchment is Master William Shakespeare. *Your* William Shakespeare.

Bloodied and bruised, hair matted, beard wild and unkempt, bleeding from two ugly-looking gashes on his forehead, he is, nonetheless, unmistakably yours, the man whom you married and for whom you bore three children.

He smiles at the sight of you but it is a smile against the odds and it is filled with sorrow.

"Anne," he says again. "My love."

"William."

"It has been a long, strange journey to come home to you."

"I know. I have seen... I have been shown a little of it."

"The news is not good. This, I fear, is now to be the end of all things."

"The void," you murmur, reaching for the strange language of the Guild. "It has reached our world. It has been drawn here by the knife? I suppose that there is nothing that can stop it now?"

Your husband bows his head. You think at first that this is regret at the scale of the catastrophe. That or else bashfulness, at having been for so long from your side.

Then he raises his eyes and you meet his gaze and understand the truth. He is neither regretful nor abashed, and what you see in his familiar features—the face of that person whom you know better than any other—is something quite unfamiliar. It is, you realises, with a shiver in your heart, pure shame.

"It has been defeated," he says. "The void. This is to be the finish of it."

"What do you mean?"

"This world is being scoured clean, my love. It is being destroyed by our own creation before the arrival of the true void."

"I do not understand," you murmur. "No, William, I don't..."

"It is the scorching of the earth, my love, as of that which is laid down to stop the progress of some inferno."

"No. No, that cannot be."

"The lattice is safe now. And millions upon millions shall live. One pinprick of a world will die, one amongst an infinity. One single star in the sky. So that all the rest may flourish and thrive."

"No."

"We took the decision together. The Guild voted and we were unanimous. The damage that the knife had wrought was too great. We had no other choice but this."

"But why?" You are protesting, but the answers are already palpably, painfully clear.

"My love, you know why we were chosen."

Tears sting the edges of your eyes. "Because here, uniquely, you never left. You never wrote. You stayed with us. With your family."

"Yes," says William. "Yes, my love."

And he steps towards you, arms outstretched. There are tears in his eyes too, although he blinks them fiercely away.

Behind him, the void—or rather, perhaps, the pseudo-void—begins once again to advance.

"Tell me," you say as your husband reaches you and enfolds you in his arms, in his warm, smoky scent. "Hamnet? Does he—I mean, in other worlds? Or is he too only with us... when you stayed?"

"I am sorry," he says. "Truly. It was the only way."

He holds you, and you hold him too, and there is a little comfort to be found in this as that great and terrible white wall draws nearer.

But then you raise your head over his shoulder and you look at that logical monstrosity and with all the passion which dwells within you, you shout out your defiance. You shout your name and that of your husband. You shout that of your daughters and that of your doomed and melancholy boy.

You shout of all the things that have made your life important, of everything that has made it count. And your last words, as the blankness washes over you and brings with it the cool sweet balm of oblivion, are those of profound and imperishable love.

On the Twelfth Night

5th of January, 1610

MISTRESS ANNE SHAKESPEARE—fifty-five and careworn, long accustomed to the cost, in all its forms, of solitude—was standing alone in her garden on the day when he came home.

She was not waiting, at least not exactly, for she had received no word of his return and she harboured no particular expectation or desire for that event. Even had she had known of it in advance, had she suspected, she never would have gone deliberately out to greet him. She would never have been before their house on purpose in anticipation of his homecoming, like some honour guard providing a formal welcome. Although the gentleman had assuredly done right by her and by the children—at least, had done so in material terms, in those grand, beneficent gestures which, like this house and its expansive garden, were visible to society at large, she had endured his absence, both physical and emotional, for long enough now to have decided that he did not deserve such tender treatment, that, in all major respects, he had become unworthy of her love and had placed himself beyond the boundaries of their marriage.

She had, of course, heard the rumours. Folks tried their best to shelter her from the worst of it but she had caught wind of enough—the love affairs (conducted, humiliatingly, in public), the boys (plentiful and diverse and not especially discreet), the liquor, the carousing, the gambling and that plethora of whores—to understand that his betrayal of their vows had been quite rigorous in its totality. When such stories came her way, she felt not shock of any kind or even dismay, for she had long known, almost since the start, of his darker, hidden nature, of his insistent lusts and his destructive hungers. Rather she felt at these revelations—overheard at market or whispered as she passed by in the street—a kind of hollowness and disappointment at the enthusiasm of his capitulation, together with a stifled despair, held in for decorum's sake and for that of her two daughters.

Yet it was there all the same, visible in the flash of her eyes when her husband's plays were lauded in her presence, there in the defiant tilt of her chin when gossip was bandied about concerning the objects of those sickly and much-repeated sonnets, there too in her pregnant silence when she was asked when exactly it was that William was ever going to come home for good. Indeed, it was with her always, her quiet rage. It was her burden and, in some obscure way, so long had she lived with it, her friend.

So it was not planned, none of it was meant or intended. But this, all the same, was how it happened.

It was dusk, that depressive hour, and Anne was alone— Susanna long having since married and moved away and little Judith soon set to do the same—breathing in cold winter air, remembering the past and, for all her material circumstances, considering also the nature of her losses.

At first, when she saw the figure in the distance, she took it to belong to some stranger, some trickster or gipsy and in all three of these things she was not so very incorrect.

But as the person draw nearer and she saw that it was a man something rose up within her, something like trepidation and something like hope.

Eventually, the silhouette resolved itself into the known and there, unmistakably, to her surprise but not, of course, to any who are schooled in the arts of narrative, was Master William Shakespeare himself, a good few years older than when she had seen him last, dressed in unfamiliar clothes, in all of his London finery which had become just a little ragged at the edges, a trifle battered and stained from his long journey.

He carried nothing with him at all and there was in his gait and in the steady and cautious manner of his approach, much of the penitent and of the prodigal.

Very briefly she thought she saw—and it must, it can only have been—an illusion generated by the drained and fitful nature of the light—a child, a small boy, walking by her bad husband's side. But this trick, this piece of optical wish fulfilment, vanished quickly so that all which was left was Shakespeare.

He raised his hand, in solemn greeting although Anne did not respond believing him, given his conduct, to have forfeited all but the most essential civilities with her.

Yet as he came nearer, she considered how uncared for he seemed, how messy was his beard, how exposed the dome of his pate.

There were some, she thought, who might imagine William to be returning in triumph, wreathed with his manifold successes, plumpened by his grand connections, strutting after his life of urban glamour. Yet as he walked to the garden gate, his face filled, she saw, with dolour and with reflective ruefulness, an old truth would be quite plain to any who witnessed his approach—that no man on earth is ever a hero to his wife.

He opened the gate and walked into the garden, his movements methodical and patient. He reached her side and for a long while neither of them spoke at all until at last, tentatively but with every motion of it filled with sincerity, he reached out and took Anne's hand in his.

"I am sorry," he said. "My God. I am so sorry."

She looked up at him and nodded once as the distance between them started to dissolve. "Come inside," she said, more softly and with greater gentleness than she had perhaps intended. "You must be tired. You must be hungry."

"Thank you," he said simply, his gratitude evidently unfeigned.

And this would have been enough—it would have been more than enough for so difficult a homecoming—but then, without quite knowing why, Anne took his other hand and she drew her husband to her and she leaned up and she kissed him once upon the lips, with unexpected passion and forgiveness.

Afterwards, they went inside and they sat by the fire and they talked of the life that was left to them, and for a little while, they thought not of the past at all, but only of the future.

That night, uncomprehendingly, Anne dreamed of the lattice of worlds, of the Scotsman's knife, of the implacable void. She dreamed of poor lost Hamnet and of history. She dreamed of possibilities and variation and change, of choices made and those not made, of those branching tributaries which hide in of every hour and in every day.

And, although the image was to her most curious and most strange, hailing as it did from some quite different time and place, on just this one occasion only she dreamed also of you.

Afterword

by Dr John Lavagnino
London Shakespeare Centre
King's College London

OF COURSE, SHAKESPEARE did it too. We've long been familiar with the way his plays adapt and extend plots from other sources and reuse prior literary materials in every way; *Monstrous Little Voices* differs primarily in choosing always to extend and enrich the old story rather than to redo it.

In his history plays, especially, we see Shakespeare not only drawing extensively on his sources but also treating his own works as the basis for further development by prequels and sequels. The First Folio and most modern editions tidy things up so that it looks as though he planned all along to write two substantial historical tetralogies, but really they were accumulated piecemeal instead. It's the histories that *Monstrous Little Voices* draws on less than any of the other plays—perhaps because Shakespeare was there first, exploiting the material and finding new possibilities himself.

In the first tetralogy—the three *Henry VI* plays and *Richard III*—*Henry VI, Part One* is actually a prequel written after Parts Two and Three. It's the last in the series, *Richard III*, that became the biggest hit and has ever since attracted far more attention. Nobody questions how much more compelling than the first three parts it is; but today only a few readers and audiences get to discover how much richer it is when experienced after those parts and with the full story in mind.

Later on, Shakespeare used existing materials all the more: the second tetralogy picks up where the anonymous play *Thomas of Woodstock* leaves off, and after *Richard II* the Henry IV and V plays rework characters and events from *The Famous Victories of Henry V*. Far more than the first tetralogy, this one varies its style and approach with the material: the carefully planned and balanced *Richard II* with its famous poetical set-pieces, the extensive comic elements in the two parts of *Henry IV*, the martial and patriotic *Henry V*; they're united by Shakespeare's skill, not by their manner. Most surprising of all, in the middle of writing this sequence Shakespeare took the character of Falstaff out of his invented role in the historical story and made him the centre of a straight comedy, *The Merry Wives of Windsor*. Not even the tidy presentation of Shakespeare's plays in modern editions can hide the way he chose to follow the same characters in very different directions; the most Shakespearean act is to do the same kind of rethinking.

Those tetralogies are Shakespeare's only intentional shared worlds; all the other plays stand alone, without any characters or events to link them. But *Monstrous Little Voices* does something Shakespeare never did, and tells new stories that make connections among many of those standalone plays. We routinely talk about the world created by Shakespeare, as though it spans all his works taken together; in this book the storytelling is supported by an experiment in literary criticism, a skilful selection and development of characters and ideas that shows just how unified that world truly is—once you make the right additions here and there.

Why does it work? Writers have often thought of extending the story of this or that Shakespeare character beyond the end of the play, but what's happening here goes much further: not just continuing the plot, but combining materials from many plays and elaborating the stories of the characters both before and after what we knew already. Those characters are the foundation of the new fiction: we learn more things about

Miranda, Helena, and many others, it's true, but it all builds on the sense we already had of their reality. We felt we knew them, and we wanted to follow their stories to the end.

And the places make a difference too: there's already an extensive world of Mediterranean life in Shakespeare plays referring to Milan, Florence, Naples, Venice, Verona, Athens, and more, all drawn together here, and making very naturally a single broad canvas for new adventures. This world gets described in physical detail for the first time, since places on the Shakespearean stage never have the realized settings of prose fiction. The theatre of his day, without sets or lighting in the modern manner, had little beyond costumes and words to evoke distant places, but landscape description has a natural role in prose fiction.

Doubling that human world, there's the world of fairies, encountered most fully *A Midsummer Night's Dream* and glancingly in other plays. Shakespeare did new and different things with his source material on this topic, and this book does too. One of the great artistic developments of modern fantasy is to make the development of imaginary worlds far deeper than was commonly done before; these stories take Shakespeare's fairies and make them a society, not just occasional visitors to our world whose ways are seen only in glimpses. Human characters in Shakespeare barely know that fairies exist: Bottom's memories of a strange romance, and Mercutio's evocation of Queen Mab, both eventually get explained away as dreams not reality.

But here, fairies are unquestionably real and could never be dismissed that way. What in *The Tempest* is just hinted at now becomes a solid and complex background. Everything we see is compatible with the events of Shakespeare's plays, but we have a new vantage point from which the fairy realm is fully visible and intelligible. It is still magical and often dangerous: from the first pages we know what is clear in Shakespeare too, that fairies have greater priorities than the human world; and to the extent they notice us, they are not concerned to make human life happier or more peaceful.

The shared ideas and approaches of fantasy fiction are an important foundation of this book's approach, just as the playwriting discoveries of the Elizabethan era were for Shakespeare. And along with modern artistic developments there are modern ideas about society and psychology: attitudes we often wish we'd see more of in Shakespeare, and explorations of territory his plays don't ever quite reach. Perhaps it is no real surprise that the happy-ever-after of so many familiar characters is not quite like that, as we discover here in reading about many of them. But if the most passionate romances sometimes peter out, the Mediterranean world and the fairy realms offer possibilities for women that English reality did not. Miranda and Helena get the kinds of careers their intelligence and resourcefulness merit; even Parolles turns out to be more of a survivor than you might have thought, and positively useful in the right kind of scheme.

The real Mediterranean world of Shakespeare's day had a far more vivid cultural mixture than his England; there is even more to draw on than he knew about. And so here the range of people and books behind and in the stories includes not only Shakespeare's favourite writer, Ovid, but also Rumi and the Ottoman emissary Esperanza Malchi. Above all there's the dramatic and dangerous world of the Medicis—a rich source for the work of other playwrights of Shakespeare's time, for Marlowe, Webster, and Middleton in particular, but not used very extensively by Shakespeare himself; the Medician theme is in any case far more productive when the settings are international rather than focused on one city or another.

One Shakespeare play, above all, is especially like *Monstrous Little Voices*, though no reference is made to it; this is *Pericles*. This play is itself a collaboration: George Wilkins is thought to have written the first two acts, which differ in manner and style from the rest of the play. But still other authors are involved: the medieval poet John Gower is a member of the cast, narrating a story that is derived in part from his writings, but that ultimately goes back to the ancient Greek tale *Apollonius of Tyre*—a source for *Twelfth Night* as well.

Readers concerned about literary propriety and order have long been highly critical of *Pericles*: it is far too entertaining. In Shakespeare's day it was one of his most successful plays, and in the last few decades, it has been performed more and more frequently, leading us to discover that it almost always succeeds in enthralling and moving audiences. What readers may think scattered and untidy is excellent material for actors. The story ranges all over the Mediterranean, with frequent journeys from one exotic place to another: ranging across Mytilene, Antioch, Tarsus, Ephesus, and Tyre, in modern-day Greece, Turkey, and Lebanon. There are encounters with royal courts both welcoming and treacherous, a large and varied cast, shipwrecks, unexpected twists of fate, and above all magic. It is a work that wants to be fantasy fiction, as it pushes the boundaries of the medium, seeming to need far more time and space than can easily be presented on stage; it wants to do everything.

Like several other late Shakespeare plays, *Pericles* returns to a plot resolution he'd used as early as *The Comedy of Errors* and found fascinating throughout his career: the astonishing reunion with those who seemed lost forever. That particular kind of wonder doesn't appear here, and indeed fits a play better than this book's new kind of exploration. Instead we get the richness of a fictional world that could continue rolling along forever, that could keep leading us to new places and startle us not by returning to our beginnings but by going on and on.

Dr John Lavagnino
December 2015

About the Authors

Jonathan Barnes was born in 1979 and was educated in Norfolk and at Oxford University. His first novel, *The Somnambulist*, was published in 2007 and his second, *The Domino Men*, in 2008. Between them they have been translated into eight languages. He writes regularly for the *Times Literary Supplement* and the *Literary Review*. Since 2011, he has been writer-in-residence at Kingston University.

Kate Heartfield's fiction has appeared in places such as *Strange Horizons*, *Crossed Genres*, *Podcastle* and *Daily Science Fiction*. She is also a freelance journalist in Ottawa, Canada. Her favourite undergraduate assignment, nearly two decades ago, was to write an entire essay about Shakespeare's uses of a single word; her word was "mount." Her website is heartfieldfiction. com and she is on Twitter as @kateheartfield.

John Lavagnino is Reader in Digital Humanities at King's College London, where he is a member of both the Department of English and the Department of Digital Humanities. He was one of the general editors of Thomas Middleton's *Collected Works* (Oxford University Press, 2007), and more recently has been working on the reception of early modern drama in the eighteenth and nineteenth centuries.

Foz Meadows is the author of two YA urban fantasy novels, *Solace and Grief* and *The Key to Starveldt*, and in 2014, she was nominated for the Hugo Award for Best Fan Writer. She is also a contributing writer for *The Huffington Post* and *Black Gate*, and a contributing reviewer for *Strange Horizons*, *A Dribble* *of Ink* and *Tor.com*. An Australian expat, Foz currently lives in Scotland with not enough books, her very own philosopher and a toddler. Surprisingly, this is a good thing.

Emma Newman writes science fiction and urban fantasy novels, along with dark short stories. *Between Two Thorns*, the first book in Emma's *Split Worlds* urban fantasy series, was shortlisted for the BFS Best Novel and Best Newcomer awards. Emma's most recent book, *Planetfall*, was a standalone science fiction novel published by Ace/Roc. Emma is a professional audiobook narrator and also co-writes and hosts the Hugo-nominated podcast *Tea and Jeopardy*, which involves tea, cake, mild peril and singing chickens. Her hobbies include dressmaking and playing RPGs. She blogs at www.enewman. co.uk.

Adrian Tchaikovsky was born in Woodhall Spa, Lincolnshire before heading off to Reading to study psychology and zoology. For reasons unclear even to himself he subsequently ended up in law and has worked as a legal executive in both Reading and Leeds, where he now lives. Married, he is a keen live role-player and occasional amateur actor, has trained in stage-fighting, and keeps no exotic or dangerous pets of any kind, possibly excepting his son. He's the author of the critically acclaimed *Shadows of the Apt* series as well as standalone works *Guns of the Dawn* and *Children of Time*, and numerous short stories.

Woodcut Illustrations

All cover and internal illustrations in this volume are based on woodcut illustrations from the fifteenth through seventeenth centuries. The source images (and the names of the artists, where known) are listed below.

Front Cover: *On Nocturnal Dance of Fairies, in Other Words Ghosts*, Olaus Magnus, 1555.

Prologue: Unattributed English woodcut, 17th century.

Coral Bones: From *The Good Womans Champion*, 1650; and from *Fortunatus*, 1554.

The Course of True Love: *The Scholar in her Study*, Iacopo Filippo Foresti, 1497; and from *On Witches and Female Soothsayers*, 1489.

The Unkindest Cut: From *Dance of Death*, Hans Holbein, c.1522.

Even in the Cannon's Mouth: From *Dance of Death*, Hans Holbein, c.1522; and unattributed English woodcut, c.1650.

On the Twelfth Night: From *Greene in Conceit*, 1598.